The
Friendship
Riddle

ALSO BY MEGAN FRAZER BLAKEMORE

The Water Castle
The Spy Catchers of Maple Hill

The
Friendship
Riddle

SET

Megan Frazer Blakemore

BLOOMSBURY
NEW YORK   LONDON   NEW DELHI   SYDNEY

First published in the United States of America in May 2015
by Bloomsbury Children's Books
www.bloomsbury.com

Bloomsbury is a registered trademark of Bloomsbury Publishing Plc

For information about permission to reproduce selections from this book, write to
Permissions, Bloomsbury Children's Books, 1385 Broadway, New York, New York 10018
Bloomsbury books may be purchased for business or promotional use. For information on bulk
purchases please contact Macmillan Corporate and Premium Sales Department at
specialmarkets@macmillan.com

The spelling bee definitions are used by permission from *Merriam-Webster's Collegiate®
Dictionary, 11th Edition* © 2014 by Merriam-Webster, Inc. (www.Merriam-Webster.com).

Library of Congress Cataloging-in-Publication Data
Blakemore, Megan Frazer.
The friendship riddle / by Megan Frazer Blakemore.
pages   cm
Summary: When her former best friend gets popular and leaves her behind,
sixth-grader Ruth prefers to be alone, studying for the school spelling bee,
until she finds a riddle in an old book.
ISBN 978-1-61963-630-9 (hardcover) • ISBN 978-1-61963-631-6 (e-book)
[1. Friendship—Fiction.   2. Riddles—Fiction.   3. Spelling bees—Fiction.
4. Middle schools—Fiction.   5. Schools—Fiction.]   I. Title.
PZ7.B574Fr 2015   [Fic]—dc23   2014030036

Book design by Nicole Gastonguay
Typeset by Westchester Book Composition
Printed and bound in the U.S.A. by Thomson-Shore Inc., Dexter, Michigan
2 4 6 8 10 9 7 5 3 1

For Matilda
Fierce in battle, sweet at heart—
I know you will succeed in
whatever quest you undertake.

The
Friendship
Riddle

ONE

Precipitate

The secret clue was written on an index card, folded in half, placed in an origami envelope, and then tucked into an old book about the Loch Ness Monster. The morning I discovered it in the library, it was snowing. That winter, it was always snowing. The snowdrifts were so high, they went right over the sills of our first-floor windows and made their own little peaks right there on the glass. It was like looking into an ant farm, and I squinted and pretended I could see faint tracks through the snow and that the ants were wearing anoraks while snowshoeing around.

These are the kinds of thoughts that make my teachers write comments on my report cards like "Mind tends to wander," "A bit in her own world," and "Reality does little to faze Ruth."

The phone rang that morning and I snuggled down deeper into my covers. The phone rang again, and then, a few minutes later, there was my mom telling me she had been called in because another doctor's flight back from some vacation had been delayed. "Barbados? Bahamas?" She shrugged. "The other call was that awful automated message about school being canceled. The person always sounds so somber, like he's calling to tell us that a former president has died or something. Who makes that call, anyway?"

I rolled over and tugged the quilt over my head. "I dunno," I said. "Good night."

"I don't think so, darling. Up and at 'em. You're going to the library."

So we got up, and Mom made herself coffee while I made us oatmeal. We sat down together, and she had a few sips of coffee out of her #1 MOM mug (Mum has one, too), and then she said, "If you were going to make an igloo, would you build up or dig down?"

I gave this question some thought. "Both."

"When Mum gets back, we should build a snow fort. As long as it doesn't get too cold, this snow should be just right for it."

"That sounds like fun," I said. And it did sound like fun. But I knew that even though in that moment Mom had every intention of making that snow fort—she was probably picturing it in her head, with windows and tunnels and everything—the chances of us building it were slim. There was always *something*.

It took us half an hour to dig out in front of the garage after breakfast and to burst through the snowbank left at the end of the driveway by the plow as it cleared the road. "We'll leave the mailbox for later," Mom said. We'd already gotten two form letters telling us about the importance of digging three feet in either direction so the mail carrier could get her car in to deliver our bills and catalogs. Mom had crumpled them up and thrown each one in the recycle bin.

We drove down the street and into town. The deejays on the radio had to take turns reading the list of school closures, there were so many of them. Our little town was all covered in snow. It clung to street lamps and hung off the edges of windowsills. It looked like a painting. Beautiful.

Maine is a big state. Probably bigger than you realize. Most people just think of the ocean, but there are mountains and forests and even cities. We do live on the ocean, though, in a little town called Promise. If you have fancy friends, they have probably been to Promise. In the summer we are overrun by people from all over the world. That's the word folks in Promise use—"overrun"—but I like seeing all the different people and the license plates from all fifty states and Canada, as well.

I like it in the winter, too, though most of the stores close up. It's quieter, but it's as if everyone who lives here has been on vacation and they all come back and they're so happy to see one another. Only they haven't been on vacation; they've just been real busy working. I'm like a hawk in a tree looking down on all of it. It's pretty from up here. The problems come when I swoop down to the ground.

Mom turned the car onto Exchange Street and then made a quick turn onto Congress Street, driving up the hill toward the library.

My moms are different from most adults in Promise. They don't work in any of the touristy places, and they don't fish. Mom is a doctor. She works in the emergency room of the hospital in Rockport. Mum can live anywhere because she works everywhere. They came here on a trip once and loved it. "So we just stayed," they tell everyone, but it's not really true. My moms aren't exactly just-drop-everything-and-leave people. They had to sell the house in Connecticut, and before that, Mom had to get her job. Plus they'd visited on a romantic vacation with just the two of them, and before they could settle down for good, they had to go back and get three-year-old me.

"If you run out of things to do in the library, I'm sure you can go up and see Charlotte," Mom said. Hope hung on to her voice like the icicles on the side of McCallister's Pharmacy.

"Uh-huh," I said.

You'd think in this tiny town in Maine, I'd be the only kid with two mothers. And I am. But there's also Charlotte Diamond, who was adopted from China by her two dads. That's how Charlotte and I met. My two moms and her two dads formed what they called the Support Group, and Charlotte and I were thrown together. We had no choice but to be friends.

Until we weren't.

It was good while it lasted. We had matching blue raincoats with whales on the insides. We liked to read. We would take out the blender that her dads used to make smoothies and mixed drinks, and we'd fill it with disgusting combinations like peanut butter and seltzer and fish sauce, and then we would see who could take even one sip (usually me). When we got to middle school, she started hanging out with the popular girls. It's not like she ditched me or we had a fight. It's like all this shifting and sorting out happened. Like we were dumped into a colander, and all of us small, less interesting pieces fell through and left the big, juicy berries inside. Charlotte is a berry.

Me, I'm a lone wolf. I'm that hawk flying above it all, the quiet observer on the sidelines. And that's the way I like it.

The funny thing is, Charlotte was the one who was nervous about starting middle school. I promised to stick by her. Does it count as breaking a promise if the other person doesn't want you to keep your word?

Mom said "Hold on" as she cruised through the stop sign and turned right onto Main Street. "Phew. I was afraid if I stopped, we wouldn't get going again."

"We could slide right back down the hill into the ocean. Or maybe the ferry would be there and it would catch us and we could go spend the day on Swift Island, just you and me."

"I'm not sure the ferry is even running today. Actually, it just occurred to me—I hope the library is open," Mom said. "If not, you'll have to come to the hospital with me."

A day at the hospital is no fun. There are only so many things you can do with tongue depressors and the little cups for urine samples.

We pulled up by a pile of snow higher than our car. "They're running out of places to put it," Mom remarked. "They'll have to dump it in the ocean."

"They can't," I told her. "It's against the law."

"Really?"

"Really. Because of all the chemicals and everything. They used to, but now I think they take it to the gully on the edge of town." I'd seen the dump trucks full of snow out the school window, driving away from the center village.

"Clever girl," she said. "So answer me this. Why is snowy-day quiet different from regular quiet?"

There had to be a reason, something to do with the snow muting the sound, maybe. "I'll look it up," I told her. "I do have all day."

"Ruth."

"I didn't mean it like that." But I had hurt her feelings, and I didn't know how to take it back. "I love you, Mom. See you later."

"Love you," she replied.

She waited and watched as I crossed the sidewalk toward the door. The snow was piled halfway up the plate-glass windows, taller than me. This was the seventh big storm we'd had that winter: we had two in November, before Thanksgiving even, three in December, and we'd already had one earlier that week, our first back from winter vacation. They were talking about taking days off our April vacation so we didn't have to go to school until July.

I pulled open the door and stomped my feet to get the snow out of my boots. A long, long time ago, the library was a Woolworth's department store. When that went out of business, the building—which takes up most of the block—changed hands several times. I love that expression. I picture the building being picked up by giant hands and cupped gently like an egg, then spilled over to another set of waiting, warm palms. Anyway, then Renys bought it. Renys is another department store, one that exists only in Maine, which is too bad for the rest of the country. You can get honey-roasted wasabi peanuts and blueberry shampoo, sturdy socks and school supplies, all at a discount. When Renys moved into an abandoned Walmart farther up the peninsula, they sold the building to the town for a dollar. Alan, one of Charlotte's dads, redesigned the whole building so the first two stories are the library and the top floor is a condo that Charlotte's family lives in. When he designed it, he kept the layout of the department store, so each section of the library takes up an old section of the store.

I found a table upstairs in the teen area (formerly women's lingerie, according to Charlotte) and started unpacking my gear. I was thinking about how I was going to look up why it's quieter when there's snow—*the sound of snow? sound dissipation in winter?*—when I saw her: Charlotte.

Mum said that when she was growing up in Northern Ireland, the Catholic kids went to one school and the Protestant kids to another, and you didn't even have a choice in it. She said I was lucky because all the kids in American towns go to the same school. I wasn't so sure.

Charlotte had her headphones on—the big, bulky kind; hers have rhinestones—and was reading one of those books with a pink cover and a skinny girl wearing too much makeup on it. I didn't expect her to be here. I figured she'd be curled up in her PJs upstairs, maybe redoing her toenail polish (she's actually quite good at pedicures, adding little flowers and sparkly stars).

I sat down at one of the computers and did a search for "quiet snow." The first hit was from the army. They have a SNOW Research Community, with "snow" all in capitals, and the page was supposed to be about snow acoustics. But when I clicked on it, I got the FORBIDDEN message. Was the military doing secret snow research? If so, they ought to come up here to Promise. We had plenty of it.

There were a lot of images and musings on how snowy days can make you relax—clearly written by people who don't live with feet of it to shovel. Then there were some of those sites where someone posts a question and others answer, and sometimes it's good, but often you're dealing with a bunch of ding-dongs with too much time on their hands. I couldn't find anything substantial, so I went to ask Ms. Pepper for help, but there was a sign on the youth services desk that said to go downstairs for assistance. So I did, and found Eliot, the reference librarian who was also Charlotte's other dad, at the circulation desk.

"Ruth!" he said, looking pleased. "How would you like to earn free books from the book swap?"

Eliot thought he had my number, but I'd seen those book-swap books. People clean out their basements and attics and bring their old, beat-up books to the library like they're doing this big, honking good deed, but the library doesn't want their old books, either, so they sell them for a quarter each or a dollar for a whole bag.

I gave him my best side-eye look, and he said, "Oh, did I say book swap? What I meant was, how would you like to earn advance copies of books that haven't even been published yet?" He picked up a stack of paperbacks from the counter behind him. "Ms. Pepper thought you might like this one in particular." He held up a book written by Harriet Wexler.

Harriet Wexler is my absolute favorite author. She writes the Taryn Greenbottom books. Taryn is the daughter of a knight and an elf, although you don't learn about her elfish-ness until book three; she looks human. Each book is basically a different quest. She's a squire, allowed to train for knighthood because her father was such an amazing fighter for the king. He's missing, though. That's the overarching saga: Taryn trying to unravel the mystery of her father. Harriet Wexler herself is a mystery. Supposedly she lives on a tiny island in Lake Champlain that isn't part of New York or Vermont but is its own entity all to itself. When she finishes a draft of a novel on her old typewriter, she takes a motorboat to Burlington and mails it off to her publisher. Other than that, she never leaves the island. There are no pictures of her on her books or online or anything, so no one even knows what she looks like. I think all of that is absolutely magnificent. I've read all her books, some of them three or four times, but I had never heard of this book, *The Riddled Cottage*.

"What do you need?" I asked.

"Now, when I explain this job, you might think it sounds boring, but you should know I don't trust just anyone with this task. I don't even let the students who volunteer as pages do it."

"You don't have to flatter me, Mr. Diamond. I'm in." When I'm at the library, I'm supposed to call him Mr. Diamond.

I didn't ask him if he ever let Charlotte do it. Eliot and I don't talk about Charlotte.

He led me deep into the stacks and gave me the shelf-reading instructions: I had to read along the shelves, looking at the spine labels and making sure every book was in the right place. Like if by accident 822.92 MAL was put before 821.1 SIR, I would need to move them into the correct positions. He also gave me a cart where I could place any books that were in the completely wrong section. The cart made me feel official. I thought it might be fun to be a librarian. Still, shelf reading was about the most boring job you could think of.

Most of the books were in order, but I did find some strange things, like a tennis ball stuck behind some books, and someone's shopping list crumpled on a bottom shelf: milk, eggs, ladyfingers, bacon.

I found some books wildly out of place, like a book on solar heating in the philosophy section. And, hiding in the mythology section, a book called *It's Perfectly Normal*, which I actually owned, since Mom gave it to me for my eleventh birthday. It was all about the body and sex and stuff. Eliot would probably think that was funny. I had it in my hands to bring to show him when I came around the corner and almost smacked into Lucas Hosgrove. He was holding a yo-yo in his hand. "I can walk the dog, you know."

"Great," I said.

Lucas had been showing everyone his yo-yo tricks for the last three weeks.

As he was preparing himself, I remembered what book I was holding. I clutched it to my chest, but it was so big that I couldn't hide the cover. So I tried to put it behind my back.

"Are you even watching?" he asked.

"I am."

"You're not."

He was right. I wasn't. I didn't really care about yo-yo tricks. But Lucas was one of those kids you're supposed to be patient with.

He did the trick again, the yo-yo swinging out in front of him, then curling back. Walking the dog was a strange name for it. Sure, when it rolls out, the yo-yo looks like a dog on a leash, but when you tug back on a leash, it's not like the dog glides back to you as if on roller skates. He might stop and look back with his tongue lolling out. If you were lucky.

"Wonderful," I told him.

"I know," he agreed, and then he left without saying good-bye.

I dropped the book on Ms. Pepper's desk, but after that I decided to just do what Eliot said and leave the misshelved books on the cart.

It was in the second row that I found the note, not too long after I put the solar heating book on the cart to be reshelved. I was supposed to read only the Dewey decimal numbers on the spine, but I couldn't stop myself from reading the titles. Most of them were bland and didn't even tell you what the book was about. But I found one called *The True Story of the Loch Ness Expedition* by Mervin R. Shuttlecock. I knew, of course, that the Loch Ness myth had been debunked. The man who took the picture admitted that he had faked it. Still, it sounded like an interesting story even though it had the ugliest cover: brown, with the dust jacket torn beneath the plastic protective coating. I slid it off the shelf and flipped it open.

The note was in a tiny envelope no bigger than a trading card. It was made out of origami paper that was black with tiny gold flowers. Inside, an index card was folded in half. One half was blank, but the other half had a seal drawn on it in red pencil. It was made to look like it had been pressed into wax, and the artist had used a heavy hand with the pencil. The center of the seal was a bird with a thin, sharp beak and a bright eye. I unfolded the card. A border was drawn around the card, a vine of green leaves and red thorns. Printed in green ink in small, even letters were the words:

For the answers you seek,
Look up.

****

"What's the question?" I asked.

I looked up, but there wasn't an answer there. There wasn't a question, either.

I was still looking up, trying to figure out the question or the answer, when Charlotte walked by the end of the aisle. She saw me, turned around, then came back to ask, "What's that?" She was wearing jeans, puffy leather boots, and a sweater that was long, almost like a dress. A school outfit. A nice school outfit. Not the sweats and turtleneck I wore.

"Nothing," I said.

Her eyes flicked from the note in my left hand to the envelope in my right. "Nothing. Okay, sure." She slipped her hands into the pouch at the front of her sweater.

She knew I was lying. She probably knew I knew she knew, but I was not going to say anything. This was my note. My mystery.

She turned on her heel as if to go. But then she stopped. She looked right at me, her brown eyes sparking like amber. "So, what does the origami riddler have to say for himself?"

———◄◦►———

That Charlotte knew something about the note stopped my heart, and it took three little elves inside me to stomp on it and get it going again. I blinked twice. I considered acting confused, but she knew me too well. Anyway, I wanted to suss out what she might know. "He says to find the answer, look up."

"The note I found was more of a riddle."

"You found a note, too?"

"Yep. In red origami paper folded into a tiny envelope."

"What did the note say?"

She slid one foot to the side and jutted her hip out. I could see her deciding whether or not to tell me, but, more than that, whether or not to let me back into her life just this little bit. "I can't really remember it all. Something about meanings."

"Where'd you find it? When?"

She shrugged, and her long, straight black hair shimmered off her shoulders. "A month ago. Maybe two. I was helping my dad weed some books, you know, stamping them 'discarded' and stuff. He gives me a nickel a book. It adds up quick. I'm going to buy tickets to the April Showers show. Melinda and I are going to go together. Her mom said she'd drive us and would let us sit three rows in front of her."

"Great," I said. April Showers was not, shall we say, my cup of tea. She played the guitar and sang songs about boys she loved and boys who broke her heart and boys who existed only in her fantasies.

"I already have thirty-seven dollars saved. I'm more than a third of the way there. Dad said he went to see Madonna when he was my age, but Pops isn't so sure. But they said I could go."

"So you opened a book and it was there? Which one?" I prompted.

"It fell out. I found it on the floor. I thought the paper was pretty. It had these gorgeous, shining dragons on it."

The golden flowers on my paper might have been pretty and shiny at one point, but they had grown dull and flat. "And there was a riddle inside?"

"Yeah. It was like a poem. 'Under cover there are stored, meanings, maybe three or four.'" She leaned in as she spoke, but then stopped herself. "Something like that, anyway. I didn't give it too much thought."

She had, though. She had because she remembered it, and Charlotte had the worst time memorizing things. In third grade when we had to memorize and recite poetry, she ended up running from the room in tears when she couldn't remember past the third line of her Jack Prelutsky poem.

"There was more?"

"A little, maybe. I think so."

"I could figure it out, I bet, if you remembered it. With both of us thinking about it, I know we could get it." We used to make up mysteries for ourselves to solve. We would hide in corners of the library and write down observations of the people we saw and then make up stories of their nefarious lives. That woman getting the book on raw foods was contemplating cannibalism. The man in the Yankees jersey was a mobster in the witness protection program. These clues, the riddle—it could be like that again.

Charlotte scuffed her furry-puffy boot on the floor, then turned and glanced over her shoulder as if one of the other berry girls from school might come around and find us talking together. Instead, it was Lucas who cruised by on his backpack with a scooter built in. Charlotte rolled her eyes at me, but I didn't play along.

"Can I see it?" I asked.

"See what?"

"The note."

"Oh, that." She waved her hand in the air. "I threw it away, I think. Maybe I have it at home. I don't know. I guess I could look for it."

"Thanks!" I tried to make my voice sound chipper, like I hadn't expected her to run right upstairs and grab the note, and maybe one of our old little notebooks, while she was up there. I kept mine in my bottom desk drawer. Did she know where hers were?

She blinked and stepped back. "Calm down, already. It's not like I'm offering you my kidney or something."

There was a time when she would have offered me her kidney. Without hesitation, and probably without even knowing that we have two of them and only need one. "Well, thank you all the same." Even without Charlotte, I wanted that clue. Taryn Greenbottom was always going on quests, always seeking something. I had not yet had a saga-worthy event in my life. Maybe this could be mine. And maybe it could be Charlotte's, too.

"Sure," she said. As she turned, her hair spun out around her like in a shampoo commercial.

"And I hope you get the money to go see April Showers. She's really, um, cool."

Charlotte waved without looking back at me.

TWO

Rivals

The Department of Public Works trucks fanned out like robots in a military strike and cleared the roads by the next morning. Mom and I had watched the dump trucks full of snow go down Main Street, headed for the edge of town, after she picked me up at the library.

So we had school. Everyone clomped inside in their big snow boots and coats, and the ground by the lockers was slick with dirty water. I walked without lifting my feet, sliding like a cat learning to ice-skate, but it was better than falling on the ground and winding up with a big, muddy puddle stain on my butt.

Homeroom was with Ms. Broadcheck. She's the special-ed teacher and a friend of Mum's, and I think that was why

I wound up in that homeroom. So she could keep an eye on me now that I was in the regional middle school with kids from Port Stewart, the other town on the peninsula with Promise, and Swift Island, right off the coast. At first I thought maybe it was because I was actually a special-ed kid—like there was something a little different about me but everyone had decided to just be nice and not tell me.

Then there were girls like Melinda who just go and shatter the whole notion of kidness for you. Melinda had bright red hair and big teeth and no freckles, which looked weird with the bright red hair. Everyone says she looks *so* Irish, when I'm the one who might actually be Irish. Northern Ireland is a part of Ireland that England owns—though it's much more complicated than that. Mum could talk about that subject for hours. Anyway, Mum considers herself Irish and says most people in Ireland don't have red hair and green eyes, but rather dark hair and blue eyes like me, but you can't stop people's misconceptions.

When I walked into homeroom, Melinda and Charlotte were sitting together in a beanbag chair, their furry boots water-stained and tangled together. Melinda was combing Charlotte's hair through her fingers. "You have the most beautiful hair," she says. "I'm so jealous. I wish I was Asian and had hair like that, too."

"Thanks," Charlotte said.

"Chinese," I said as I put my book down on the table away from the cacophony of boys. "She's Chinese."

Melinda looked up as if she hadn't given me the once-over when I came in. "Chinese *is* Asian."

"But not all Asians are the same," I told her. "There's Japan and China and Korea and—"

"I was there for the Asian unit in humanities. Thanks for the refresher."

"That's why you should know better."

"It doesn't matter," Charlotte said. But it used to matter to her a whole lot. Melinda looked me up and down and said, "You wore that shirt on Monday."

Had I worn this red turtleneck on Monday? I might have. If I didn't know, how did Melinda?

"Oh," I said. "Well."

"Did you wash it?" she asked.

"Wash it? Oh, sure, of course. Washed it, dried it, the whole nine yards. I even used one of those little bags of lavender so it smells nice. Wanna sniff?"

I reached out my arm, but Melinda turned up her nose, which was good, because I hadn't actually washed it, and as I reached out my arm, I saw a little spot of pesto (green with a ring of oil around it) from dinner on, yep, Monday night.

I slid into my seat across the table from Lucas and next to Lena Fernández del Campo; it's the longest and most glamorous name I've ever heard. She had dark hair cut just below her chin, and on the underside, behind her ear, she had dyed a streak of bright red. It was like a campfire that seemed to have been extinguished, but then you turn over a log and it's still burning red. She didn't even look up from her tablet, but she whispered, "I like your shirt. Laundry is overrated."

"Thanks," I whispered back, blushing that she saw through my lie. I picked up a Rubik's Cube. Ms. Broadcheck had all these little toys around, I guess to keep the special-ed kids focused. Ms. Broadcheck says some kids need something to distract them in order to pay attention. Lucas can't keep his hands off them. He *is* a special-ed kid, the gifted kind. He was sliding the pieces around on one of those puzzles that you have to shift the squares to get them to line up.

"Done!" he called out. "See!" He stood up with the puzzle over his head like it was the Stanley Cup. "Nine seconds. That's a new record. I own this puzzle!"

I swiveled around in my seat and said, "Hey, Charlotte, did you find that note?"

Charlotte looked up at me with her brown eyes widened and gave a subtle shake of her head. Too late.

"What note?" Melinda asked.

"It's just a note," I said.

"Ruth's mom asked for a recipe, actually, and I was supposed to bring it in, but I keep forgetting."

"Right," I said. "I meant a recipe, of course. Not a note."

"A recipe for what?" Melinda asked.

"Hey, Ruth," Lucas interrupted. "You done with that Rubik's Cube?"

"Monkey bread," Charlotte said without hesitation.

"Monkey bread? What's that?" Melinda asked.

Alan used to make monkey bread when I would sleep over at their place. You take balls of dough and cover them in butter and sugar and then stack them up and bake them. When you eat it, you just pull off pieces. It's a big, sticky, delicious mess.

"Just a thing for breakfast. It's kind of gross, it's so sweet. Ruth likes it, though. Your mom was going to make it for you for your birthday, right?"

"Hey, Ruth, are you using that Rubik's Cube?"

"Right," I said again as I slid the toy over to Lucas.

"Awesome! Do you think I can solve *this* in nine seconds? Someone time me."

Lucas was standing right behind my chair, his hands lightly holding the Rubik's Cube. I could hear his foot tap, tap, tapping on the ground.

"Is your birthday coming up?" Melinda asked. "Are you having a party?"

"It's a few weeks away," I said. "And I haven't thought about it yet."

"Come on, Ruth. Time me. The world record is five point five five seconds."

"You need to have a twelfth birthday party. A boy-girl party."

Charlotte was pressing her thumb into the beanbag chair. "I don't think Ruth's moms will let her have a boy-girl party. Do you, Ruth?"

I shook my head.

Melinda laughed. "I always forget that Ruth has two moms and you have two dads. That's so weird. No one in Port Stewart has two moms or two dads. Not weird like bad, of course. Just weird."

"Weird like how?" I asked.

Lucas tapped my shoulder. "Ruth, come on."

"Don't get all defensive," Charlotte said. Her frown was like a toy boat sinking in the bathtub. "She said not weird like bad."

"I know. I just meant not weird like how?"

"Weird like different. Unusual. Relax," Melinda said.

"Ruth!" Lucas whined.

I spun around. "What?"

"I need you to time me. I'm going for a record."

"I don't have a watch," I told him.

"Use your phone."

"I don't have a phone. Anyway, they aren't allowed in school."

"I have a phone," Melinda said. "You want me to time you, Lucas? Do you?" She used a sickly sweet voice like she was talking to a baby.

"Yes," Lucas practically sighed.

"Okay. On your mark, get set, go."

We all watched him as he spun the sides of the Rubik's Cube. He moved his lips in-out, in-out, in-out with each spin. Slamming the toy on the table, he cried out, "Done!"

"Nine point three seconds," Melinda said. "Maybe next time."

"Let's go again," Lucas said. "Right now. I'm ready."

But at that moment, Ms. Broadcheck finally came into the room. If she really wanted to look out for me, maybe she should've been on time once in a while. She shook off her oversized coat. "What about all this snow, huh? I was up at five, and I still couldn't get it all out of the way to be here on time." She combed her fingers through her hair, which always stood up like reddish-brown cotton candy swirling around her head. "So sorry to be late when we have so much to do."

She ran through a litany of announcements: upcoming band concerts, the trip to the soup kitchen, the arts committee looking for people to perform at a coffeehouse, and "Last but not least, sign up for the spelling bee!"

She waved a paper and then put it down on the table between me and Lucas. "Our school spelling bee will be next month. The winner goes on to the Knox County Bee, and from there to the state bee and from there"—she took a deep breath—"to the Scripps National Spelling Bee in Washington, DC! You can win thirty thousand dollars and a whole set of encyclopedias—you know, when I was a kid, we used to pore through those things; you guys don't know what you're missing. Anyway, last year everyone who went to the state bee got a free e-reader."

"Whoop-dee-doo-dah," Melinda whispered so low that Ms. Broadcheck couldn't hear.

I didn't care what Melinda thought about anything, but especially not about the spelling bee. Mum and I watched the Scripps National Spelling Bee on television every year. We took turns standing up and trying to spell the word before the contestants. Mum blamed her problems on the difference between American and British spellings, but I did well. Really well. The year before, I made it all the way to the second-to-last round before I missed a word. The second-to-last round! I had my pencil out and I was reaching for the sheet when Lucas swooped in and grabbed it from me. "Don't even bother signing up. I am going to crush everyone. Crush them."

"Lucas," Ms. Broadcheck said in a warning tone. "Modesty. Respect. Humility." This was Ms. Broadcheck's mantra for Lucas. They'd been working on it all year, but he didn't seem to get it. Once he told her that he just didn't feel comfortable lying, even if it made people feel better.

"Anyone else?" Ms. Broadcheck asked.

I bit my lip. The thing of it was, Lucas was probably right. If he wanted to win, he would. His mind didn't seem to let anything go—nothing factual, anyway. So what was the point if I couldn't even make it past the school bee? It would only be a big letdown for Mum.

"Ruth wants to," Charlotte said.

"Is that so, Ruth?" Ms. Broadcheck asked.

I shook my head. "I was thinking about it, but I don't think so."

"She knows I will crush her."

"Not necessarily," Ms. Broadcheck said, but no one believed her, least of all me.

"That's okay," I said. "It's no big deal."

"Why don't you just write your name down, and if you change your mind, you can erase it. You can take the weekend to think about it."

Charlotte gave me just the smallest of nods, and I guess that was enough, because I wrote my name on the line under Lucas's. He wrote his name in all caps, so big that it took up two spaces. I wrote mine in tiny lowercase letters just to balance things out.

THREE

Illuminati

The school cafeteria smelled like old hot dogs and pizza and was so loud, you could drive a ride-on snowblower in and no one would notice. I used to eat lunch in the school library, but then they made a rule that you couldn't have food in there because one day Mrs. Abernathy came in and found two dead mice. I don't think this was conclusive evidence that the mice were lured there by food. What did they die of, anyway? Maybe they ate mouse poison somewhere else in the school and wandered into the library with their last, gasping breaths. Or maybe a cat caught them and deposited them there as a gift for Mrs. Abernathy. Our cat, Webster, puts the animals he kills on the welcome mat of our front door.

Still, mice in the library meant no food in the library, and so I had to go to the cafeteria.

Mom said I was still finding my place in this bigger school, and Mum said it would get better in high school. Really comforting. Ms. Broadcheck kept telling me to go sit with a group of girls who were already a cohesive unit of four. Like they wanted someone new. Although, I noticed, Lena was sitting with them today. Lena seemed to sit at a different table every day, though she never landed at mine. Anyway, they were island girls who took the ferry back and forth to the mainland for school, and they only ever talked to each other. Even if I made friends with them, it wasn't like I could go visit them. Mom and Mum would never let me take the ferry by myself.

So I sat at a table in the back corner. It was fine. Just the way I liked it. I had the Harriet Wexler book that Eliot gave me even though I didn't finish all the shelf reading he wanted me to do. It was one of her Taryn Greenbottom books. In this one, Taryn had to travel from her own king-dom to one nearly thirty leagues away. To do so, she had to go through the Forest of Westbegotten, a dark, dreary, and dangerous place. I hadn't gotten that far yet. She was still preparing by feasting with her fellow squires. Taryn's favorite food is cheddar and onion, eaten between slices of fresh bread. The male squires drank mead, but she chose apple cider.

I felt a special kinship with Taryn that day because I had

brought a cheese and chutney sandwich. I was reading and minding my own business when Charlotte walked past. She never came by this part of the cafeteria, but she didn't come to see me. I thought maybe she was going to say something about that morning, maybe an apology for being so weird about the note. Instead she just walked on by.

Lucas sat at a table a couple over from mine. He sat with the smart boys, but with a few seats between them and him. He had moved up here from down in southern Maine, where he went to a private school. He told us that the lunch was much better there and that he had hard-boiled eggs and Rice Krispies and dessert every day. I watched as he dumped a sugar packet onto his ham and cheese sandwich. He read a graphic novel while he ate. He read so much that Mrs. Abernathy actually took him aside and told him that the books were getting in the way of his making friends, and at the very least he should put down the book while walking and eating. He stopped reading while he shuffled from class to class, but had not yet taken the second half of her advice.

The smart boys were arguing about the practicalities of the time stop in the first Andromeda Rex book. I could hear them all the way over at my table. Adam, with his long-sleeve polo shirt tucked into his khaki pants, stood up and hit the table. "It is simply scientifically inconceivable."

Dev tugged at Adam's sleeve to make him sit down. "Don't cause a scene."

"That's why it's called science fiction," Coco replied. He

had a flop of brown hair that was always getting in his eyes. He was the smartest of the smart boys, and his name wasn't really Coco. It was Chris. But I guess his big sister couldn't say Chris when she was little, so she called him Coco and it stuck, and he was so smart and kind that he didn't even get made fun of for it.

Coco glanced up and saw me looking at him and smiled, so I looked back down at my book. All the squires had gone home except for Taryn and Benedict, squire to the royal Sir Gandriel. He begged her not to go on the quest, and it seemed he was just about to declare his love, but Taryn stopped him. "Pretty words are wasted on me," she said. "I leave in the morrow. Without a quest, I am nothing. I am no one if I do not seek."

That was why I loved the Taryn Greenbottom books: Harriet Wexler didn't mess them up with any of that boy-girl stuff. There's nothing worse than reading along with a good action-adventure story and then *BAM!* Love story.

Charlotte, who adored love stories, was back at her table. She sat between Melinda and Mitchell, who was the most popular of all the popular boys. His dad was a fisherman, and Mitchell started going out on the boat with him this past summer. He came to school in the fall with a nose red and peeling, hands calloused, and shoulders broadened. In Promise, he'd always just been Mitchell, quiet and still, but then Melinda saw him and declared him positively adorable, and the next thing you knew, quiet, still Mitchell became a star with his own orbit. He had gravitational pull. And that gravitational pull seemed to be working its power over Charlotte: she sat so close, you couldn't even put a quarter between them.

I checked my sandwich. Three more bites and then I could leave the smelly cafeteria and go to the library. I had a space right below the twisting staircase where I liked to sit and read. I could usually get there with twenty minutes left before fifth period.

One bite.

"Hey, Ruth." It was Coco.

I still had a mouth full of sandwich, so I just nodded. He beckoned me over. Only two bites left. Maybe one and a half if I crammed. I stood up, swallowed hard, and walked over to their table. "Have you read Andromeda Rex?" Coco asked.

"Only the first two," I replied. I had thought they were okay, but then I went online and read that the author, Timothy Desmond Green, had called Harriet Wexler a "no-talent, derivative" writer whose "act of being a recluse is just a posture designed to garner the affections of moon-ing preadolescent girls." I wouldn't ever read another one of his books.

"Not an expert," Adam said without looking at me. "I told you."

"We're talking about the first book," Dev said. Then, to me: "Sorry. He's rude. No excuse for it, really. It's just the way he's made."

"But she doesn't have the whole context," Adam replied. He glanced past me at the rest of the cafeteria.

"You know how Andromeda stops time so he can go and change things? Move them around and all that? Do you think that's in any way possible?" Coco asked.

I reached back in my memory to try to recall what I thought when I read the book. "I don't know," I said. "But I don't think so."

"Ha!" Adam said. "Told you. She doesn't know anything about it."

"Why don't you think so?" Coco asked.

"Well, if time isn't linear, I mean, that's the whole idea behind time travel, right?"

"Obviously," Adam said. "If you are going to travel through time, it's not just front and back. There are alternate time lines and so on and so forth."

"So on and so forth?" Dev asked.

Adam tugged on the end of his sleeves. "We don't really have the time here to go into a full discussion of the physics of time travel."

"Or maybe you just don't know," Dev said.

I interrupted their bickering. "The point is, let's say time is a wheel that's spinning. But it's not just one wheel—it's a lot of wheels side by side. So if you stopped the one you were on, the other ones are still spinning. You might stop it here, but not there."

"That's *one* theory of time travel and time manipulation," Adam said, still adjusting his shirt cuffs. "But that might not be Timothy Desmond Green's version. You have to work within the confines of the book, you know. Remember, Coco, we talked about that at Brain Camp."

"Brain Camp," Dev said with disgust. "It wasn't even camp. It was like—summer school."

There was a big science company on the peninsula—they made medicines and vaccines, I think—and they had a camp where their experts taught classes to kids. It could be their field of study, or just something they were passionate about. I had taken one on genetic engineering in the hopes of learning how to build an army of genetically superior animals, but all we did was talk about Punnett squares and the ethics of parents choosing, say, green eyes for their children. The teacher was a young woman with long brown hair and hipster glasses who referred to all of us as "dear" and "honey." She worked in the lab, testing their products on mice, and I sometimes wondered if that was how she talked to the rodents.

"Our teacher said that when you are looking at the science of science fiction, you need to consider the world of the novel as well as the confines of science. And Timothy Desmond Green is very clear about how time works in his books, and so—"

"The question is whether it's possible at all, not possible in the books," Dev interrupted.

I started to say that I wasn't really sure, but then Coco said, "I think Ruth's explanation makes sense."

"It sure does," Dev said, grinning, but I knew it was just because he liked getting the upper hand over Adam. Sometimes it seemed the only thing that tied Adam and Dev together was Coco, each of them pivoting around him like the ends of a kayak paddle.

"What does Lucas think?" I asked.

"You try asking him," Coco said. "He's lost in that book."

"Hey, Lucas?" I tried to make my voice like Melinda's when she talked to him, but I just couldn't make it that syrupy. "Have you been listening? What do you think?"

He lifted his gaze from the book. His glasses were crooked across his face, and he had a little bit of mustard on his cheek. "I think I'm going to crush you in that spelling bee."

FOUR

Physique

Ms. Pepper's laugh was like wind chimes in the summer, but she wasn't free and easy with it, so I was glad my story of how I had found *It's Perfectly Normal* buried in the mythology section elicited a little tinkle. But then she cleared her throat and said, "Have you read it?"

"Pardon me?"

"It's very informative."

"I know."

"You can check it out if you'd like. I still have it right here."

"I have my own copy."

"That's fantastic!" She had earrings shaped like Curious George and the Man in the Yellow Hat, and they danced on her ears as she nodded enthusiastically.

"Sure," I said. "It's not really relevant to my life right now."

"Not relevant?" The characters swung back and forth like they were on a teeter-totter. "It's about the human body!" Her voice went up in volume and pitch. "Ruth Mudd-O'Flanahan, you have a glorious body!" I swear, her voice echoed around the room.

Body, body, body.

I checked over my shoulder to see if anyone was around. Charlotte passed by. She pretended not to have noticed me, but she had a little smirk on her lips. Would she tell Melinda about this? Would my glorious body be the butt of jokes all over school?

"Thanks, Ms. Pepper," I said. "I'll take that under advisement."

"I mean it, Ruth. Never be ashamed of your body."

I never said I was ashamed of my body. "That's good advice," I said. "You know, I'm supposed to be helping Mr. Diamond with a project. That's how I found the book in the first place."

"Well, if you find any more of our juvenile books out of place, you let me know."

"Sure thing," I said.

She gave a sharp nod, and George seemed to wink his monkey eye at me.

Ears still red as hot rods, I went back to shelf reading for Eliot. I was in the seven hundreds, the arts, when I found a book on Romanian operas. I didn't know that there were any Romanian operas, let alone a whole book on them. My sperm donor dad put down opera as an interest, and so I thought genetically my own love of it was inside me somewhere. As much as I've tried to listen, I hadn't discovered it yet. Maybe my love was for Romanian operas.

It was on the very bottom shelf, and as I bent over to pull it out, I must admit I was thinking that this would be the perfect spot to hide another note. I mean, Romanian opera? Not exactly a high-interest topic. Plus the spine was all weathered and tattered.

I pulled it out, carefully, carefully. A piece of paper spun out of it, and my heart beat like those windup chattering teeth bouncing all over the place. The paper was no wider than a staple and dotted with holes. It was the edging of old computer printer paper. You used to have these long reams of continuous but perforated paper that was fed through the printer by pins. Once you printed your page, you tore it off like a paper towel from a roll, and then ripped off the dotted edges.

I recognized it right away because my grandmother—Mom's mom—still had that kind of printer and when she printed, she didn't bother to pull off the edges, so I always ended up tearing them off for her and I tried to use them to make crafts, but they weren't very useful, so most ended up in the recycle bin.

My humanities teacher, Ms. Lawson, would call this "diverging from the task," but I think it's interesting. Maybe it's not 100 percent relevant, but it's not *ir*-relevant ("ir" as a prefix making the word its opposite).

So anyway, I picked up this paper. Even though it was not in an origami envelope, I still had hope. It was twisted and I smoothed it out.

Nothing.

I felt as let down as a balloon nearly out of helium, hovering inches above the ground.

I needed to see that other note. I needed to see Charlotte.

"Charlotte?" Eliot echoed my question. "Well, if she's not upstairs, I suppose she's gone into the back room. You can go look for her."

The back room was where the library staff had their space. There were supplies for cataloging books, and a little kitchenette where they could reheat their lunches. Charlotte and I used to spend all sorts of time there, back when we were friends, but I hadn't been in ages.

"That's okay."

"It's really fine," Eliot said. "You can grab me some rubber cement when you go to check for her."

I scratched my lip. Charlotte had told me it was a bad habit because it looked like I was picking my nose and that I really needed to stop before middle school. I mostly had. Mostly.

"Okay," I said. "I'll be right back with the rubber cement."

I pushed open the door and it creaked. The building

was so old that sometimes it creaked a symphony. I figured I'd just go in, grab the rubber cement, then head back out, and forget about even looking for Charlotte. But she was in there, and the door was so loud that she looked up when I came in, right in my eyes, and I couldn't just pretend I didn't see her. Could I? No. She wanted to pretend she didn't see me. I could see it in the way her eyes shifted left and then down and then back up at me as if I were a train wreck and she couldn't quite look away. "Hi, Charlotte," I said.

"Hi, Ruth," she replied.

"Your dad needs some rubber cement. I'm getting him some rubber cement."

"It's right over near the paper cutter."

"I know."

She flipped the ends of her hair over her shoulder. It was a practiced gesture. I wondered if Melinda gave her lessons. I took a few steps toward the counter. It was none of my business anymore what Charlotte did with her hair or anything else.

"You really should do the spelling bee," she told me.

I turned to face her, but I couldn't figure out just what to say. She looked like the old Charlotte. Her cheeks were pinkish and she wore her dad's earflap hat, even though it was really dorky, because it was so cold in the back room.

"It's just that you've always wanted to do it. And I know Lucas has that crazy memory, but spelling bees are as much about luck as skill."

"There's a lot of skill involved."

She pursed her lips but kept going. "I mean, who knows what word he might get, and what might trip him up. All I'm saying is that you shouldn't let Lucas scare you off from something you want to do. That's all I'm saying."

"Thanks," I said, though I wasn't sure what I was thanking her for. It wasn't exactly a huge vote of confidence.

She picked up a colored pencil and sucked on the tip, but she didn't start drawing. I used to give her ideas and she would draw. Like I would say, "That falling leaf could have a whole colony of miniature elves on it," and she would draw it, and it would be beautiful. Every vein on the leaf would be just right, and each elf would have a different face and expression. We said that when we grew up, we would make books together that I would write and she would illustrate.

"Ms. Pepper is pretty weird, huh?"

I blushed. "I was afraid you might have heard that."

"You do have a glorious body." She giggled. She wasn't teasing, though. Her eyes flashed at mine and it was like we were at one of our old sleepovers, with our parents downstairs drinking wine, their voices coming louder and louder while we planned our own grown-up parties.

"As do you," I replied.

She shook her head. "Ruth Mudd-O'Flanahan, don't you ever forget that you have a glorious, miraculous body."

"And yet one that is perfectly normal."

"Perfectly, gloriously normal."

We were both giggling then, holding our sides, when Ms. Pepper pushed through the creaking door. She beamed at both of us, and that was enough so that we were in peals of laughter. Charlotte laughed so hard that she snorted, and that set us off again. I bet she never snorted in front of Melinda. She got laughing so hard, she wasn't even really making a sound, just wheezing.

Ms. Pepper grabbed her cup of tea from the counter and the rubber cement and went back out into the public part of the library. She shook her head as if questioning her career choice.

It took us a few minutes to calm down. We didn't look at each other. We knew from past experience that would only set us off again. My side ached and my cheeks were sore.

"I was actually wondering if you had a chance to find that note, the one in the book?"

She was still looking down and away from me. "Oh, that," she said. "Sorry, I forgot all about it."

"That's okay."

She shaded something on her drawing. "I'll look tonight if I remember. I'll bring it here to the library to give to you. Will you be here after school again?"

"Probably."

"Okay, then I'll give it to you here. At the library."

"You said that."

Her lips tightened.

"And you only ever found the one?" I asked.

"Yes."

"I just thought it was odd that there were only two notes."

"I would have told you if there were more."

"I know."

"I did remember something about the book. The cover was red, but it was so old and dirty, it looked brown. It didn't have a dust jacket, and the fabric over the cover was faded around the edges."

"That's a lot!" I said. "Thanks."

She colored for a moment longer. "You know all of this is probably nothing. These notes."

"Sure, of course."

"We're too old for mystery games, Ruth."

"I know," I said. She hadn't looked up at me once since we stopped laughing. "I should probably get your dad the rubber cement."

"Ms. Pepper already did."

"Right. Well, I should probably get back outside, anyway. My mom will be here soon."

"Bye," she said.

"Bye."

I hesitated, but there was nothing more to say. Nothing at all.

FIVE

Neologism

Bandersnatch."

It was Coco. "Excuse me?" It was Monday morning, and I was clutching a stack of *Cobblestone* magazines that Ms. Lawson asked me to organize for her. Her room was full of bookcases overloaded with books, the history and social studies books jammed together with the fiction.

"Bandersnatch. Ask me the definition."

"What's the definition?"

"It's from Lewis Carroll, and it's a grotesque and strange creature."

"Okay," I said. He was grinning, so I felt pretty sure he wasn't teasing me. But he had also called me grotesque and strange. Maybe.

"It was on the Scripps spelling list last year. More precisely, it was the word that my sister got wrong in the state spelling bee."

The girl who'd gone from our middle school the year before had been tall and willowy with bright blond hair. I hadn't realized she and Coco were related.

"I see," I said. Although I didn't.

"I thought I could help you study."

"Study?"

"For the spelling bee." He reached up and scratched behind his ear. The skin on his neck had started to flush.

"Oh," I said.

"If you want to, I can quiz you."

"I think I've got it." I spread the magazines out on a table in the back of Ms. Lawson's room. She let me come in here during study hall since she didn't have a class. Officially I was her student aide, but mostly it was just an escape. I wasn't sure how Coco knew to find me there.

"I helped my sister study."

"And she spelled 'bandersnatch' wrong."

Coco's skin turned pink starting at his cheeks and diving down to meet the red on his neck.

I kicked my boot into the floor. "Anyway, my mum is going to help me." She had about flipped when I'd told her that I had signed up for the spelling bee, and promised we could watch *Akeelah and the Bee* for inspiration as soon as she got home.

"Oh," Coco said. I didn't know someone could make such a little word sound so forlorn, like the sound of the lighthouse on one of these snowy winter nights.

"Except she's British, so sometimes she gets confused. Because, you know, some words are spelled differently. And she always says 'zed' for *Z*." I was babbling. Taryn Greenbottom never babbled. I clamped my mouth shut.

"British?"

I slid an issue from March on top of one from May. "Technically, yes. She's from Ireland, but Northern Ireland, and they're British, but she considers herself Irish. The whole island is smaller than Maine, and there are two different countries on it."

"I know. It's kind of like Hispaniola with Haiti and the Dominican Republic."

"Exactly."

"I like geography," he said.

"Me, too," I agreed.

"But not as much as spelling?"

"Not as much as spelling."

"Well, if you want help—"

"She'll help me," I said, too hastily.

"I could help you at school."

That actually sounded useful. Who knew when Mum would be home to study with me? And once she got home, she'd just be off again a few days later. "Don't you want to help Lucas?"

"Lucas?" Coco furrowed his brow.

"He's your friend, isn't he?"

"Not really. I mean, I like him fine, but I wouldn't call him a friend. Anyway, he's a genius. He doesn't need help."

"Oh." Another foghorn sound.

"I mean, you're smart, too," he said.

"I know."

"Okay," he said.

"Actually, maybe I could use help. My mum travels a lot. And since you have experience—"

"Emma did go out in the fourth round of the state tournament."

He was still smiling, so I smiled back. "I think we'll be okay."

"So," he said. "Your word is 'bandersnatch.'"

"Country of origin?" I asked. That was what the spellers always did on television. It drove me and Mum crazy because we knew they were just stalling. "Spell it or smell it," she would say, which didn't make much sense but always made me laugh.

"British, I think."

I took a deep breath. "Bandersnatch. *B-A-N-D-E-R-S-N-A-T-C-H*. Bandersnatch."

———◄○►———

Ugly books. That was about the only clue I had to go on. The book I found the note in was ugly, and the book Charlotte found her note in was so ugly that they were going to remove it from the library. Ugly like a bandersnatch. I pictured a grotesque figure with spiky horns and torn wings, sharp teeth and drooling mouth, hunched over an old book.

The conversation with Coco had been about the strangest I'd ever had. I'd thought about it all afternoon. He and I had barely spoken all year. In the fall we'd been paired up for an assignment in math—finding the area of irregular shapes—but that had only lasted for a period and I don't think we said much more to each other than "Draw a line there," and "I guess that gives us forty-seven." But now in two days he'd sought me out two times. He had probably realized that I had no friends and was trying to be nice. That was the kind of guy Coco was. With a guy like that, one who was nice to everyone, well, it hardly mattered if he was nice to you, too.

After school I went back to the library to search the stacks. This time I started at the end, in the 900s, which is the history section, pulling out the ugliest books I could find. Books with no dust jackets, books with hints of mold, books with renegade dust bunnies on them. Some of the dust bunnies were so big, they looked like they had grown teeth, which made me think of those stories where people have tumors in them and when they are pulled out, they have teeth and hair and sometimes even legs and hands. It's not like there was another person inside them—the tumor itself grows these extra bits.

Mum told me about those tumors—teratomas is what they're called—even though Mom said I had enough trouble

with my own imagination, and that I didn't need to have
gruesome reality added to it.

I shouldn't have said I would study with Coco. I was a
lone wolf prowling the halls of Frontenac Consolidated
Middle School until I could have an island in a lake just like
Harriet Wexler. I was as solo as Han Solo. I was a one-woman
band. I decided I would tell him the next day that I didn't
need his help, after all.

My fingers started to turn grayish brown from all the
dust, and I was beginning to doubt there were any more
clues to find. I'd pulled out seventy-three books before, in
the 821s, I picked out a book of poetry by someone named
J. Samuel Samuelson. When I flipped it open, I saw the telltale origami envelope.

I told my heart not to race. This could be as big a disappointment as the printer paper.

The envelope was wedged into the book, and it tore a
little and left a thin line of red behind when I pulled it out.
The origami paper was so dry, I was afraid it would disinte-
grate before I removed the note. But I got it, and pulled out the
index card. The same red seal with the sharp-beaked bird on
it. I'd really and truly found a second clue! I unfolded the card.
This one had a border made of stones that pressed against
one another. At the top was a drawing of a sculpture of a
man's head. Floating above the head was a golden crown. The
picture made me think of Charlotte, and the way she could
use her colored pencils to make her drawings alive. I read:

Our <u>Great King Ferdinand</u> joined the warring masses,
And to honor him we pass him as we run to all our classes.
But if you stop and listen to the marble man,
He will tell you where to look, ye miners with a pan.

"My <u>knight</u> in dingy armor
Move as by your plan,
Then by crook or <u>rook</u>
Straight as you can."

* * *

I understood the first part. Ferdinand Frontenac wasn't a king. He was a settler who united the British, French-Canadian, and American Indians on the peninsula. That was why the schools were named after him. Our mascot was the beaver because he traded their fur. There was a statue of him in the school. That had to be the marble man.

The rest was just gibberish. "Miners with a pan"? Like the gold rush? We studied that in fifth grade, and there was nothing that connected that to Ferdinand Frontenac. And the quote at the end: What could that possibly mean? It seemed like it was giving me a direction, like it was telling me to make a plan and keep going, straight and steady.

I had to remind myself that the notes weren't talking to me. I didn't know who they were talking to. They had to be for someone, didn't they? I wanted it to be me.

◄○►

Mum called us over the computer from Texas that night. She looked all grainy and jumpy on the screen. Behind her was a framed print of a cactus. It's funny how hotels don't change much from city to city, state to state: beige walls, white sheets, shiny desk. You've got to look for the little details to see the differences: a cactus print instead of a photograph of a skyscraper, pink coverlet instead of brown.

"I should be home tomorrow," she said. "As long as the weather holds there."

Mom and I were eating dinner while we talked with her. I wound the spaghetti around my fork. "Good."

"We can study for the bee."

"I've started," I confessed. "There's this boy, Coco, at school who is going to help me."

Mom's eyebrows jumped up her forehead like jacks out of boxes.

"And I can help you." The connection made Mum's accent harder to understand. It almost sounded like she said "An I can't help ye."

My mouth was full of spaghetti, so I nodded eagerly. I didn't want Mum to think that studying with Coco meant I didn't trust her to help me. Swallowing, I said, "I've got the Spell It! study site bookmarked on the computer."

"Let me know as soon as your flight is confirmed," Mom said. "I'm on call tomorrow. We need to make plans for Ruth."

"I'm fine here by myself," I said.

They didn't even bother to answer.

"I think we're looking at another snow day," Mom said.

"Here's hoping I get back in time to enjoy it. Maybe we can go snowshoeing."

"Did you know that in Africa, girls are getting married by my age? They run their own households," I informed them.

"Africa is not a country," Mom said. "And every country is different. But in the countries where girls marry young, they usually become part of a larger family unit, with older women to help guide them. No one your age is running a family."

I wondered if that was true, absolutely. Somewhere, somehow, there was a girl my age on her own and looking out for a family. "All I'm saying is that you can leave me alone for a night. I'll be sleeping. What can happen to me when I'm sleeping?"

Mom looked at Mum on the computer screen. "Not up for discussion," she said. "Why are you bringing up Africa, anyway?"

"We're starting the unit on Africa in humanities. Today we went over the map."

Mom's face lit up. "Did you talk about Côte d'Ivoire?"

"Not yet."

"Tell Ms. Lawson I can come in and talk about it. I can do a slide show. You know that's actually part of the mandate of the Peace Corps—to share the foreign culture with Americans. In fact, I'll just e-mail her myself."

"When?"

"Tonight after dinner."

"No. When are you going to have time to come in and talk to the class about the Ivory Coast?"

"I'm sure we can work out a time," Mom says. She slid a meatball to the side of her plate, then used her fork to cut it in half. "This is a big unit, isn't it?"

"Most of the trimester."

"Then we'll surely find the time."

"Tell them about the guinea worms!" Mum said.

"The point is not to gross them out," Mom replied. "I want them to see what a beautiful country it is."

"The guinea worms will hook them, though. Ha, hook them!"

Guinea worms are long, thin worms that get inside you and lay their eggs. Their eggs. Inside you. Then, when the egg hatches, the worm has to get out. So it works its way out of your skin, usually on your leg. The place where it comes out gets big and red and swollen and painful. But you can't just yank the worm out, because then it might break and burrow back into your flesh. No, you have to pull it out a centimeter each day, and wrap it around a toothpick that you bandage to your leg.

I pushed my spaghetti away.

"You've got to know your audience," Mum said. She winked at me. Or maybe it was just a flicker of the screen. Sometimes I pretended she was a robot version of my mum, and these little tics were glitches in the system.

"I think I have photographs in the attic. I'll have to scan them."

"Ms. Lawson may not want you to come."

"Of course she will. I have firsthand experience."

Mum bore her gaze into me across the miles. "It won't do any harm to ask," she said.

No harm.

Mom reached over to the computer. "I love you, honey," she said. "We've got to clean up from dinner, and I want to send that e-mail."

"Love you both," Mum replied.

"Good night," I said, but Mom had already clicked on the red hang-up icon and was opening her e-mail.

The one good thing about her fixating on coming into my class to speak was that it made her forget my mentioning Coco. That was a close one. In fact, just to make sure I escaped a third-degree grilling on the Mom-B-Que, I grabbed my plate and glass, popped them into the dishwasher, and said, "Off to study science."

"Mmm-hmm," Mom said.

"I have to memorize the classification system."

"Sounds lovely."

"Good dinner," I told her.

"Thank you," she replied, her gaze trained on the screen.

I backed out of the room just to keep an eye on her. She was a fast one, that Mom, and I wanted to be ready to sprint should she look up at me with those inquisitive eyes.

SIX

Chauvinism

Ms. Broadcheck came tumbling into homeroom with a stack of papers. "Everyone has to take the test!" she announced. "The spelling test. The spelling test." She shook off her coat. "I'm sorry I'm late. My dog pooped in my shoes. Not these shoes, of course. My other shoes."

Melinda wrinkled her nose. "In them or on them?"

"In them, on them, around them. But we don't have time to talk about my dog's gastrointestinal distress. Not enough kids signed up for the spelling bee, and we think there might be some secret spellers lurking about, so everyone takes the qualifying test. The top four for each grade will compete in the school bee."

Secret spellers. Each night they tucked themselves away

in their attics spelling words like "hibachi," "begonia," and "hoomalimali." Maybe they were the smart ones. Maybe I should remain a secret speller, too.

"Do I have to take the test?" Lucas asked.

"Everyone has to take the test," Ms. Broadcheck answered.

"But everyone knows I will own them. I will rule the spelling bee. This is a waste of my time." I didn't want to be like Lucas—known for the wrong reasons. Better to be unknown.

"You *don't* know that, actually, Lucas. Which is what I said during the faculty meeting when some teachers thought it was unfair to change how we qualified students for this. I think it's unfair that some of you might not even know you're good at this. This might be fun for some of you and you don't even know it. Like, well, sometimes I wonder if maybe I was destined to be an Olympic athlete but just never found it. Like maybe I am a world-class luger. Or curler. And I just never got the opportunity. Well, one of you might be a world-class spelling bee-er, and here is your chance to be discovered."

"I don't want to be discovered. You can't force us to be in some lame-o spelling bee," Melinda said.

But then, Melinda thought she knew me, didn't she? Better to be known the way you wanted to be known than the way someone like Melinda decided you were. I wouldn't allow myself the fantasy of a total shift—my classmates lifting me up on their shoulders in victory—but maybe it would afford me a modicum of respect. ("Modicum" was one of Mum's favorite spelling words—such a big word for something small.) There was some honor in being good at something.

Ms. Broadcheck sighed as she placed a sheet of paper in front of each of us. "No one is going to force you to be in the competition. Should you prove to have one of the top four scores, you may abdicate."

I didn't think anyone was too concerned about Melinda having one of the top four scores.

"Abdicate. *A-B-D-I-C-A-T-E.* Abdicate," Lucas said. "It can also mean 'to disown,' like giving up a child."

"Interesting, but not relevant, Lucas," Ms. Broadcheck said. "Come on, now, we don't have much time."

Ms. Broadcheck read each word and gave the definition from Webster's dictionary, the official dictionary of the Scripps National Spelling Bee, and we wrote them on our papers. "'Trajectory.' 'The curved path along which something— such as a rocket—moves through the air or through space.'" Pencils scratched across the paper. This one was easy. "'Ninja.' 'A person trained in ancient Japanese martial arts and employed especially for espionage and assassinations.'"

"Can you repeat the word?" Lucas asked.

"It's 'ninja,' Lucas."

"That's right. I'm the spelling ninja! I will assassinate you with my skills."

"We don't have time for outbursts. You're going to be

late for first period. The next word is 'inane.' 'Empty, insubstantial.' Secondary definition: 'lacking significance, meaning, or point; silly.'"

"This test is inane," Melinda said.

"No. More. Outbursts."

We went on and on. Forty words in all. My hand was tired by the end of it. I checked over my sheet. There were only two that I was uncertain about: "mammoth" (*is there a double* m *in the middle?*) and "adamant" (*or "-ment" or "-mint"?*), but I still thought I'd done a good job. Good enough to be in the top four, I hoped. It would be mortifying to be cut before the bee even happened. Mum would be so disappointed. She'd e-mailed me that she had printed out lists of words and we were going to start studying that night when she got home.

I handed my sheet to Ms. Broadcheck, who took it with a wide smile. "Chin up, Ruth, honey. You're going to be fine."

Ms. Broadcheck shouldn't make offhand comments like that. They feel like promises, but there's no way to keep them.

———◇———

Some kids hate gym class, but I'm pretty fast and can actually throw a ball, so I didn't mind as long as we weren't playing volleyball, a game invented with the sole purpose of torturing schoolchildren. It was the locker room that I hated. At Frontenac Consolidated Middle School, the locker room is a really an oversized hallway that's divided by a bank of lockers.

Getting ready, you have to rush because the boys walk through the girls' locker room to get upstairs. They're supposed to wait before they come in, but sometimes they forget. I always tried to get a locker on the side behind the bank of lockers. Trouble is, so did all the other girls. We were all rush, rush, rush as we got ready to go up to the gym. But after class, once the boys passed through and Ms. Wickersham was back in her office, all bets were off.

All the other girls wore bras. Even Lena, who had nothing much that needed to be supported. Even Charlotte, who was smaller. But I didn't.

"Is it true that your moms won't let you get a bra?" Melinda asked me.

I glanced at Charlotte. She dug in her locker for her deodorant.

I pulled my undershirt on over my head. "No," I said. "That's not true."

"Huh," Melinda replied. She made a big show of adjusting the lace on the edge of her bra. It had to be padded. Charlotte shimmied into her shirt. "So it's your choice, then?" Melinda asked me.

"Yes," I told her.

"Huh," Melinda said again. "You know that's weird, right?"

I pulled my turtleneck on. "I don't need a bra. Half the girls in this room don't need a bra."

"Do you hear that?" Melinda asked. "Ruth just called half of you flat-chested."

"I did not—"

"You said half of them don't need bras. It's the same thing. Right, Char?"

"Right," Charlotte agreed. If she had hesitated, I might have been able to forgive her. And then maybe I wouldn't have said what I said next. But she didn't, and I did.

"Charlotte doesn't need a bra, that's for sure," I said. "She was thinking of stuffing with cotton balls before we started middle school, but I talked her out of it."

"Ruth!" Charlotte cried.

I narrowed my eyes at her.

"Ruth," she said again, her voice softer. "Tell the truth."

"Are you lying about Charlotte?" Melinda asked. "You really are a jerk, aren't you?"

I tugged my hair into a ponytail—loose and low, not high and mighty like Melinda's—and grabbed my bag out of the locker. I was not going to say anything else. Not one word more.

SEVEN

Serendipity

Ms. Broadcheck had a new winter coat. It was white-and-black houndstooth, and she tied it tightly up above her belly. I wondered if she knew that wasn't where belts go. It was a very fashionable coat, but she wore it with L.L.Bean boots, the kind with green rubber bottoms and leather up top.

She shook it off and underneath she was wearing a dress. Ms. Broadcheck almost never wore dresses. This one had a belt above her belly, too. So odd. She started digging through her tote bags. She always carried at least three. "I know I put them in here," she mumbled. We all watched her, this swirl of kinetic energy. She lifted books from the tote bags. Books we might like to read, like *The Westing*

Game and *A Wrinkle in Time* and *Hatchet*, and even a book by Harriet Wexler, which wasn't my favorite one, but still good. Then she started taking out books with boring titles like *Reaching Every Child* and *Your Student, Your Task*. All the while she repeated, "Where are they? Where are they?"

Finally, Charlotte spoke. "Do you need some help, Ms. Broadcheck?"

Ms. Broadcheck looked up like she forgot we were there. "Help? Oh, no, Charlotte. I just packed my shoes to wear today, and I can't seem to find them."

"The shoes your dog pooped in?" Melinda asked.

"Why, yes, actually, though of course they've had a thorough cleaning."

Melinda still wrinkled her nose.

"They're my favorite non-clog shoes," Ms. Broadcheck went on. "And now it seems I'm stuck wearing this dress with these old boots of my husband's."

"You have a husband?" Lucas asked.

"Lucas," Melinda cooed. "That's not the kind of question you ask."

"Why not?"

"Yes, I have a husband. You know, when I was in college, the fashionable girls wore these boots. Not the girls who all dressed the same, mind you, the ones with their own sense of style. Like Lena."

Lena herself wore ballet shoes. Not ballet flats, which Charlotte taught me is the name for dress shoes without a heel with a round toe, but actual pink ballet shoes. "I can dig it, Ms. Broadcheck," she said. "You've got to loosen them up, though." She walked over to Ms. Broadcheck. "Unlace them and pull them loose and then let the laces hang down." I wondered if Lena would tell her to slide her belt down, too.

"They're already two sizes too big, Lena," Ms. Broadcheck said. "I only grabbed them because I couldn't find my own boots. And because I was sure I packed those shoes." She dropped down into her chair. "Oh, well, it is what it is."

"Who are you married to?" Lucas asked.

"Mr. Broadcheck, duh," said Mitchell. I liked Mitchell better when he wasn't adorable.

"Actually, his name is Mr. Kendall. I kept my name."

"You could have been Kendall and you kept Broadcheck?" Melinda asked. "Why?"

"I suppose because I've always been Simone Broadcheck. I'm not sure who Simone Kendall would be."

"She sounds glamorous," said Melinda. "I'm going to marry someone whose last name starts with *M*. So I can be Melinda *M*-something. Like Melinda Mitchell."

"That's my first name," Mitchell said.

"I wasn't talking about you," Melinda said. But she giggled. And he smiled. And Charlotte looked away.

"Anyway," Ms. Broadcheck said. "Marriage is not the planned topic of discussion for this morning." She pulled a piece of paper from her desk and shook it dramatically. "The spelling bee qualifying results!"

I wrapped my hands around my Harriet Wexler book as tightly as Taryn held her sword.

"Though of course I had no part in the outcome, it still makes me very proud to say that three out of the four sixth-grade finalists for the spelling bee come from this very homeroom."

Melinda gave three slow claps. Ms. Broadcheck ignored her. "A drumroll, please." Lena slapped her hands on the table. "In first place in the sixth grade, we have Mr. Lucas Hosgrove."

"Own it!" he exclaimed.

"In second place, our very own Ms. Ruth Mudd-O'Flanahan."

I smiled, but I also tried to wrestle it down, so it probably looked like some weird, twisted scribble of lips. I just didn't want Melinda to see that it mattered to me. Lena said, "All right, Ruthy!" No one ever called me Ruthy.

"And in third place, Dev Gupta, who is, of course, not in this homeroom, but whom we will support nonetheless. And finally . . ."

Lena banged her hands like crazy. I didn't care who it was. I could take anyone else in this homeroom. Lucas was the one I really needed to worry about.

"Ms. Charlotte Diamond!"

Our reactions were right across our faces. Charlotte's mouth in an open O. Melinda smirking. Me, I'm sure my jaw dropped and my eyebrows went up. I snapped my mouth shut right away, but I knew Melinda and Charlotte saw. Melinda saw everything.

It's okay, I told myself. *It's okay because Charlotte is not going to do it. She won't do anything that Melinda deems dorky.*

"Ms. Broadcheck," Charlotte said, her voice quavering. I let out my breath. One competitor down. I knew it was not the spirit of good sportsmanship to win by abdication. Mum, whose flight had been canceled due to an engine malfunction, would be disappointed in me if she could read my thoughts from hundred of miles away. But it wasn't like Charlotte would have been a real competitor, unless she got some easy words and I got hard ones. Eliminating her was eliminating the luck factor.

"We're going to need a copy of that word list," Melinda interrupted. "We have some studying to do."

My head swiveled on my neck like the Tin Woodman. Melinda was going to coach Charlotte?

"Oh, actually—" Charlotte began, still trying to quit.

"You are going to rock this spelling bee, Charlotte. It's going to be awesome. I mean, you live in a library, right? You will be the prettiest girl to ever win a spelling bee."

"Right," Charlotte agreed, and then, more sturdily: "Where can we get the list?"

———◦———

Coco and I were going to meet at the library to study during study hall, but now that Dev was in the spelling bee, I figured that was off. So I stayed in Ms. Lawson's room to help her arrange her bookshelves, theoretically. Actually, I was curled up on Ms. Lawson's ratty old couch reading more Harriet Wexler while Ms. Lawson graded papers at her desk. She had very short hair that was gray and black, or salt and pepper as Mom would say, which always made my mouth feel furry. She held a red pen in her left hand—she once said that the move away from red-penned correcting was the first sign in the decline of public education—and wrote with firm pressure on our papers, frequently shaking her head from side to side.

Taryn had left the lovelorn Benedict at the edge of the Forest of Westbegotten and had just entered the woods. The woods were not so bad in the daytime, but still she kept her hand on the hilt of her sword. As she walked, she heard footsteps behind her, but every time she paused to look, they were silenced and she saw no one. She told herself it was just an echo or a trick of the mind. Walk. Footsteps. Nothing. Walk. Footsteps. Nothing.

"There you are!"

My legs shot out in front of me.

Coco.

"I was waiting in the library for you. Did you forget?"

"No, I just thought that since Dev was in the bee now, you wouldn't want to help me."

"Why not? I said I would."

"But that was before he qualified."

Coco gave a half shrug. "Adam will help him."

I raised my eyebrows. "Adam?"

"It'll be good for them. Anyway, I'm backing the winner."

Ms. Lawson gathered her papers in her hands and tapped them on her desk. "I agree, Ruth," she said. "With Coco helping you, this could be an unbeatable team."

"See?" Coco said.

"Though I'm a little surprised you didn't qualify yourself, Coco."

Coco's cheeks burned. "I guess spelling isn't genetic, after all."

"Maybe not." Ms. Lawson pursed her lips. "Some of the words you got wrong on the test, though?" she prompted.

"I guess I got confused. Nervous. I got nervous and that's why I wouldn't be good at the bee."

Ms. Lawson stood up. "My room is open to you as long as you want to study. I'll be in the teachers' room if anyone needs me."

"I'm not a shoo-in," I said as soon as Ms. Lawson was out of the room.

He put up his hands. "Don't tell me that Lucas is going to win. Step one is to banish that attitude."

"If he's seen a word, he knows it. And we have the list, so he will have seen all the words."

"Everyone makes mistakes." He held up the printout of the study words. "These words are just the start. The final list may contain words that aren't here."

"I know."

"This is probably a better place to meet, anyway. You want to be able to practice projecting. Let's get started."

"Are you really sure about this? I don't want you to lose your friend."

Coco smiled. "Dev wouldn't ditch me over this."

"And you really think Adam will help him? I mean, the other day at lunch, about the time stop thing—"

Coco shook his head. "Dev's still upset about Brain Camp. He really wanted to go, but his parents wouldn't let him. That's where I first met Adam, in that science-fiction class. I actually signed up for one on anatomy, but that one was filled up. Anyway, my mom says that Dev is confusing the two—he's mad at Adam because he's mad about Brain Camp."

"What do you think?" I asked. I wondered if Alan and Eliot were giving Charlotte some silly story like that about me.

He shrugged. "Dev and I go way back. Adam, my help-ing you with spelling, none of that's going to change our friendship. I mean, we were friends in preschool."

"So were Charlotte and I," I said.

"Charlotte Diamond? Really?"

"What's the first word?"

"Um, how about 'aviary'?"

"Okay. A-V—"

"No!" Coco shook his head, the flop of hair swinging from side to side. "You have to say the word first."

"You don't actually," I told him. "Not at the local level, anyway."

"But you will when you make it to the Scripps Spelling Bee. And, anyway, if you've heard the word wrong, the judges can correct you before you start to spell."

I liked how sure he was that I would not only win our school bee but also make it all the way to Scripps. "Okay, I guess. Aviary. A-V-I-A-R-Y. Aviary."

"You need to ask for the definition or country of origin, too."

"Did I get it right?"

"Sure, but you should still ask."

"Why?"

"Because you might think you know, but not really know."

"That's just stalling."

He shook his head. "Country of origin is really useful. It helps you know the root words."

I frowned.

"If this were a sports movie, I'd say, 'It's my way or the highway!' you know. I'd be the crusty old coach pulled out of retirement, and you'd be the young whippersnapper with an attitude, and I'd train you into shape, and you'd make me realize that my heart wasn't so hard, after all."

"Wow. That was detailed."

"My dad likes sports movies. A lot."

"Does he know you're coaching me and not your sister?" I had seen the final list, and Emma was one of the eighth graders to qualify.

He checked the list. "Your next word is 'alabaster.'"

"Alabaster," I began. Then I stopped myself from spelling it. "Country of origin?" I asked.

He told me Middle English.

"Alabaster. *A-L-A-B-A-S-T-E-R*. Alabaster."

"Great!"

We went through a dozen more words. I didn't get any wrong. "You're really good at this."

"The practice still helps."

He glanced down at my book. "Harriet Wexler. She writes all those fantasy books, right?"

"It's more than just fantasy," I told him.

"What do you mean?"

"A lot of fantasy is about the world and the creatures and all that. But her worlds are simple. It's the characters that are complicated."

"I see," he said. And I thought that maybe he did, which was refreshing. Charlotte had once said, "I don't get it. An elf and a human had a baby? How is that even possible?"

I went on: "I think maybe it's more like the quest. The adventure. I don't know, they just make you think, think about what you would do, what your quest would be."

"Do people go on quests anymore?"

I wished we did, but he was right. "That's why you need to read about them. It's the same as a series like Andromeda Rex. I mean, it's not like you really think you're going to have a world with time stops and teleporting through wormholes and all that, right?"

"Well, that's science fiction," he said.

"But they're both fiction. They make you think about things, but they aren't actually real."

"But science fiction *could* be real."

"Maybe. But the authors are just guessing, don't you think? No one knows what's really going to happen in the future."

He pushed his floppy hair out of his eyes. "Adam and Dev and those guys don't really talk about books like this. They just talk about what's cool and how they would rule the world if they could stop time or time travel. Adam read *When You Reach Me* and all he could say in the end was that if he figured out how to go back in time, he would bet on all the World Series games."

"I don't know Adam very well, but he seems pretty financially oriented."

Coco laughed. "You could say that. Anyway, it's nice talking to you about books. Maybe I could borrow one of those Harriet Wexler books sometime."

"This one?" I asked.

"Maybe when you're done—"

"'Cause I got this one from Eliot—Mr. Diamond—at the library. It hasn't even come out yet."

"I thought you might have others at home."

"I do."

"Okay."

"Oh!" I said, feeling like a dunce. "Well, sure, I could bring you one. What one do you think you would like? The Taryn Greenbottom series is the best, but some people like *A River Slowly* better. That's a stand-alone book, and it's more science fiction. It's about time travel, too. You might like that one."

"Whichever. They both sound good."

"Okay."

"Okay."

"Do you like riddles?" I asked. I didn't know why. I had no intention of telling anyone else about the notes in the books.

"Sometimes. I don't like dumb riddles like that one about a stranger coming to the door asking for food and you have peanut butter, tuna, and pickles. What do you open first?"

"The door," I replied.

He grinned. "Of course you got it! I said pickles because you could give the strangers a pickle while you tried to figure out what to give him for a real meal."

"I didn't mean that kind of riddle."

"What kind did you mean?"

"Nothing," I said. I pointed at the book cover. "It's just that this book is called *The Riddled Cottage*, and it got me thinking about riddles. We should get back to studying."

He stared right in my face for a minute, and I wondered

if he could tell I was lying. Not lying, exactly. I had started down one path and then made a right turn. My riddles. My mystery.

"'Didgeridoo.'"

"What?"

"An aboriginal wind instrument from Australia."

"Is that on the list?"

"No. I just like it."

"Are there any alternate pronunciations?"

"I don't think so, no."

"*D-I-D-G-E-E-R-I-D-O-O.*"

"Ha! Stumped you!"

"Is that the old, crusty coach coming through?"

"Nah." He smiled. "I just wanted to make sure you weren't totally perfect."

He smiled at me again and so I smiled back.

And then the bell rang.

———◄○►———

The next afternoon, when I returned to Ms. Lawson's room for the spelling bee participants' meeting, the four eighth graders had already claimed the couch. Coco's sister, Emma, sat to the far left, twirling her blond hair in her fingers and occasionally sucking on the ends. I didn't have any friends there, of course, so I took a seat next to Dev. He had a notebook in front of him with the words "spelling bee" written in straight, square letters. He bounced his pen on the paper,

making the button on the end click, click, click like a playing card in the spokes of a bicycle wheel. I imagined the
letters were little soldiers marching to this furious beat.

"So," Dev said, but then his voice trailed off. It was like he
knew he should say something to me, but didn't know what.
Was he angry, I wondered, that Coco was working with me?

"So," I said back. "Do you watch the bee?"

He hesitated. "Well, yes, I went with—I mean, wait, do
you mean the county bee? Or the one on television?"

"The one on television. The Scripps National Spelling
Bee."

He shook his head. "I never expected to be here," he
told me. "I don't actually know what I'm doing here at all."

"Secret speller," I murmured.

"What?"

"Nothing. Just something Ms. Broadcheck said. About
secret spellers. It doesn't matter."

Dev nodded, though, as if he understood. "When Ms.
Lawson said we had to take this test, I figured Coco would
be here."

"Because of his sister?" I prompted.

"Sure, I guess. And his brother, Clint. But more just him.
You know, Coco."

I didn't really know Coco, but I supposed it didn't surprise me that he'd be expected to do well on the test. He
was probably the smartest boy in our grade. Smartest after
Lucas, anyway, who at that moment was crouched on the

chair of one of Ms. Lawson's chair-desks reading a graphic novel about Zeus and biting his fingernails.

As if he could sense me looking at him, he raised his eyes to look at me. "I'm going to write my own graphic novel of Greek mythology. I'm just checking out the competition." Then he ducked his head again. I heard a snicker from a seventh-grade boy who was so big, his legs stretched way out into the aisle in front of him.

Dev placed his pen down in the center of his notebook. "Last year I went with him to watch Emma, and he was right next to me writing the words down in a book for her. Only he wrote them before the spellers said them. And he got them all right. Every single one. So how come he isn't here?"

I didn't have a chance to ponder the question. Dr. Dawes, our principal, and Ms. Lawson came into the room together. Ms. Lawson carried a stack of papers. As she began passing them around, I realized Charlotte wasn't there. So maybe she had dropped out, after all. Good.

"Welcome, spellers!" Dr. Dawes exclaimed. "This is going to be an exciting few weeks for you!"

I don't know if she expected us to break into applause or war whoops of excitement, but we remained silent. The big seventh grader—Max, I think that was his name—scuffed his work boot against the floor. That was about it.

The door opened, and there was Charlotte, small and tentative. She surveyed the room. There were two open seats in the circle that Ms. Lawson had created. One next to me.

One next to Lucas. I saw her weighing her options. Her gaze drifted over to the couch. She was small. She might be able to fit there. If they let her in. She took a deep breath and then slid into the desk next to mine. I guess that meant I was the lesser of two evils.

"Hi," I whispered.

"Hi," she whispered back.

And suddenly my mind exploded with a new vision, warm and familiar as the summer sun down by the water, racing together toward the ice-cream stand. Charlotte and I could do this together. We could quiz each other. I could teach her the tricks I had learned from years of watching the bees on television. She would help me to be more poised in front of the crowd. I could practically feel our shoulders pressed together as we studied the word list, her long black hair falling down toward the paper. And when we weren't studying, we'd be chasing the clues in the books. She was curious. She had to be. It wouldn't be like old times. Not exactly. But maybe it could even be better.

Ms. Lawson put a packet down on Charlotte's desk. "Sorry I was late," Charlotte said.

Ms. Lawson just nodded.

Dr. Dawes explained how the school bee would work. It would be a morning assembly, which made Maybe-Max groan, and ask, "Really?"

"Yes, really."

Dev wrote the words "school assembly" in his notebook.

Then, underneath, he wrote: "Wear tie." His pen hesitated over his paper before he added: "Ask Adam how to tie a tie?" Then he crossed that last bit out with a single straight line.

"In your packet you'll find all the rules of a spelling bee," Ms. Lawson said. "I will be the head judge, and as you all know, I am a stickler, so make sure you know those rules. I am fond of you all, of course, but I'm not going to bend the regulations for you. No mumbling. No backtracking. No corrections. Got it?"

We nodded. Dev wrote down: "Read all rules. Follow precisely."

"What if we run out of words?" Lucas asked.

"Wouldn't that be wonderful!" Dr. Dawes said cheerfully. "But I don't think you need to worry about that. The list is quite long."

"It happened," Lucas said. "In Kansas. At a county bee. They went through so many rounds, they used up all the words the spelling bee people had sent them, and then they went to the dictionary. And it went on so long that they sent everyone home and had to finish it another day."

"I suppose we'll tackle that problem if we come to it," Ms. Lawson said.

"I just think you should have a contingency plan in place. I know a lot of words." He pushed his glasses onto his face with the heel of his hand. "Then again, what am I saying? I could spell all day. The question is, can any of these people keep up with me? And the answer is, I think not."

"Lucas," Ms. Lawson said.

"Humility," Lucas mumbled back to her without much conviction.

Charlotte played with the staple in her packet, wiggling it back and forth like a loose tooth. We could study in the library, I decided, after school. I went there most every day anyway to wait for my mom. And of course that would give us plenty of time to look for clues, too. And it would mean she wouldn't have to give up any time with Melinda, though I hoped—well, it was too much to hope, wasn't it, that she would give up Melinda altogether.

Dr. Dawes and Ms. Lawson explained some more about the bee and the best ways to study. Dev wrote it all down in his neat handwriting, and I did feel a little bad for stealing away the person who could really help him. Maybe if things were going well with Charlotte, I could tell Coco that he should go help Dev, after all.

When they finished, I reached down to pick up my backpack, then turned to ask Charlotte if she wanted to meet me at the library to study, but she was already hustling to the door. She had left her packet on the desk, though, so I wrote her name on it. I started to put it into my bag to give to her in homeroom, but Ms. Lawson saw and said, "Thanks, Ruth. I'll make sure Charlotte gets that tomorrow."

"Okay," I said. "That's probably for the best."

I walked out of the room as solo as I had come in.

EIGHT

Behoove

Friday in the locker room, Lena wasn't wearing a bra. She flipped off her T-shirt for gym class—it was an old one with a faded Wild Thing doing the Wild Rumpus on it—and pulled on a shirt and then a sweater. Melinda noticed. She wrinkled her nose, that's how I knew. But she didn't say anything.

"You didn't have to do that," I said to her in the hall.

"Melinda is a witch," Lena said. "She's a witch and the word that rhymes with it."

"'Twitch'?" I asked.

Lena raised her eyebrows as if she had misjudged me, and then saw that I was joking. "Actually, I was thinking 'stitch,'" she said.

"Or 'switch.'"

"'Fibbledegitch.'" She grinned.

"Still, you didn't have to do it for me."

"Maybe I didn't do it for you."

"Oh," I said. And blushed.

"Or maybe I did," she said back. She was smiling. She didn't make any sense at all. "You know, women used to burn their bras for women's rights."

"I know," I said.

Lena put her hand up in the air. "Solidarity, sister."

Somehow I didn't think our not wearing bras was going to bring down the tyranny of Melinda. Lena wrapped a silk scarf around her neck and tied it in a big, beautiful bow all while we walked to our lockers.

I jammed my bag into the narrow metal space and took out my lunch in its insulated bag from L.L.Bean. I had to beg Mom not to get it monogrammed with my name. Lena had her lunch in a hand-sewn fabric bag. I went to my usual table and she sat down next to me. I guessed it was my turn in the rotation of where she sat.

Coco glanced over at us from his table with the boys.

"Who do you think the cutest boy in sixth grade is?" Lena asked me.

Well, that was an abrupt disappointment.

"What?" she asked.

"All this boy-girl stuff."

"I think it's Coco. Don't you?"

I glanced at Coco. He had warm brown eyes, and I thought his hair would be soft to touch.

"I don't know," I said.

"And I think Charlotte is the cutest girl. She must be like a million times cute, because she's next to Melinda all the time and that makes anyone look ugly."

"She's not that cute," I said.

"You guys used to be friends, right?" Lena asked.

"Sure," I said. "I guess. My moms and her dads are friends."

She nods. "I shouldn't have asked that. About the cute boys. I don't have a lot of girlfriends. I have three older sisters. Twins and one in between them and me. They talk about boys all the time. I guess I thought that's what we're supposed to talk about."

This raised a million questions in my head: Who are your friends? Where are they? Are we friends? "What do you want to talk about?" I asked her.

"What are you eating?" she asked.

"Peanut butter and Fluff," I said, wishing this had been another chutney and cheddar day. Lena's was in a little tin bowl and I couldn't quite tell what it was. It looked lumpy and not at all appetizing. "You?"

"Chicken garam masala. I got the recipe from Dev's mom, but I don't think I made it right. I didn't have all the spices she put down, so I had to improvise, like on those cooking shows."

"You made it yourself?"

"My sister Vera helped. I like to cook, but she actually

wants to be a chef. Well, actually, she wants to be a restaurateur. I don't think restaurateurs actually cook. She says when she gets older she's going to turn the Salt and Sea Shack into a real nice sit-down restaurant."

"I love the Salt and Sea Shack!" I exclaimed. It was out by the piers and you could get the best fried clams and milk shakes.

Lena rolled her eyes. "You and every yokel who makes his way up the coast."

I reddened.

She didn't seem to notice. "You'd feel differently if your whole house smelled like oil and sour clams."

"Your family owns the Salt and Sea Shack?"

"Third generation," she said. She twisted her hair and the streak of red flashed for a moment.

"I like the red in your hair," I told her.

"It's a compromise," she replied, letting her hair fall back down. "It's all my mom would let me do. I wanted to dye the ends red all around, red and orange so it would look like coal on fire."

"That's what I thought when I saw it!" I said. "Like it was a log in a fire, only you can't see that it's still hot until you turn it over."

"A secret fire? I kind of like that." She smiled to herself. "Coco's watching you."

"What?"

"Don't look. He stopped watching."

"He's helping me with the spelling bee. He probably just wants to know if we're going to practice today."

"Are you?"

I shook my head. "I want to get that science homework done before the weekend."

"Wanna do it together during study hall?" She paused. "Are you in study hall?"

"I usually go to Ms. Lawson's room. I'm her student aide."

"What does that mean?"

"I help her out." I poked at my half-eaten sandwich. "Though really most of the time I just read."

"Cool. So, do you?"

"Do I what?"

"Want to work on the science together?"

I hesitated. I don't like working with other kids on schoolwork, because, frankly, they are usually just too slow. And, anyway, this entire conversation had been utterly perplexing. Half the time she was being nice, and the other half she seemed to be insulting me. "Maybe."

"Hey, it's no great shakes or anything. I was just asking."

"No, we can. I just need to tell Coco."

"So go tell him."

"Right now?"

"Yes, right now. But first wipe the peanut butter off your face."

————◁◦▷————

Coco, Adam, and Dev were huddled around something in the center of their table. When I got closer, it just seemed to be a plain plastic cup of water, about half-empty. Coco lifted his head and looked up at me through his brown hair. A grin spread on his face, and I was afraid I was about to be asked to settle another bet. "Ruth!" he said. "Hi!"

"Hi," I said. He kept staring up at me and I realized that it was still my turn to talk. "I, um, I came to say I can't study for the spelling bee today."

"Oh," he said. The smile faltered.

"Tomorrow I can."

"Tomorrow is Saturday," Adam said.

"Right. Monday, then."

Coco stared at the cup of water.

"Yeah, Lena wants me to help her—I mean, Lena and I are going to do the science homework together."

Coco picked up a packet of salt, ripped open the top, and dumped it on the table. "Well, that makes sense."

"If you're looking for someone to study words with—" Dev began.

"What are you doing?" I interrupted.

"I'm going to balance this cup on its edge." Coco's eyes were focused on the cup, and his hands hovered just beside it.

"We're each going to give him a dollar if he can," Adam said. "And if he can't, he has to give each of us a dollar. You want in?"

I shook my head. Looking back over my shoulder, I saw

Lena. She leaned her elbows on the table with her chin in her hand and was watching the whole thing like it was a silent movie.

Coco took the cup and tilted it on its side so the water nearly touched the lip, then placed it down in the pile of salt. Slowly, like how we approached our old cat, Webster, when it was time to take him to the vet, he removed his hand from the cup. It held still on its edge. He leaned forward, pursed his lips, and blew the salt away. The cup didn't move at all.

He held his hands above his head. "That's a dollar from each of you!" he exclaimed. Then he looked up at me. "Smart move not betting against me!" His smile stretched from ear to ear.

"How'd you do that?" I asked.

"A magician never reveals his tricks."

"It's not magic; it's science," Dev mumbled.

"Either way, it's my trick," Coco said, then turned to me. "But I'll tell you if you win the spelling bee."

"Okay."

Lena was still watching us. It was a good thing she couldn't hear me and my dopey reactions.

"We could all do science together," Coco said.

"Well, I—"

"I thought we were going to work on that together," Adam said.

"We are," Coco said. "With Ruth and Lena. Right, Ruth?"

"Right," I agreed.

"Great!" he said. "See you in study hall, then."

He looked back at the cup, which was still balanced on its edge like the Leaning Tower of Pisa. I guessed that meant we were done, so I started backing away. When I was a few steps back, I said "Bye" in a soft voice, then spun and strode back toward Lena, who seemed as pleased with the whole interaction as Coco was with his cup.

NINE

Metamorphosis

Mum was supposed to be home for twenty-four hours that weekend, but they were forecasting more snow, so she flew from Texas to Seattle for her next appointment. Once Charlotte asked me, "What exactly does your mum do, anyway?"

I didn't really have an answer. As far as I could tell, she went to conferences and trade shows and taught people how to use software in order to sell it to them, and then went to their business or wherever and taught them how to use it some more. Sales and training is what she called it.

Evidently, whatever it was she sold was not needed on the coast of Maine.

Mom tried to overcompensate. I woke up Saturday morning and smelled pancakes. Not just pancakes, but blueberry pancakes made with blueberries we'd picked over the summer and frozen. There was bacon, too, from pigs raised on Swift Island, and orange juice and hot chocolate with whipped cream. "Wow," I said when I shuffled downstairs.

"I was just feeling a little festive this morning," she said.

She dropped three pancakes onto a plate and made a frame of bacon around it. She put it in front of me with a flourish. I doused it with maple syrup and started eating.

I was about a third of the way through the second pancake, my mouth full, when she cleared her throat. "There's something I need to talk to you about," she said, then took a drink from her coffee cup.

"What?" I said through the pancakes.

"Ruth," she said. "It's a little bit awkward. Really it's my fault. I should have been more open about all this."

I swallowed. "What is it, Mom?"

"I think you're getting old enough for a bra."

I couldn't help but look down at my chest. It was a straight line down from where my neck hit my body to my waist, as if I'd been cut from one smooth piece of paper. "Not necessary," I said.

"Well, sure, maybe not completely necessary, not yet. But you'll grow. I was a late bloomer, too."

I raised my eyebrows. It was Mom who carried me in her belly, but they never told me whose egg it was.

"I'm not sure about Mum. We can ask her when we video-conference tonight."

"That's okay."

"Oh, she won't be embarrassed at all. She's much better about this sort of thing than I am. Which is funny, I suppose, since I'm the doctor."

"No, I mean, that's okay. I don't want a bra."

She fingered a piece of bacon. "Are you sure?"

"I'm sure."

I thought of Lena and how it was like our thing now: two bra-less girls. I didn't know if I wanted to have a thing with Lena or not, but I wasn't ready to cut off that option.

"Do other girls wear bras?"

I sighed. Mom could not be more obvious. Charlotte. She was talking about Charlotte. I could just see her running into Eliot and Alan and them telling her how they went shopping for a bra for Charlotte. It would be a great, uproarious fish-out-of-water tale, and Mom would be laughing, but the whole time she'd be thinking, *I haven't gotten a bra for Ruth! I must get a bra for Ruth!*

I took another bite of my pancakes. It nearly lodged in my throat when I realized a much worse scenario: Charlotte told her dads I was one of the only girls in the sixth grade who wasn't wearing a bra.

"Some do," I said. "But not all."

"Okay." She still held the bacon, flipping it from side to side on her plate.

"Okay," I agreed. Conversation over.

"Maybe we should go and buy one or two just in case."

Conversation not over.

"We could get training bras. They're like undershirts, but they cut off right below your breasts."

"I know what training bras are."

"It's just that with this weather and my schedule, I don't know when we're going to have another chance."

Oh, my God, it's a bra emergency!

Mom caught me smiling. "So we'll go?" she asked.

I had wanted to go to the library to see if I could find another note, or maybe even cajole Charlotte into giving up the one she had. But Mom's face looked about as excited as it did when I came down the stairs on Christmas morning. "Sure," I said. "We'll go."

◄◊►

When we got on the highway going down toward Topsham, I figured we were going to go to Old Navy, or, preferably, Target, where we would go to the underwear section lodged between women's clothes and the baby food, and I'd grab a couple of training bras and we'd go to the checkout, where I'd make sure to pick the line with the middle-aged woman and not the teenaged boy and then we would be on our way. Maybe I would be able to convince her to take us to the movies or one of those big chain restaurants with limitless bread.

Instead she brought me into a lingerie store for a bra fitting.

"There's nothing to measure," I said.

"You don't need to be embarrassed."

"I'm not embarrassed. I'm just stating a fact. I thought we were going to get training bras."

"When I got my first bra, my mother brought me to Town Shop on the Upper West Side. The *New York Times* did a feature on them."

I'm pretty sure a *New York Times* feature is what first brought my moms to Promise.

"So it's like a rite of passage?" I asked. "When I get my period, are you going to make me go sit in a hut in the woods until it's over?"

Mom's face blanched. "Period? Oh, that will be coming soon, I suppose."

"I'd rather do one of those go-out-in-the-woods-and-hunt-a-wolf things that boys do."

"Ruth, honestly, I'm just talking about getting a bra that fits you well."

"At least I didn't say I wanted to go through the Spartan rite of passage."

"A bra that fits you will give you confidence in your lovely body."

I wondered if she had been talking to Ms. Pepper. *My glorious body.*

"In Sparta, the boys had to murder someone."

"Yes, I know. And it was usually a slave and nothing to be glorified."

She navigated through racks of lace and ribbon like we were on a television race show and if we were the first ones to the fitting department, we would win a special prize.

The prize, as it turned out, was an old woman with cold fingers who wrapped a tape measure around me and tick, tick, ticked her tongue on the top of her mouth. It was like she had a little computer in there and she was type-typing away, sending my measurements off to the bra-computer in the sky, which would surely come back with a message of DOES NOT COMPUTE.

"Our training bras come in pink, white, and flesh," the woman said.

"Whose flesh?" I asked.

"Ruth, don't be sassy."

"I'm being serious. Not everyone has the same color flesh. Charlotte wouldn't be that color," I said, pointing to a beige bra hanging on the rack. It looked big enough for three women.

"That's taupe," the woman said.

"Pink," Mom said, and the wrongness of this choice startled me.

"No," I said. "White."

"How about one of each? For variety."

"Sure," I agreed. It's not like I was ever going to wear them, anyway.

When the woman went to get the bras, Mom turned to me. I expected her to tell me that while she admired my sense of equality, a lingerie shop might not be the best place to discuss the nuances of labeling something flesh-toned. Instead she said, "Does Charlotte wear a bra these days?"

These days?

"I don't know. I haven't asked her."

"You haven't noticed in gym class or anything?"

So Charlotte had told her dads that I didn't wear a bra yet. She must have.

"Mom, I just change and go. The locker room smells, and the boys come through."

"The boys?"

The woman came back carrying three bras. They were about as bland as could be. I wondered where Melinda got her lacy ones. Probably her mom took her to Victoria's Secret, which, I decided, would be the only thing more horrible than being here.

Mom and the woman waited and stared at me. "Um," I said.

"We'll wait out here," the woman said, and snapped the curtain shut.

I lifted my undershirt off and pulled the white bra off its tiny hanger. I shimmied it on over my head.

"What do you mean, the boys come into the locker room? Have you told the gym teachers?" Mom called from the other side of the curtain.

"They know," I said.

"How's the fit?" the bra lady asked.

The fit? It was like one of my undershirts, but instead of going over my belly, elastic encircled my torso.

"Fine," I said. "These will be fine."

"They know? Are they doing something about it?"

"It's the only way to get to the gym," I told her as I took the bra off. "The way it's set up, the boys have to go through the girls' locker room to get into the gym."

The bra lady returned to the room just as I had my arms straight over my head, my chest exposed. "Back on," she instructed.

I decided not to argue and slid the bra back on. She tugged at the elastic band with her bony, icy fingers and did some more tick-tick-ticking.

"And the boys come through willy-nilly?" Mom asked.

"They're supposed to wait."

"Frontenac Consolidated School?" the bra lady asked.

I nodded.

"It was the same way when I was there. It was the high school then, though."

"So it's been that way for decades and no one has done anything about it?" Mom asked, shaking her head. Her eyes were flashing.

Oh, no.

"It's nothing," I said. "The boys wait outside. And we all

just hurry because you don't want to be the one that's holding up the whole class. The boys get antsy."

"I just think that's simply unacceptable."

Bra Lady raised her eyebrows.

"It's fine," I told my mom. "Really."

But Mom's radar had detected something to be outraged about, and she wouldn't stop until she had fixed it. It would be just like the yogurt incident in third grade. Mom found out that every day the vegetarian option for school lunch was yogurt. Just yogurt. It didn't matter that I was not a vegetarian and that I didn't buy school lunch; she still made this huge fuss about it. The cafeteria workers rolled their eyes every time they saw me coming, and I bet if I had eaten there, they would have spit in my food.

<o>

Mom washed the bras, let them dry overnight, then put them back on their tiny little hangers and hung them in my closet. Sunday afternoon I sat staring at them, contemplating the tiny-ness of the hangers. They must have special tiny hanger machines, so maybe they needed tiny people to run them—or children. Maybe these were made in one of those countries that still use child labor, like China. If she hadn't been adopted, Charlotte could have been making these hangers.

That wasn't actually my thought: it had gotten lodged in

my brain by Melinda, who'd said it when we were discussing child labor as part of current events in Ms. Lawson's class. Melinda said that Charlotte's parents had rescued her from the floor of some factory, which was stupid because Charlotte was adopted as a baby. Then Charlotte explained how in China people were only allowed to have one baby, and most people valued boys more than girls, so a lot of girls were put up for adoption, or sometimes killed. Melinda started crying and threw her lanky arms around Charlotte as if Charlotte had just, in that very moment, been saved from the clutches of death.

Mom came in and sat down beside me on the bed. "Do you think that tiny hangers are made in sweatshops?" I asked her.

She tucked her legs up and considered the question. "Ruthabella, I think far too many things are made in sweatshops."

"Were there sweatshops in the Ivory Coast?"

She shook her head. "Not that I saw. It's more an agrarian society. Kids definitely worked long days in the field. Most of our cocoa comes from there. And coffee. Some of the farms were great. Others, not so much, and the kids there, well, they were certainly exploited. They took us to visit a cooperative farm. Well, it wasn't so much a farm. The farmers brought their beans there to be processed. I ate a raw cocoa bean." She grinned. "It was disgusting. Bitter."

"Bitter," I repeated.

"Do you think it would be possible to roast cocoa beans and make a drink?" she asked. "Something like coffee?"

"Maybe."

"With sweetened condensed milk. That would be delicious." She closed her eyes as if dreaming about cold days building snow forts, then coming in and sipping on the fair-trade chocolate drink straight out of her own imagination.

"I wanted to talk to you about your birthday." And like that, we were back to reality.

"What about it?"

"Alan and Eliot told us that a lot of the kids are having boy-girl parties now. Mum and I talked about it, and while I'm not entirely sold, we do think it would be nice for you to have a party." She scooted back a little on the bed.

Of course Charlotte told her dads that. She knew it would get back to my moms, and, she hoped, I would have the party, and she and Melinda could do all the truth or daring or whatever with the boys.

"We don't really have room here, but we could do it at the hospital. They have a big room for classes and staff meetings."

"You want me to have my party at the hospital?"

"Did you have someplace else in mind? When I was growing up, kids had them at a roller rink or a bowling alley. Do you want to go to the bowling alley?"

"No."

"Good. We'd probably have to rent out the whole thing in order to have enough lanes."

"How many people do you think I'm going to have?"

"If it is going to be a boy-girl party, we thought it made sense for you to invite the whole class. We're not convinced that you've given—that people have had a chance to really get to know you, the real you."

"They know me fine."

Mom smoothed her hand over the quilt on my bed. "I'm not sure that's true, honey."

"Why can't we just do what we've always done? I like that. It's a tradition."

"Something special with Charlotte?"

"No. Not Charlotte."

"Someone else?" Her voice radiated hope. Like if it were one of those graphic novels that Lucas liked so much, the letters would be all caps and drawn in wiggly lines with sparkle dashes coming off them.

"I'm not really sure . . ."

"How about Lucas?"

"Lucas Hosgrove?"

"Maybe after your playdate, you'll realize—"

"Playdate?" I interrupted.

"I told you about that."

"No, you didn't."

She tucked her hair behind her ears. "Didn't I? I really meant to. Well, you are going there tomorrow."

"No one has playdates anymore."

She frowned, but I could see she was determined not to let it bother her. The edges of her mouth twitched like live wires after a thunderstorm. "Fine, then. You've been invited over to Lucas's house."

I groaned. "No," I told her. "My answer is no."

"I've already said yes for you," she replied, lips still sparking. "His mother called up during the week and suggested the two of you get together. Since you are both going to be in the spelling bee, she thought that was something you had in common, and I agreed. Great friendships have been built on less."

I wondered if Lucas's mother had called Charlotte's family or Dev's. I couldn't imagine Charlotte going over to Lucas's house. She would find a way to die of embarrassment. "He's my top competition," I said.

"You can help each other study."

"Why would I help my top competition study?"

"Well, I am sure you can find something else you have in common."

I looked at my Harriet Wexler book on my nightstand. She was deep in the forest, hungry and alone. I thought that I should get back to her and help her on her way.

"So you'll ride his bus home tomorrow," she said.

I groaned again. "Can't we postpone it?"

"I don't see why you're being so difficult about it."

"He wants to annihilate me. That's his plan for the spelling bee. To crush me."

"I'm sure that's just talk. What's that called? Trash talk? It's all just part of the game."

"Okay, but let's say this plan of yours works and he and I become friends, then I have to go against him in the bee. I don't want to like him. I need to be fierce against my competition."

Mom gave an exasperated sigh, and it was like all the frustration marched right off her tongue and parasailed its way toward me. "It's just a school spelling bee, Ruth. Don't let it rule your life."

I lifted my Harriet Wexler book and started reading. *Just a school spelling bee?* That didn't even warrant a response.

"Ruth," she said.

"Lena," I said. "I want Lena to come for my birthday. And I want to go somewhere with good food."

Mom's eyes positively lit up, and she jumped off the bed. I knew she was going to go right to the school directory to look up Lena and send an e-mail off to her parents. Before she went out the door, she spun back, leaned over, and put a kiss right on the top of my head.

TEN

Mahal

Lucas's mom seemed relatively normal for a woman who thought it was okay to invite near strangers over for playdates. She offered us milk and cookies, which, come to think of it, was awfully suspicious, like she might actually be a robot intent on world domination and this was her acting the way television told her a typical mom should. They were store-bought cookies, the kind that come in a bag and are hard and uniformly round. I hated those cookies. Mum likes them. She likes all the American snack foods, especially Twinkies, which I guess you can't get in Ireland.

Lucas's mom put the plate of cookies down and gave us each a plastic cup of milk. If I were Lucas's mom, I'd probably use plastic cups, too. He shoved three cookies into his mouth, gulped his milk, and then said, "Come on."

His house was a raised ranch, which Alan, Charlotte's architect dad, claimed was an architectural curse that has been foisted on the people of Maine, but Lucas's house felt cozy.

I followed him down carpeted stairs to his bedroom. I knew it was his because it had a fake license plate that said LUCAS on it, and stickers from computer games and graphic novels. He pushed his glasses back up his nose. I'd never been in a boy's bedroom before. I hoped this wouldn't get back to school somehow. I already had to listen to Melinda humming "Ruth and Lucas, sitting in a tree" all day.

Lucas pushed open his door. The curtains were drawn and it was dark inside, but I could make out shelves taking up the whole back wall and they were filled with aquariums. Some were dark and some had eerie green lights in them.

"Come on," he said, from inside. He dropped down on the floor and picked up a graphic novel called *Cardboard* that had a picture of someone with huge eyes on the front. "I have lots of books if you want to read."

"What are those?" I asked. "Pets?"

"Pets?" he replied, indignant. "Those are insects. I study them. I'm an entomologist, a person who studies bugs, not words. That's an etymologist. Or maybe I'm just trying to confuse you in case those words come up in the bee."

"I know the difference between an entomologist and an

etymologist, and even if I didn't, I wouldn't get the word wrong in the bee, because I could ask for the definition and then I could put it together."

"Sure," he said.

I crossed the room to look in the aquariums. There were white maggots crawling over something fleshy looking. I stayed away from that one. In another, there was a chrysalis hanging from a leaf. In a third, a praying mantis, green and delicate, stared back at me. "What do you study?"

"The insects," he said without looking up from his book.

"What about them? Like what they eat?"

He put down his book, annoyed. "What they eat, what they do, how they react to various stimuli."

"Stimuli? Like what?" I couldn't help but picture him pulling the legs off daddy longlegs.

"Lights on, lights off. Water. Heat."

"Isn't that torture?"

He half stood, half leaped to his feet like a jack-in-the-box with a hitch. He picked up a binder. "I write it all down in here. Everything I do comes from *The Amateur Entomologist*, so you know it's all okay."

"Do they do anything interesting?"

"Everything they do is interesting!"

He pointed to the praying mantis, which continued to stare at us, rubbing its front legs back and forth. He waved his hand in front of the glass and the insect seemed to disappear, then reappear in a different part of the cage. "Fast, huh?"

I nodded.

"My favorite are the bees. I had a hive at our old house. I'd watch them coming and going, doing the work for the queen, buzzing and dancing. Mom said we couldn't bring them with us, though, because this house is too close to town and people wouldn't like us to have bees. I still have some honey, though."

He told me about swarms, medicated syrup, and mite treatments, and how you get the queen in the mail in a small box. All the while I pictured him walking up to the hive, the bees crawling over his skin-and-bones body, and he trusts, just trusts that they won't sting him.

"I cried a little when I left my bees behind, but one of my old teachers offered to take them."

"That's funny," I said.

"How is that funny?"

"Not that you cried. I mean about the—"

"Do you mean honey is funny? Because it rhymes? Rhymes aren't necessarily funny, you know."

"No, I meant that you keep bees and you're into spelling bees."

"I'm not especially into spelling bees. I just like winning."

My mouth opened a little, and I closed it right up. Mum's mother has an expression about how you shouldn't leave your mouth open, because you'll catch flies. In this room, who knew what all else might land in there. "You don't care about the bee?"

"Nope," he said. "I'm still going to crush you, though." Then, after a brief hesitation, he added, "Sorry. My mom said I should be nice and try not to intimidate you about the bee."

He wasn't intimidating me. He was angering me. Exasperating me, to use a spelling bee word. He didn't even care about the bee, just winning—no matter what the contest. Rubik's Cube, spelling bees, map quizzes in Ms. Lawson's class—it was all the same to him: he wanted to win just to win.

On a shelf above his desk were butterflies pinned inside wood-and-glass cases. "Where do you even get something like that?" I asked.

"I made them!" He trotted over next to me. "I catch them outside and then put them in one of these." He held up a glass jar with a white cotton ball in the bottom.

"You just wait until they run out of air?"

"Of course not." He twisted open the top and held it out to me. I breathed in and then rocked back. "Formaldehyde. I always have a couple of jars ready. You never know what kind of specimen you might find. I found that blue one outside our house when we first moved in. It was flitting around a peach tree. Isn't it beautiful?"

The pin was pressed right through its thorax. I closed my eyes, but it didn't stop me from imagining the beautiful butterfly flitting around the bushes outside Lucas's house, only to be unceremoniously dumped into a stinky glass jar. It was probably good that Lucas didn't talk about this hobby at school.

I turned around and examined the insects some more. There was a large beetle, its shell an oily yellow and blue. When I peered closer, it skittered away. "So this is what you do on a playdate?" I asked.

"I've never had a playdate," he replied.

"Not a big bug-hunting crowd at your last school?"

He pursed his lips.

"Insect hunters," I corrected myself. "Entomologists."

"My dad used to say that entomology was wasted on the young."

Used to say. I didn't ask.

"So what do you want to do?" he asked.

"I don't know. Normally you talk or play something."

"Do you want to play chess?"

"I don't know how."

"It's easy." He stood up and went to the wall opposite the insects. This one was filled with books. He yanked out a thin brown one—so ugly, my heart actually fluttered that there might be a note in it—and tossed it to me. *Essential Chess.* While I flipped through it, he pulled out a board. "I'll be black," he said. "Which means you can be white."

"I've figured out that much, thanks."

"It means you go first. It's an advantage." He set up both sides of the board. Naming the pieces as he did so. "King, queen, pawn, knight, bishop—"

"What's the castle?" I asked.

He groaned.

"What?"

"It's not a castle. It's a rook."

"A rook?" My body leaned in toward him. "A rook and a knight?"

"Yes." He seemed perplexed. "And a pawn and a bishop and a king and a queen."

I found the pages that told me which ways the pieces can move.

He beat me in five moves, but I was distracted. *My knight in dingy armor . . . by crook or rook.*

"That's just the way the spelling bee is going to go."

I closed the book. When I left, I took it with me without even asking.

◄◇►

"How was the playdate?" Mum asked, her face pixelated on the computer.

"He has a room full of bugs and he crushed me at chess."

"Sounds like a regular date, not a playdate." She laughed.

"But I did get to eat store-bought cookies, so it wasn't all a loss."

"Oh, the horror!" Mum cried out, putting her wrist to her forehead. "Store-bought cookies? Don't tell your mom!"

"I'm right here," Mom said from the stove, where she was stir-frying vegetables and tofu. She'd read that we should start eating more vegetarian meals. "And Ms. Hosgrove said it went very well."

"It wasn't so bad," I said.

"The bugs?" Mum prompted.

"He's an amateur entomologist. He has all these different kinds. Praying mantis, maggots—you know, bugs. But you have to call them insects or he gets mad."

"Understandable," Mom said. She pushed a pile of snow peas from the cutting board into the pan.

"Hey," Mum said. "I'm going to go to the library when I'm out here in Seattle. They have over a million books and they get moved around by a robotic system. And the stacks, they go round and round so they never stop, you know. I'll take some photographs for you."

"I'd like to see the robots."

"They aren't exactly robots, I don't think. I mean, not like our Hoover robot." Mum called the vacuum a "Hoover," which I guess was an old vacuum brand. "Anyway, I have the spelling list here. Do you want to go a few rounds?"

"Sure," I said. Coco and I had practiced that afternoon, and I was doing pretty well, but a little more practice couldn't hurt. "'Succotash,'" she said.

"Succotash," I repeated back to her.

"Ask me to use it in a sentence," she said before I had a chance to start spelling.

"Can you please use it in a sentence?"

"Suffering succotash, I sure do miss you guys!" She tilted

her head back and laughed, and the camera on her computer couldn't keep up with it, so on-screen she jerked around from fuzzy to focused.

"Mum," I said. "You are a dork."

"Dinner's ready," Mom said. She walked over behind me and brought her own face into our frame. "We'll talk tomorrow, hon," she said to Mum.

"Grand," Mum said.

"Hey, Mum," I said.

"Yeah?"

"I sure do miss you, too."

———◄◦►———

Charlotte caught me in the hall before homeroom. I already had my Harriet Wexler book out, ready to sink into a chair and keep reading. I was at a very exciting part. Taryn was trying to forge a stream, but her horse lost its footing and she slid off. Turns out it was more river than stream and she was being washed down, bouncing from rock to rock. The description went on for two pages before she was washed up on the shore.

Charlotte said, "Come here a sec," and led me to a nook under the stairwell. I hesitated before going in. It could be an ambush.

Or it could be that Charlotte had brought the clue she had found, and she was going to ask me to help solve the rest with her. If she asked nicely, I just might say yes.

I tucked around the corner and found Charlotte tugging on her hair and wearing skinny jeans and those stupid fluffy boots. "I heard you went to Lucas's yesterday."

She was invited for a playdate, too. Her dads must be making her go and she wants a preview.

"Yep," I said. Let her discover those bugs on her own.

"You shouldn't do that."

When we were seven, we rode our bikes through town, down by the water. A dog charged out of the yard of a rental property. It was long and lean with muscles as tight as a racehorse's. It bounded straight toward her with teeth bared and drool spewing. I pedaled hard in front of her, then spun my bike out so my back wheel hit the dog and sent him mewling back home. The hit shook my bike, my hands, my bones. Through her tears, she had said, "Why'd you do that? You shouldn't hurt a dog."

She stomped her boot to loosen some snow that was stuck onto the suede. "You can't just go to Lucas's house."

"Why not?" I knew why she thought I shouldn't—the rumors that would start, his social leprosy—but I wanted to hear too-kind-to-hurt-a-raging-dog-Charlotte say it.

"You just shouldn't," she told me. "I'm trying to help."

I turned toward the hallway. Could I just walk away?

"If you would just be a little more normal, Ruth, it wouldn't be so bad. You'd see. Melinda's really nice—if you would just—" She stopped. "Never mind. Forget it." She turned and left me there standing in the dirty puddle of water that had melted off our boots.

I wanted to be angry, but my heart was pitter-pattering because Charlotte had maybe just told me she still wanted to be my friend.

ELEVEN

Contrapuntal

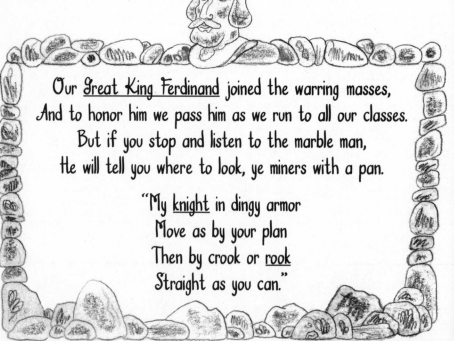

Our <u>Great King Ferdinand</u> joined the warring masses,
And to honor him we pass him as we run to all our classes.
But if you stop and listen to the marble man,
He will tell you where to look, ye miners with a pan.

"My <u>knight</u> in dingy armor
Move as by your plan
Then by crook or <u>rook</u>
Straight as you can."

****

I stared right into the nonexistent eyes of Ferdinand Frontenac. He seemed to be sleeping, dreaming of his glory days as the great unifier of the peninsula.

The squares on the floor were made up of four smaller squares, two feet by two feet in total. I flipped through Lucas's *Essential Chess* book to the page about how knights can move. They make L shapes. I turned so my back faced the statue, moved two big squares to the left, then forward one. I was about to move forward like a rook, but then I stopped. If Ferdinand was the king, then I should start where the knight would start on a chessboard.

From the gym down the hall, I heard the thump, thump, and squeak of basketball practice. Charlotte was in there. She'd tried out for the team with Melinda, and both had made the cut, though Melinda was on the traveling team, and Charlotte was on the more-junior varsity team, only they didn't call it that, since they didn't want to make anyone feel bad.

I flipped back in the book to the diagram of how the chessboard was set for the start of the game. The knight was to the right of the king, with a bishop between them. I moved so there was one square between me and the statue. I wondered if Coco played chess. I could ask him, but then he might want to know why, and I didn't want to share these clues with anyone. If I found a couple more, I could bring them to Charlotte. Or maybe this would be my solo expedition, like Taryn in *The Riddled Cottage*. Either way, I didn't want anyone else involved, not even Coco.

"What are you doing?" It was Melinda, because of course it was Melinda. Her ponytail was high on her head, and she was wearing a white sleeveless shirt and bright pink short shorts that matched her pink-and-white basketball shoes. In her hand she held a shining mouth guard.

"The latest dance craze. Chess hop. Haven't you heard of it?"

She rolled her eyes.

"My New York City friends told me about it." I didn't have any New York City friends, but I could. My moms still had friends down there, and some had kids. I even knew their names if Melinda pressed me.

Melinda, though, looked me up and down. My flannel button-down was not tailored to hug every potential curve. It was a man's shirt, from L.L.Bean, with the sleeves rolled up. I wore it over old sweatpants that were a little tight and a lot short but long enough to tuck into my snow boots. Lena approved, but Melinda sniffed out the truth: I had been late for school and my weekend clothes were close at hand.

"Charlotte says you're all right, but I think she's got you all wrong."

I couldn't stop myself. "She said that?"

Melinda smirked. She was the kind of girl you should never show a weakness to, and now she had me.

"Because I think she's a—" I couldn't bring myself to say the word Melinda threw around so easily in the locker room. "Traitor."

Melinda laughed. "I'll be sure to tell her that."

I flinched but didn't tell her not to, because then she'd have me two times over. She spun so her ponytail whipped around, and marched back to the gym.

I stood there wondering how she was going to relay this conversation to Charlotte. I would come off weird, for sure, even weirder than I had actually acted. She would definitely tell Charlotte that I had called her a traitor, and probably embellish it with a few more details. I blew my hair out of my eyes with an exasperated sigh. Stupid. It was stupid to ever open my mouth around Melinda.

I picked up where I had been when she'd interrupted me. I moved like the knight, then I became the rook. Rooks can go in any direction (forward, backward, left, right), as far as they can until they bump into something. So I walked straight forward. I could see the side door of the school in front of me. I didn't know what I expected to happen. A loose tile I could pry up? A clue to drop from the sky?

Of course neither happened. I went back to where the knight turned into the rook and tried again. This time to the left. I brushed by the door to the main office. It was not the same as running into it, but maybe this was what the clue meant. So I opened the door. Dr. Dawes, the principal, was still there, in a back office working with a low light. There was a display of old yearbooks, and I paged through them quickly. Nothing but falsely smiling face after falsely smiling face. When we did school pictures this year, I didn't smile. The photographer tried in a halfhearted way to cajole me, but I remained straight-lipped. Mom made me get retakes and so I grinned like a monkey. She wasn't happy about that, but she still framed the biggest one and hung it up above the couch in the living room with one of those gallery lights shining on it. I think she was trying to embarrass me, but it wasn't like I had anyone over. The mice and spiders could laugh all they wanted.

Next to the yearbooks was a stand with some brochures. Nothing. A display case with history and awards. I peeked around looking for a telltale envelope shoved somewhere.

"Oh, hello, Ruth. Can I help you?" Dr. Dawes asked.

I shook my head. "I'm okay."

Dr. Dawes hesitated. "So, what are you in here for?"

"Oh," I said. "I wanted to check the lost and found."

Dr. Dawes pointed to a box by the door. "What did you lose?"

"My retainer."

I didn't wear a retainer.

"Oh, dear!" Dr. Dawes exclaimed. She hurried over to the box and started digging through. "I know how expensive those can be. Did you ask in the cafeteria?"

I shook my head again.

She held up a wrinkled sweatshirt that I knew belonged to Charlotte, but I didn't say anything. She stacked all the clothes on her thigh as she crouched next to the box. "I don't see it," she said. "But listen, I can send an e-mail out to teachers."

"It's okay," I said.

"Really, I would like to help you find it."

"You know, the more I think about it, the more I think I just forgot to put it in this morning."

She cocked her head to the side. "You sure?"

I nodded.

She dropped the clothes back into the bin, and then, in one quick motion, stood and put her hand on my arm. "How are you doing, Ruth?"

"Fine. It's really no big deal. I'm practically done with it."

"I meant in general. You feel like things are going okay?"

"Sure. I'm excited about the spelling bee."

She nodded and pursed her lips in a way that showed me she was really listening. I didn't think it was an act, but she still looked a little ridiculous. "And friends? Are you making some good friends here?"

"I'm making friends." I was making acquaintances, really, like Lena and Coco, but didn't want to get into it with Dr. Dawes.

"I've seen you chatting with Lena. And I heard Christopher is helping you to study for the bee."

"Yes."

"He must be a good help. Spelling genes run in that family."

"He is. Dr. Dawes?"

"Yes, dear." She leaned in.

"I need to get going."

She stood up straight. "Of course, Ruth. See you tomorrow."

"See you tomorrow."

I eased out of the office and made sure she had gone back to her desk before I tried one last time. Going backward as the rook would just bring me to the wall, so I went right. It brought me to the door of the gymnasium. Through the small window I could see the girls' basketball team practicing. Charlotte dribbled the ball in place while wearing a yellow pinny. Melinda was talking to her. She leaned in close and whispered something into her ear.

I'd have to check out the gym another time. No clue was worth walking into that lion's den.

———◦———

Mom had to work late, so after school I went to the library. First I checked my e-mail. The account had been a "gift" for my eleventh birthday. Charlotte had gotten the same, and nearly all my e-mails had been from her at first. Now I only ever bothered to check because I was a member of the Harriet Wexler fan club, the Greenbottoms, and they sent out a monthly newsletter that I hoped would have arrived. Instead I had an e-card from Mum. It was one of those retro ones, with a bee holding a bouquet of flowers. The caption said:

"You get my heart buzzing!" Mum's message said: "Sorry I cannot be there to help in person. STOP." For some reason, Mum thought it was funny to send me e-mail messages that were like old telegrams. "Here is a link to help you study. STOP. Will arrive by soonest aeroplane. STOP. Much love, Mum." She never wrote "STOP" after she signed off, because once I told her it looked like she meant she was going to stop loving me.

I clicked on the link. It went to Word Central from Merriam-Webster with a bunch of games that you could use to study spelling. Before, it would have seemed like fun, but after a few sessions with Coco, it almost seemed like a sad way to study. I would go back later, I decided, and try some of the games then.

Next I pretended I was still doing the shelf reading for Eliot, but I was just looking for more ugly books that might have notes in them. In the 500s, I found a book called *Chemical Equations and YOU!* It had a puke-green cover with bland red type. When I pulled it out, I saw that the cover had a picture of a test tube with a man and a woman swirling out of it surrounded by smoke. The woman wore a big flower in her hair and the man had an eye patch. I was flipping through it, sure that a book this ugly must have a note in it, when someone said, "Oh, hi, Ruth, I thought that was you!"

Coco.

He carried a stack of books from the tween/teen area and

had his hat pulled on so low that it hid his chocolate-brown hair. "Hi," I said as I twisted my head to read the titles on the spines. He had the latest Andromeda Rex book (*yuck*), but also two by Harriet Wexler, and one called *Corpses and Skeletons: The Science of Forensic Anthropology.*

"*Corpses and Skeletons?*" I asked.

"Yeah!" He tugged the book from the bottom of the pile. "Ms. Pepper got it for me. It's a little old. Hopefully they'll put out a new edition soon." He stared at the cover with admiration, but when he looked up and saw me staring at him, he gave a sheepish smile. "Forensic anthropology, it's, like, studying the remains of people to learn about history. It's really cool. Not gross."

"I don't mind gross things," I said. "In fact, Charlotte and I used to mix up really gross concoctions and then drink them. Only she could never do it. Only me."

"Really?" He sounded a little impressed. "Anyway, it really isn't gross. It's what I want to be when I grow up, I think."

"So, like, you'd go around and look at old bodies?"

He nodded. "That's how I got interested in geography. But you can do it anywhere. Like, remember when they were digging up Stewart Street, down by the edge of town, and they found that old cemetery? Well, they had to call in all these forensic anthropologists to figure out who the bodies were and how old and everything."

It turned out it had been a graveyard for people too poor to pay to be buried. They'd moved all the bodies into the graveyard up the hill.

"They let me come and watch them. It was amazing."

"That does sound cool," I said. Because it did. "How'd you even get interested in that?"

"Well, you know, I liked dinosaurs a lot as a kid."

"Who didn't?" I asked.

"Right. Exactly. But then one day I guess I wondered if anyone studied human bones the same way, and it turns out they do, and that was even more interesting to me." He shrugged. "Anyway, what about you. What are you looking at? Find something good?"

I held up the book. "Oh, this? No, I don't think so."

"Why does that man have an eye patch?"

"I'm not sure."

He shifted his books from one hand to the other. "I didn't know you liked chemistry."

"Chemistry? I don't. Not particularly, anyway. I'm looking for ugly books."

"Ugly books? Why?"

If there was anyone I would tell about the notes, it was Coco. He would probably like the mystery and would be good at figuring out the clues. Probably. Or he might think it was a silly waste of time, and then he'd just flutter off like geese flying down south for the winter. "I'm helping

Eliot—Mr. Diamond. I do that sometimes. Help in the library."

"Ms. Lawson. Mr. Diamond. This town couldn't survive without you," he said. When he smiled, his eyes crinkled and you almost couldn't see them anymore.

"You have cat eyes," I said.

"What does that mean?"

"They go away when you smile."

"Oh." Now he frowned.

"It's not bad."

"Is it good?"

"It's not good or bad. It just is."

He shook his head. "Anyway, Ruth, I heard your birthday was coming up."

"Yeah." I nodded. "Next month. Why?"

"Well, Melinda said you were having a boy-girl party with the whole sixth grade."

"I'm not having a boy-girl party. I'm not having any sort of a party."

"Oh, well, that's too bad. I thought it sounded like fun."

"You like boy-girl parties?"

"I've never actually been to one."

"Me, neither," I said. "But they sound terrible. Dancing and boys trying to stick as many marshmallows as they can into their mouths and spin the bottle."

Coco blushed. "I don't think they have spin the bottle at every party. You wouldn't have to have spin the bottle."

"I'm not having a party," I told him again. I had thought that he was smart—that was what everyone said—but now I was starting to have my doubts.

"But if you did, you wouldn't have to play spin the bottle. It's your party. You could have whatever games you wanted."

I imagined my classmates outside in the snow, running around while I sat in a treestand shooting a Super Soaker at them. I would fill it with grape Kool-Aid and shoot it straight at Melinda in her all-white winter coat. That's the kind of game I would want to play.

"I guess so," I said.

"Okay," he said.

"Okay."

"Five."

"Five?" I asked

"That's how many marshmallows I can fit in my mouth. We did it at Adam's party. He can do seven."

"No surprise," I said.

He smiled. "If you did have a boy-girl party, and you invited me, I would come."

"But I'm not."

"I know," he said. "Bye, Ruth."

I thought about calling after him and telling him that maybe the man had an eye patch because he'd been in a terrible chemical accident and had burned out his eye. The woman was his lab partner, and she wore the flower in her hair to cover up the smell of singed eye-flesh, and also so that he would always be able to find her so they could continue their important work into chemical equations. I wondered what his reaction would be. But he was gone and I slid *Chemical Equations and YOU!* back on the shelf.

TWELVE

Debacle

Mom sent the e-mail to every parent in the sixth grade. And some in seventh, too, if she knew them. The subject: *Girls' Locker Room Issues.*

In it she explained the fact that the boys had to traipse through the girls' locker room to get to the gym.

In theory they wait outside the girls' locker room until someone gives the all clear and then march through and up the stairs to the gym. Calls to appropriate teachers were not returned.

I knew this because Melinda had a printout of the e-mail, and she read it to Charlotte as they sat, legs intertwined on the beanbag chair in Ms. Broadcheck's room. "I don't know

why your mom is so upset," she told me. "It's not like anyone wants to see you naked."

Charlotte folded the piece of paper. "It *is* a little strange
when you think about, how the boys come through our
locker room."

"But not something to make a big deal about. Right,
Mitchell? I mean, it doesn't bother you to have to wait,
right?"

Mitchell shook his head but kept his eyes on the mag-
netic blocks he was using to build a tower.

"It's not like you want to come in and spy on Ruth?"

Mitchell glanced over at me. His cheeks were red. In
first grade he didn't know how to read yet, and during quiet
reading time, he would sit next to me and I would whisper
the words of my book to him. He was littler then, with small
fingers whose nails had white half-moons at the base. "I just
want to play ball," he said.

"See?" Melinda said, as if this proved her point. "Total
overreaction. You didn't tell me how weird her moms
were."

I didn't tell her that Mum wouldn't do this sort of thing.
Mum would come to school, have a look around, devise a
plan to fix the problem, then bring that to the gym teachers.
First, though, she would check to see if I wanted any help.

If Mum were home, none of this would have happened.
But now she was in Seattle with the million-book robotic
library.

Charlotte folded the paper into smaller and smaller pieces. "Yeah," she said. "Anyway, Melinda, where'd you get that shirt? I really like it."

———◀◦▶———

Ms. Wickersham asked to see me before I went into the locker room. She sat on the edge of her desk and held a basketball in both hands. It had signatures all over it, and I wondered who they belonged to. Maybe it was members of the WNBA. That would be cool. Probably it was just the girls' basketball team.

She cleared her throat. "Let me begin by saying I'm sorry."

I blinked.

"I try to give you girls your privacy, but I understand that means I might be missing something. It's a fine line, these days, that we walk. I know—the research shows this—that bullying occurs in the locker room at an alarming rate, all over the country, I'm talking."

Her sentences never seemed to end, but to fold in on one another, and I wasn't quite sure what she was saying, so I just nodded.

"And I thought I could hear anything that happened from my office, even with the glass, you know, the windows, sound travels through them, so I thought I could hear both within the locker room and coming from without. But it seems I've missed something."

"What's that?" I asked.

She squeezed the ball. "You tell me, Ruth, I was hoping that's what would happen."

I scratched at some dry skin through my shirt. I tried to think about when I'd been bullied, which was every day with Melinda, so it was hard to think of which one particular incident would have caught Ms. Wickersham's attention. "I'm not sure I know. Do you mean about the bras?"

"The bras?" She held the basketball to her stomach and leaned forward over it.

No, not the bras. Stupid. "Or something else?"

She didn't talk. She was going to wait me out.

"Some of the girls wear them and some don't. It's no big deal."

"And the boys mentioned this?"

"No," I said.

"The trouble I'm having, Ruth, is, you know, I have this e-mail, we all got this e-mail, and I just wish you had told me, sorry, no, it's not your fault, but if the boys are bothering you—"

"No," I said. "They aren't. I mean, it's a little stressful to have to get changed so quickly, and it's annoying when they are yelling outside."

"So they haven't come in?"

I shook my head.

She spun the basketball in her hands. I thought of the cafeteria workers. Was she going to spit on the ball and then make me shoot baskets? She stood up and walked around her desk. "I can offer you another place to change. Someplace else could work, the bathroom, or here, no, the windows, we've already discussed the windows."

"I don't need another place to change."

"Did something happen, Ruth?"

"Nothing happened. It's just my mom—she didn't know about the locker room, how the boys come in, and when I told her, she freaked."

"It's not an ideal situation, I know."

"Please don't make a big deal out of it."

She tugged on her ponytail. "It already is a big deal, my dear." She gave me a sad little smile and walked to the far side of the room. "I can offer you this," she said, pulling open a door. There were bins full of balls: soccer, basketball, softball, and more. A stack of orange cones listed to the right.

"A closet?"

"It's spacious. No one goes in but me."

"I don't need to—"

"Dr. Dawes asked me to work out a solution for you."

I sighed. "Let me get my things from my locker."

"Okay. The boys are waiting. I'm going to go let them through, and then you change and come on up and join us."

Every boy stared at me sitting in Ms. Wickersham's office as they walked through the locker room and headed upstairs. Even Coco. He didn't smile.

And when we played basketball, not one person passed me the ball, even with the three-pass rule.

———◄○►———

Lena followed me into the closet after class. "Whoa, private digs," she said. "Hold on."

A moment later, she came back in with her stuff. "You don't mind, right?"

I shook my head, but I was racing to get changed.

When we stepped out of the closet and joined the line waiting to leave, I said "Oops," to no one in particular. "I think I left my ponytail holder upstairs." I had. Purposefully.

"I can loan you one," Lena said.

"I'll just run up."

"It's just a hair elastic," she said. "No big deal."

"No. I'll go."

Before she could argue, I raced up the stairs and back into the gym, which smelled of rubber and sweat and sorrow. I needed to get to the bookshelf tucked into the back corner of the gym. I grabbed my elastic from the bleacher where I'd left it, then slid over to the bookshelf.

It was all sex-ed books.

I guess I was expecting sports books, like *How to Shoot*

Baskets Like a Pro. Books I've seen kids carrying, but from a section of the library I'd never been to.

I took a deep breath and began flipping through them. Nothing, nothing, nothing.

And then I saw it: when I picked up a particularly large book titled, simply, *Sex*, I revealed the corner of an envelope peeking from the back side of the shelf. Putting the sex book down, I peered over the back of the shelf and saw the envelope held on by yellowing tape. I freed it, turned, and nearly walked smack into Charlotte and Melinda.

I tucked the envelope behind my back, but I think Charlotte saw it. Maybe.

Melinda saw the books.

"So," she said. "Doing a little research?"

"I forgot my elastic," I told her.

"And that book just jumped right off the shelf?" She smirked. She always smirked.

"Yep. Guess so."

I bent over to pick it up. Melinda had her foot on it. I didn't have any interest in the book—at all—but I still felt bad for it with her salty, muddy sole all over it.

"Let's go," Charlotte said.

"Wait, I want to hear what Ruth's learned about *S-E-X*."

Country of origin? Can you use it in a sentence?

I held up my elastic. "Found it," I said. I gathered my

hair at the nape of my neck and begin twisting the elastic around it.

I heard clomping feet and when I looked up, there was Lena trotting across the gym in her black lace-up boots—Ms. Wickersham would have a fit—"There you are!" she called out.

"She's looking at the sex books," Melinda said as Lena came up to us.

"And?" Lena replied.

Melinda cocked her head to the side. She'd never taken on Lena before, and I wondered if she had simply never bothered or if there was something about Lena that scared her a little bit.

Lena took me by the hand. She looked from Melinda to Charlotte and then back to Melinda again. "Anyway, Ruthy, can we go over that science unit again? I'm nervous for the test."

She looped her arm through mine and led me out of the gym. I felt bad about leaving the book on the floor, but not bad enough to go back for it.

"Thanks," I said when we were in the hallway.

"What was that all about? And don't say it was a hair elastic. I just dove into a pit of hyenas for you. Piranhas, even."

The envelope was in my back pocket, probably bent. My stomach lifted and hovered, like when you're at the top of the roller coaster, about to rush over, wishing you could turn back. I pulled it from my pocket, opened up my palm, and showed it to her.

———◄○►———

"And how many of these have you found?" Lena asked after I told her about the notes in the books.

"This is the fourth one. Well, this is the third one I've found, but Charlotte says she has one, too. Not that I'll ever see it."

"Come on, then. Open it up."

My fingers tightened on the envelope. "Not here."

She tugged me into the girls' bathroom. It was pink-tiled with cracked mirrors and a lingering smell of cigarettes from when this was a high school.

She leaned back against a chipped sink and looked at me. I knew I should open the envelope and read the clue, but I hesitated. "Well?" she prompted.

I pulled the card out of the envelope. "They always have this seal," I said. I ran my thumb over the drawing of the bird that seemed to be in the red wax.

"It looks real," she said. Her hand hovered toward the card, but I didn't let her touch it.

I unfolded the card. The border was red, white, and blue ribbon, with black ink used to make the colors seem bolder. For the picture, a bright British flag, the Union Jack, waved in the breeze. A light seemed to shine on it from below, and the whole thing gave me a sense of vertigo, as if the flag might wave its way right out of the drawing.

Don't you love those crazy Brits?
Jumpers for sweaters and spots for zits.
And when they want to change their suits,
It's in a box, not a booth.
Be a hero, make the call.
Steepest streets might make you fall.

*****

"Whoa," she said.

"See. They're all different kinds of riddles." Mixed with the queasy feeling was something like a thrill of finally—*finally*—having someone who thought the clues were as amazing as I did.

"I do love those crazy Brits with their accents and stammering. I keep telling my mom to hire British workers in the summer, but she likes the ones from Germany. Do you watch

Doctor Who? It's this great British show with time travel—you'd like it."

I knew all about *Doctor Who*. It was Mum's favorite show.

"I like the young one with the floppy hair. He's got great big eyes, kind of like Coco's. See, I told you you'd like the show."

"I don't—"

"My sister Vera, she likes one from the old show, from like the seventies or eighties. He wears this long scarf and has huge curly hair. I don't get it, but I'm learning how to knit so I can make her a scarf like that for Christmas."

"Christmas already went by."

"For this year."

"How do you know she'll still like him?"

"My sisters don't change much."

"I don't like Coco."

She raised her eyebrows. "You only spend every last minute with him. It makes it practically impossible to be your friend."

I only spent one period a day with him, and not even every day, since we only had three or four study halls a week, depending on the schedule rotation. "I don't— Wait, what do you mean?"

She regarded herself in the cracked mirror and smoothed out a bit of her hair. "Anytime I want to find you to study or eat lunch or sneak into the bathroom during class, you're studying spelling with him."

"I didn't realize—"

"But not today!" she interrupted.

"Because we're in the bathroom," I said. "Oh, God, we need to get to class!"

"We'll tell Ms. Lawson I got my period. I can cry on command if I need to."

"But—wait." The information was coming at me so quickly, I couldn't even think. "Have you gotten your period already?"

She blew her bangs out of her eyes. "Three months ago. It sucks. Have you?"

I shook my head.

"Lucky."

"Let's go," I said. "And you'd better start crying now."

"This afternoon," she said. "Can you meet me? We'll ponder it all afternoon, and then once we've figured it out, we'll go to Sea Street and look."

"Why Sea Street?" I asked.

"That's the steepest street in town. My sister Lucia was walking down it over the weekend and fell flat on her butt. She had a big wet spot and wanted me to walk behind her in case anyone drove by and saw it and thought she had wet her pants."

"Did you?"

"Once the price was right." She pointed at the T-shirt she wore for a band I'd never heard of—the Velvet Underground. I thought it was a band, anyway. But maybe it was a store. There was a picture of a banana on it.

"Not today. I could do it tomorrow, maybe. I guess."

I inched toward the door.

"Great. I'll have my mom call your mom and you can stay for dinner. Okay?" she asked.

"Okay," I agreed, but it felt a bit like she was taking something from me. Something that was only mine. And Charlotte's.

THIRTEEN

Kith

The light snowflakes that started to fall as school let out turned into a heavy storm, and Mom was stuck at work. Her voice sounded crackly over Eliot's cell phone as I stood in the lobby of the library, looking at the snow falling in the glow of the streetlight. "I need you to go to Charlotte's house tonight," she said.

"Maybe Eliot can just drive me home."

"Ruth, please don't argue with me. The roads are terrible."

"We need to feed Webster."

"He'll be okay for tonight." Only her voice dropped out on "tonight." "Listen, I know you and Charlotte haven't been as close as you used to be, but it's only one night. You'll be okay. I talked to Eliot and he agrees."

So it was done. "Okay, Mom," I said. "See you tomorrow."

I wandered back into the library and found Eliot moving buckets around the lower level. "This building," he said with a sigh. "I told Alan when he first looked at it, there are some things that aren't worth fixing. The only good thing is that none of the leaks are over the books."

I took a bucket from him and we walked farther into the stacks. "So I guess I'm going to your house tonight," I said.

"Yep," he replied. "We can make up the guest room for you."

I never used to sleep in the guest room. I'd sleep in Charlotte's room, in my sleeping bag or even right in bed with her. "Thanks."

"Closing time is in fifteen minutes. You can head up now or wait for me."

"I'll wait," I said. I placed my bucket in a far corner where there was a slow but steady drip-drip-drip.

———◄o►———

As long as Alan and Eliot were around, it was easy. We talked to them and they talked to each other and to each of us, and if you were from the outside, you might not have noticed that we never once spoke to each other, not even to ask the other to pass the butter.

After dinner, though, we sat alone in the television room. Only the cable was out, so we weren't watching anything. We were just sitting there. We had our homework, and we were both doing the science worksheet, but we certainly weren't working on it together.

We were side by side and alone. At one point that would have been comfortable, but now it felt like little robots were building a wall between us, brick by snowy brick.

I saw her list of spelling words sticking out of her binder. It was flipped over to the page of challenge words. Melinda would be terrible to study with. She wouldn't be able to pronounce any of the words or have any tricks to help Charlotte remember how to spell tough words. I ought to have offered to study with her, but I didn't. I didn't say anything.

Bedtime was worse. I didn't have any pajamas, of course, so I had to borrow some of Charlotte's. And get a spare toothbrush from a bin in her bathroom closet. All these things used to be normal. Sometimes we'd come over as a family and it would get late and we'd all just stay there—my moms and me. I wouldn't even ask Charlotte what to borrow; I'd just take it right out of her drawers.

The kicker: Alan had three models for a bid he was working on spread out on the guest bed, so I had to sleep in Charlotte's room.

Alan brought in an air mattress, and the motor to blow it up was so loud that none of us could talk. I wished we could have that motor going all night. When Alan left, it was quiet, but neither of us slept. I heard Charlotte turning over and over and over.

"Can you stop moving so much?" I asked.

"Can you?"

"I'm not moving much. The air mattress is just noisy."

"Whatever." She sat up in bed and looked out the window. "We're not having school tomorrow, so I'm not sure it even matters if we don't get to sleep." Outside, the wind blew the trees and made them creak like old doors. "Did you ask your mom to send that e-mail? About the locker room?"

"No."

"Oh. Okay." She tugged on her blankets. "I'm glad she did. I hate that locker room. I hate how the boys can come through. Toby says you can see in, just a little bit."

"Really?"

"He says they try to guess who they are seeing."

I shivered. I couldn't imagine Coco or Adam or Dev playing that game, but maybe . . . maybe.

"They can always tell when it's me, I bet."

"Why?"

"Because of my hair. My skin." She reached her arms out in front of her and splayed her fingers wide. "Do you think they'll do anything about it?" she asked. "What did Ms. Wickersham say to you?"

"Nothing," I said. "I mean, I don't think there's anything they can do. That's why I have to change in the supply closet now. I tried to tell Mom that."

"She's just trying to help."

She settled back down onto her pillow. On her ceiling, she had ribbons twisted together going from end to end.

She had started clipping things to them. I saw them for a flash before we turned the lights out. Pictures of people—not me—and little mementos.

We were quiet for several moments before she asked, "Do you like Coco?"

"No," I said.

"He likes you."

I shook my head. "He's just helping me with the spelling bee."

"He likes you," she said again, sounding a little bit mystified.

"Do you like Mitchell?" I asked.

She didn't answer right away. She was going to lie to me. I could feel it. And then, I supposed, I would know our friendship was truly over.

"Yes. But he likes Melinda."

"Are you sure?" I used to catch Mitchell looking at Charlotte in class sometimes, even way back when I was still reading to him.

"Yes."

"Did he tell you that?"

"No. I can just tell."

I thought of Melinda and Mitchell and Charlotte. I couldn't tell you which of the girls he liked. "I could find out for you," I told her.

"No!"

"Sorry."

"Even if he did like me, what would it matter? Melinda likes him."

"So?"

"So, if Melinda likes a boy, that boy is hers."

"What about what you told me about Lucas? About how I shouldn't let him keep me from the bee?"

"That's totally different."

"Why?"

"Because Melinda is my best friend."

She said it so easily, without even thinking about how that might sound to me. I knew, of course. Knew that I wasn't her best friend anymore, that I had been replaced. But she had moved so far on that she didn't even think to try to shield me.

"She's helping you study, right? For the bee?"

"A little. Not like you and Coco or anything."

"I thought you were going to drop out."

"You don't have to worry about me, Ruth. You're the star, not me."

Outside, an owl hooted.

"You could probably see her house from yours, you know. It's on the other side of the inlet."

"The hills would be in the way," I told her.

I heard her move on her bed. "It's this little cottage on a cliff. I guess it used to be someone's summer guesthouse." She cleared her throat. Maybe she wasn't supposed to tell me that. "Anyway, it makes her lonely."

"What? Being so far out?"

"The water. She says it makes her lonely."

I wasn't sure why she was telling me this. Did she want me to feel bad for Melinda in her little cottage over the bay?

The moon was obscured by clouds, and we were just fuzzy lumps to each other. There was so much I wanted to ask her when we couldn't really see each other. Did she really like Melinda, or did she just like being popular? Did she really think that anyone could like Melinda more than they liked her? Did she miss me?

Instead, I curled myself into a ball. The air mattress squelched beneath me. At the same time, she pulled her covers over and heaved a sigh.

"Sorry," I murmured.

"Yeah," she said. "Me, too."

FOURTEEN

Amenable

Charlotte was wrong. We had school after a two-hour delay. I'd escaped down to the library, where I resumed my search for an explanation of the quietness of snow with little luck.

All the periods were short, but Coco and I still met to study. I waited in Ms. Lawson's room, and he came in with Adam trailing behind him. I raised my eyebrows, and Coco shrugged. "All I'm saying, Coco, is that I think we should set up a scrimmage."

"A scrimmage?" Coco asked.

"Yes. Your contestant and mine. One on one. It will help them both. And between you and me, Dev could really use it."

Coco hefted up his backpack and put it on one of Ms. Lawson's desks. He made a noncommittal *Mmm* sort of noise.

"I mean," Adam went on, "he knows all the words. But speaking them, he gets all jumbled up. No matter how many times I tell him to just calm down and spell, he can't."

"Well, how are you telling him?" Coco asked.

"What do you mean?"

"Are you telling him like you're talking to me? Or are you in Adam the Genius mode?"

I snickered at that, which made Adam frown, but he kept talking to Coco. "I try to explain it in my most patient voice."

Coco shook his head. "Well, there's your problem right there. When you use your patient voice, you sound like you think the other person is an idiot."

"Well, most people are idiots," he said. "Present company excluded, of course."

Coco looked over at me. "I think we're doing okay as it is, but if Ruth wants to scrimmage, we can."

"Um," I said. Lena, Coco. Now Dev and Adam. There were getting to be a few too many people around for me to maintain my lone-wolf status. "I don't think so."

"The speller has spoken," Coco said.

"Great," Adam said, throwing his hands into the air. "Maybe you should get Ruth to write your friend recommendation for that camp."

"Adam—" Coco said.

Adam shook his head, calming down as quickly as he'd gotten riled up. "You're right. I don't want you to see what a tremendous competitor he's become, anyway. And we'll write your stupid recommendation, too. It will tell the story of this spelling bee and how you are gracious in defeat."

When Adam left, I said, "What was that all about?"

"That was Adam."

"But the camp? The recommendation?"

"Oh, that." Coco grinned. He dug into his backpack for our spelling list and pulled out a stack of blank index cards, just like the ones the clues were written on. "I'm applying to go to this camp down at Harvard."

"Harvard?"

"It's a new program at their museum of natural history. It's an anthropology camp."

"That's so cool! I mean, that's perfect for you, right?"

"Yeah, but you know, it's really just a weekend. When I'm in high school, I want to go to Bone Camp at the University of Arizona. That's actual forensic anthropology. But this is cool for now. Anyway, we should get studying. I thought today we could work on homonyms."

"Okay."

"So anytime it's a homonym, if you recognize it, you need to ask for the definition. Sometimes they will just give it to you but not always."

"I thought I was always supposed to ask for the definition."

"You are. But you don't always follow the rules. This is like a rule squared."

"An exponential rule," I said.

"If you don't follow it, you'll be thrown into the Pit of Lostness," he said.

I grinned. The Pit of Lostness was from the Taryn Greenbottom books. Everyone in the universe feared it, especially since the great Lord Charlesmoore had vanished and was feared swallowed by it. "Okay," I said. "I promise."

We practiced a few rounds until the bell rang, and Coco began packing up all his stuff. When he was done, we headed together toward the door. "So I'll see you tomorrow, right?" he said.

"Right," I agreed. "And Coco?"

"Yeah."

"If Adam flakes or gets mad again, I could write that recommendation."

Coco's smile flashed across his face at the same time as his cheeks flushed pink. "Thanks, Ruth. I just may take you up on that."

———◦———

Lena found me there in the hallway, still with a smile on my lips. She asked me about it, and I told her that I had just rocked the homonyms.

"Sounds super-thrilling. Now, let's get going, or we're going to miss the bus."

We took the school bus to the library and hopped off, just like I did every day. But instead of going in, we trudged through the hard-packed snow away from the library. She kicked a little ball of snow in front of her, and it scurried along like a white tailless mouse. "Does Charlotte really live above there?"

I nodded.

"That's cool. I would love to sneak down in the night and just pluck any book I wanted."

"I don't think she does that."

"What's the story with you two, anyway?"

The story? There was a whole book of stories. A whole library. "We used to be friends and now we aren't. Can we talk about something else? Did you do any pondering?"

"Sure. And all my time spent on *Doctor Who* message boards and watching BBC America has paid off. Do you know what they call a sweater in England?" she asked.

"A jumper," I told her. It had taken years for Mum to drop that one. She kept a lot of her British phrases but tried to change the ones that were confusing. Now she reserved it for Irish fishing sweaters with their intricate patterns.

"A jumper! Isn't that weird? People are always talking about wearing jumpers, and I picture them in those little-girl dresses, which I could totally rock, by the way, and I think I may wear one tomorrow."

"You use a lot of words," I said.

"Wait till you hear my sisters. Anyway, of course you know their word for zits?"

"Spots," I said.

"Exactamundo. So the clue is just showing different words for the same thing in American English and, um, English English."

"So we just need to figure out what we call a booth that they call a box," I said. I was starting to wish Mum hadn't dropped so many of her British expressions. What had she ever called a booth?

A clump of snow fell from a tree onto the sidewalk. I sidestepped it, but Lena clomped right on top of it. "Well, it says to change your suit, so maybe it's like a changing room, like at a store," she said. This made me think of the bra lady's frigid fingers, and I shivered.

"But we call that a room, not a booth or a box."

We turned onto Sea Street. The brick sidewalks were shiny with ice that was broken up by blue crystals that melt tiny holes in it, but do little else. "If you fall," she said, "I'll walk behind you—don't worry."

"Okay."

"Maybe it will materialize right in front of us like Doctor Who's TARDIS."

"All wavy lines and wind?" I asked.

"Yep. And out will step the young doctor, who'll whisk me away from all this."

"What if it's the older doctor and he's here for your sister?"

"Well then, I'll pretend to be Vera and go with him anyway. It's only a matter of waiting out his regenerations or whatever they're called."

"You want to leave that badly?" I asked.

She stopped walking and turned so that we were staring eye to eye. "I want to leave this town more badly than a Santoku knife wants to gently slice a tomato. I want to get off this peninsula more than a dog wants the fleas to jump off his back, more than a baby wants a bottle, more than Melinda wants to rule the world with a bunch of demonata to follow her every wish. And you should, too."

"Why? It's nice here."

"Says the girl who is harassed on a daily basis."

I stomped on some ice at the edge of the sidewalk. "It's just a matter of waiting it out, right? And it will take a lot less time than waiting for a fictional character to regenerate."

"It's not just about the moment. It's like, when I'm sitting in Ms. Lawson's class and we're going over the maps, it makes me think about how big this world is. It seems like a waste of a body to stay in one place."

I'd never thought of it that way.

But she had more to say. "As for you, I mean, I don't think there's anyplace where you'd be Miss Popularity or anything. You're always going to be your own kooky deal."

"Kooky?"

"Yeah, you know, not of the normal variety—"

"I'm perfectly normal," I said, then snorted, thinking of Ms. Pepper and my glorious body and how Charlotte and I had laughed.

"Case in point: I thought you were getting mad, but then you started laughing."

"I *was* getting mad, but then I thought of something else. Anyway, why wouldn't there be a place for me to be Miss Popularity?"

"Would you want to be Miss Popularity?" she asked.

"I just don't think it's a very nice thing to say."

"What's nicer than being honest?" she asked.

Before I could think too much on this, a streak of something red and blue caught my eye. "Lena, look!"

We stood outside of Pledge Allegiance Comics. Superman flew across the window.

"You into comics?" she asked. "I like some. I'm not really into the superhero stuff, but, you know, whatever floats your boat."

"Be a hero," I said. "Change your suit!"

She looked at me, at the window, then back at me, though now her eyes were flashing. "Superman changes into his suit in a phone booth! A telephone box in England. I totally should have known that. The TARDIS is a police call box."

"But where is there a phone booth? I mean, do they even exist anymore?"

"Um, Ruthy, take a look." She pointed: nestled in between

the Promise Cupcake Factory and Pledge Allegiance Comics was a bright red phone booth, just like the ones in England.

"How have I missed this all my life?" I asked.

"You and me both," she replied. "You don't think it really just app—"

"That's impossible, Lena." Who was kooky now?

We stood there staring at the booth. It had been painted recently, maybe this past fall. Snow was piled on top of it, but the doorway had been cleared out. "Come on, then. Open the door," she told me.

So I did.

——◦——

I wish I could say we opened the door and fell down a rabbit hole into an unknown world of pink magic kittens and golden unicorns. Or that there was a time lord waiting for us. Or even that the phone booth didn't smell like pee. But it did.

It was just a normal phone booth, I guess. I'd only ever seen them on television. There was a phone in one corner, and a shelf below held a phone book with its pages curling back. That was the first obvious place to look. I pulled it out. It was from 1993. That was promising. But when I flipped through it, there were no origami envelopes tucked between its pages.

"Hey!" Lena exclaimed. "Look at this."

"What did you find?"

I followed her extended index finger. "For a good time call Francesca. That's my mother!" She giggled.

"How do you know?"

"How many Francescas do you think there are in this town?"

"Why aren't you mortified?"

"You haven't met my mother. This is about the funniest thing I've ever seen." She took out her phone to snap a picture. "I'm sending this to my sisters."

I read the other graffiti. There were numerous people who you could call if you were looking for a good time. Also, there were quite a few people who would do unspeakable things, allegedly. And there were lots of initials who loved other initials.

"It really smells awful in here," she said.

I nodded in agreement.

"So what exactly are we looking for, anyway?"

"Another clue, I guess."

The booth was small and there was barely room for both of us. I shifted around her and she bumped up against the wall.

"Hey, now!" She giggled. "So are those rumors about you true, after all?"

"What rumors?"

"That you're a lesbian. Like your mothers."

My shoulders drooped. "How can there be rumors that I like Coco *and* that I'm a lesbian?"

"Gossip is an illogical beast," Lena told me. "Oh, hey,

don't be all sad about it. It's no big deal. You know it's just Melinda being jealous."

"Jealous?"

"You were Charlotte's friend first. You don't give a crap what anyone says."

"I do give a crap."

Lena tilted her head to the side. "Then you, my dear, have one fantastic poker face."

I leaned back. We *were* just a little too close in here. I slipped on melted snow from our boots and rocked back, catching myself on the shelf and knocking the phone book down. It flipped open to an earmarked page in the yellow pages: TOWING to TOYS. On an ad for a game store I'd never heard of—Wizards and Warcraft—there was a drawing of a wizard crouched over a board and rolling a set of dice. It looked familiar somehow. Written around the edge of the ad were the words:

The Raven's author __ __ __

Walked down the road, abbreviated so we're told. __ __

The bus came by and one departed,
That is to say, he got this. __ __ __

Come on now, it's time to play.
When water's cold it is this way. __ __ __

Put the pieces together, then roll your die.
Natural 20! Flying high!
Find the boxes, nearly there:
Level up to 7, here is there.

* * * * * * *

Lena read it along with me. "What in the heck does that mean?"

"I have no idea," I replied. "But it's definitely a clue." I had four clues now. Maybe I didn't even need the one Charlotte had found.

"Good. Let's get out of here. It stinks." She grabbed the page and tore it from the phone book.

"Lena!"

"What. The store doesn't exist anymore. No one is using the phone. I bet this doesn't even work." She lifted up the receiver, and we both heard the dull sound of the dial tone.

She held the phone and we stared at it. Then it started to ring.

"It's ringing," she whispered. "Ruthy, the phone is calling someone. All by itself!"

"I know!"

What would Taryn Greenbottom do in a situation like this? Stay calm! Stay calm!

"Did we find it?" Lena asked. "I mean, did we solve it?"

"I don't know!"

Five rings. Six. Seven.

Then a strange set of three tones.

"Aliens!" whispered Lena.

"If you would like to make a call," a cheerful female voice came through the line, "please hang up and try again. If you need help, hang up and then dial your operator."

We gaped at each other with eyes wide as the message started again.

Lena slammed the receiver back onto its hook, then fell out of the booth laughing. I stumbled out after her.

There was a man outside Pledge Allegiance Comics shoveling the sidewalk. He had a long *Doctor Who* scarf just like the one Lena wanted to make. When he saw us, he raised his bushy eyebrows, which just made us laugh more. We clutched our sides as we half ran, half slid down Sea Street to Lena's house.

When we got there, our sides and mouths and cheeks all hurt. Lena's sister Vera was at the table. "Oh, hey," she said to no one in particular. "Weird Lena just brought home a weird friend. What a banner day this is."

And all we could do was laugh some more.

—⟨o⟩—

"Dinner guest!" Lena yelled.

"Dinner guest!"

"Dinner guest!"

The call went from room to room of Lena's bungalow down off Commercial Street by the wharfs and just around the corner from the Salt and Sea Shack.

Lena turned to me. "When one of us has a friend over for dinner, we get the real food."

"What do you get the rest of the time?"

"Fried clams," Vera said from the kitchen table, where she was playing with her phone.

"Every night?" I asked.

"Fried clams, fried haddock. Lobster rolls if it's raining."

"Or unless Vera or I cook," Lena said.

"Really?" I asked.

Lena's mom joined us in the kitchen, wiping her hands on her jeans. She rolled her eyes at Lena and Vera but extended a hand to me. "Francesca Filipepi-Fernández del Campo. It's a mouthful. Call me Franny. You must be Ruthy."

"Ruth," I said. "Yes."

"Welcome," she said, then, turning to Vera: "Get a lasagna from the freezer."

"I'm not sure if I can stay for dinner," I said. "My mom said five thirty, but, well, sometimes she's late."

Lena's mom nodded. "I talked to her. You're good for dinner. And don't listen to these girls. We have a good dinner every night, and when was the last time you girls had clams? Not since the summer? And you know what, you should consider yourselves lucky! People in Ohio, they'd kill to eat the way you girls do."

Vera pointed at her chin. "Girls in Ohio would die with these zits."

"I don't see anything," I told her.

"Vera has microscopic vision," Lena told me. "It's her superpower. Come on. We can boot Lucia off the computer and use it for our research. She's just looking up fan fiction for some stupid television show she watches about vampires and mermaids and guardian angels."

Lucia was hard to convince, but we got her off the computer by offering to do her dish duty that night. The room was filled with cardboard boxes. Lena looked like she was seeing them for the first time. "We moved over the summer. Height of the season. This room became like the drop zone. Someday we'll clean it out."

"You lived in Port Stewart before?"

"The thriving metropolis, yes. When this place came up for sale, my parents decided to move to be closer to the shack. Okay." Lena cracked her fingers. "Where do we start?"

"Do you think it's cheating to use a computer?"

She hesitated. "Okay. Read it to me again."

I unfolded the yellow piece of paper and read:

The Raven's author __ __ __

Walked down the road, abbreviated so we're told. __ __

The bus came by and one departed,
That is to say, he got this. __ __ __

Come on now, it's time to play.
When water's cold it is this way. __ __ __

Put the pieces together, then roll your die.
Natural 20! Flying high!
Find the boxes, nearly there:
Level up to 7, here is there.

＊＊＊＊＊＊＊

"I wonder what those dashes mean," I said.

"Dashes or underscores?" Lena asked. Then she mused, "The Raven's author?"

"Poe," Stella, Lucia's twin, called from across the hall.

"What?" Lena asked, sticking her head through the open doorway.

"Edgar Allan Poe," Stella said. She poked her own head out her door. Her long black hair fell down her shoulders in curls so impossibly beautiful that I would believe she had her own hair styling team tucked away in her closet. "He wrote 'The Raven.' Duh. And you're welcome."

"Stop eavesdropping," Lena replied, a phrase I can't hear without picturing the eaves of a house tumbling down as a nosy neighbor hangs out her window. She shut the door. "All right. Edgar Allan Poe." She wrote it on a sheet of paper. "Do you think it's *A-L-L*-A-*N* or E-*N*?"

"I'm pretty sure it's an *A*."

"You are the speller. Hey, what do you and Coco even do to study?"

"What do you mean? He quizzes me, helps me remember rules and tricks and stuff."

"All that time and it's just words, words, words?"

"Yep. What's an abbreviation for 'road'?"

"*R-D.* And you know that. Message received. Don't talk about Coco. Which, by the way, indicates that there is something to talk about, but we aren't talking about it. Totally cool. Next hint."

"'The bus came by and one departed. That is to say, he got this.' To his destination?"

"Off," she said. "When you depart a bus, you get off." She added the word to her list, and below it, she wrote "ICE." "That's what water is when it's cold."

"You don't think it could be frozen? Or slushy?"

"You're overthinking this. Let's see. We're supposed to put the pieces together. Edgarallanpoerdoffice."

"Office!"

"But what about the first part. Even if we just use 'Poe,' that doesn't make sense. It would be 'POERD.'"

"What if it's not as simple as *R-D*? What are some other words for 'road'? Highway? Lane?"

"Street," she told me. "Man, all that spelling bee study has you avoiding the simple words, hasn't it?"

"Street is abbreviated *S-T*," I said. "Post! The post office! And look, now each answer fits on the dashes—the letters, like Hangman."

"We have to go to the post office!"

We both turned our heads to the clock. It was five fifteen—too late to go tonight.

"Let's do the rest of the clue. This is fun. We could be detectives when we grow up. You'd be the no-nonsense, by-the-book one, and I'd be the sassy and unconventional one who runs in high heels. You know, on the TV shows the actresses aren't actually running in heels. They wear sneakers and are just shot from the ankles up."

"Interesting but not relevant," I said, echoing what Ms. Broadcheck said to Lucas.

She sighed. "Actually, I think I may have a talk show. Then everything I say will be interesting *and* relevant. "Okay. 'Level up.' That sounds like a video game," she said.

"You play video games?"

"I've been known to rock the vids," she replied. "'Natural twenty,' though, I have no idea what that is. I think it's okay to look it up." She started typing. She had her knees drawn up to her chest, which lifted the ends of her pants. I could see a collection of small, circular scars that she'd connected like a constellation with black lines.

"Blackflies?" I asked, pointing.

"Blackflies, mosquitoes, you name it, I'm a magnet. And I can't not scratch, so I'm a walking scar. I used to tell myself they made a map."

Charlotte and I used to sit side by side squeezing each other's hands so we wouldn't scratch our bug bites.

I wondered if there would come a time when every little thing didn't remind me of her.

"Here we go. In Dungeons and Dragons, when you roll a twenty on a twenty-sided die, it means you rolled a natural twenty."

"That means nothing to me," I said.

"I don't know anything about Dungeons and Dragons, either," she said. "But I know someone who does."

◅◦▻

Mom was so excited that I'd gone over to a friend's house—on my own without her interference—that she called up Mum so we could all talk about it. What could I say? That we'd found a phone booth and tore out a page from the phone book?

"Her family runs the Salt and Sea Shack," I said. "But we had lasagna."

"Oh, I love lasagna!" Mom said, as if I had announced we'd had steak tartare or crème brûlée, like it was a rare treat.

"Is she a speller?" Mum asked. Now her room looked more modern, with a glass-shelved bookcase and a flat-screen TV behind her.

"No," I said.

"Good. You wouldn't want to go up against a friend."

I gave Mom a meaningful look, thinking of how she had sent me to Lucas's house, but Mom was frowning and shaking her head at Mum, and I realized they were thinking of Charlotte. "She likes to cook," I said. "But she didn't make the lasagna. Her mom is Italian, I guess."

"Did you get the link I sent you?" Mum asked.

I nodded. I still hadn't played the games, though. "Yep. Thanks."

"When I get home, it will be spelling boot camp. You will be untouchable!"

"Of course, you have been studying," Mom said. She waved her hair in the air in a spiral. "With the boy..."

I wasn't about to fall into that trap, not even to supply Coco's name. "Did you know that there was a spelling bee where the kids knew so many words that they had to leave the list and go to the dictionary, and even then they had to stop and then start again on another day?"

"That is a fascinating story," Mum said. "But nothing you need to worry about." Then she clapped her hands together. "Oh!" she said. "Look at this. I got it at the Seattle library." She held up a package with a figurine of a woman dressed in a blue jacket and a long skirt. She held her finger up to her lips. "Librarian action figure! For Eliot!"

I didn't have the heart to tell her that he already had three. They stood like tin soldiers in his office at the library. "Where to next?" I asked.

"I'm driving down to Eugene, and then on to Portland Junior." Mum always referred to Portland, Maine, as Portland the First, and the one in Oregon as Junior since our Portland came first. "But then I should be flying home to you."

"Good," Mom said. "This trip seems even longer."

"Interminable," Mum said. "Spell it, Ruth."

I thought about the root of the word. "Terminus." "The end." "Interminable. *I-N-T-E-R-M-I-N-A-B-L-E*. Interminable."

"Good girl, Ruth!"

"I miss you, Mum," I said.

"I miss you, too, sweetheart."

Her image on the screen flickered. "It looks like we're losing you, hon," Mom said.

"I've got to dash to a meeting anyway. Talk to you soon." She kissed her hand and then blew it at us. Mom pretended to catch it, snapping her hand closed, then pressed it onto my cheek.

FIFTEEN

Synergy

On Monday, Coco brought in a game he'd made to help us study. He wrote a bunch of words on cards, and then places of origin on pieces of construction paper that were sun-faded around their edges. Old English was on green that was nearly yellow at its borders, and Latin was on red that had faded to pink on its frame. It made me think of the notes with the intricate borders around their riddles, and once again I thought of telling him about the clues but stopped myself. He shuffled up the index cards, and then I was supposed to put them on the right place of origin as fast as I could.

"I still don't understand the point of this," I said as we were setting up for a second round. It had started snowing again, softly this time, the flakes drifting sideways and up outside the window as much as they were falling down.

"Spelling isn't just memorization. It's patterns. The more patterns you have, the easier it will be for you to figure out a word you don't know." He handed me the stack of cards. "Go!"

I put "ramen" onto Japan, and "muumuu" onto New World (it's Hawaiian). "Gruff" was Dutch. The next word stopped me: "robot." I held the card in my hand. "I know how to spell 'robot.' I'll never need to figure it out."

"Patterns," he said again. I tapped the card against my lip, then put it on the Latin pile. He shook his head. "Slavic," he said.

"Really? Slavic?"

"Czech, actually. '*Robota*' means 'compulsory labor.'"

"Why don't you do the bee?" I asked as I put "saboteur" into the French pile.

"I wasn't one of the top finishers in the grade."

"You should have been," I said. "Ms. Lawson said so. Dev, too. At the meeting of the participants, he said he couldn't believe he was one of the top finishers and you weren't. He said when you guys went to watch your sister last year, you knew all the words up to the very end."

"One more." He nodded at the card in my hand.

"'Bratwurst.'" I placed it on the German pile.

"Good." He gathered up the cards. "You know my sister,

Emma, won the school bee last year. That was small fries,"
he said. "My older brother, Clint, went to nationals."

"Really?"

He shuffled a new set of cards, making a shrifting sound
that reminded me of the ocean. "We all went down to Washington, DC, with him, stayed in a hotel, met a lot of the other
kids. There was a boy from Alaska who had a bear tooth
around his neck. He said he caught and killed the bear
himself."

"That was just a story, right? To scare the other kids?"

Coco said, "Maybe, but he looked like he could kill a
bear. Anyway, my brother did all the pretests, and he was
one of the kids who wound up onstage—on television—and
he got his first word wrong. And he had to sit up there
through round after round, and then we drove back home."

He tapped the stack of cards.

"So what are you saying?" I asked. Was he afraid of fail-
ing? Of having to sit up there, feeling a thousand eyes on
him? "Just because your brother and sister flubbed, that
doesn't necessarily mean it would happen to you."

His hands shuffled the cards slowly. "It might. The reason they messed up—"

"Of course it might," I interrupted. "Anything *might* happen, but if you prepared yourself as well as you're preparing
me—it just seems unlikely."

"They were prepared. Trust me. It's more complicated
than that."

I furrowed my brow. "The past, it doesn't determine what's going to happen in the future."

Coco smiled. Or, anyway, his lips turned up, but his eyes turned down and lost their shine. "That's what my dad always says about sports. Baseball especially. He says the past isn't destiny. That statistics are *de*scriptive, not *pre*scriptive."

"That's different, though. I mean, if a baseball player never hits the first pitch, like their batting average on first pitches is 0.075 or whatever, then chances are he isn't going to hit the ball. But your brother and sister—well, first of all, it's not a big enough sample size. And second, they're them, not you."

"You like baseball?" he asked. Was he missing my point or changing the subject?

"My mom really likes it."

"The British one?"

"No. The American one. Don't tell anyone, but she's a Yankees fan."

He laughed and handed the cards to me. "Are we going to study or what?"

"Sure," I said. "Let's study."

After the next round, while he sorted the cards again, peering carefully at each one, I asked, "Did your parents say anything about the e-mail my mom sent?"

He rolled his eyes before he could stop himself.

"What?" I asked.

"My mom gave me a big lecture about privacy, about

respecting people's bodies—all of that. I told her I never go in until Ms. Wickersham blows the whistle. It was nothing."

"I didn't tell her to say anything."

"I know."

"I have to get changed in the supply closet now."

The red spread across his cheeks. He held one of the cards against his lips. "I was just thinking that maybe I should do something like this with root words. Would that help?"

"I don't know. Maybe. How did you know I didn't tell my mom to send the e-mail?"

"Because you're smart. Way too smart to do that."

I nodded, but what he said didn't slip by me. "Because kids think it's stupid, right?"

"Stupid," he said as if pondering the word. "Country of origin?"

"Ha-ha."

He wouldn't look at me, only at the cards. "Anytime something makes your parents stop what they are doing and talk to you about boy and girl stuff, that's not anyone's favorite, right?"

I took the stack of cards from him and began sorting. "Can you really put five marshmallows in your mouth?" I asked.

"Maybe more," he boasted, though I thought it was a strange thing to be boastful about.

"It's seems impossible. Let's say each marshmallow is a one-inch cube." I drew a cube on a piece of scrap paper.

"At least an inch. We'd have to measure to be sure."

"Let's say one for the sake of argument. So that's a cubic inch multiplied by five. The volume of the inside of your mouth is five cubic inches?"

He gaped his mouth wide.

"That's three, maybe four, max."

"They compress," he said.

"So it's not really measuring the volume of your mouth, or whose is biggest—greatest, I mean." It seemed important to use the right term with Coco. I didn't want him to think I was stupid.

"Adam has the biggest mouth, but not the greatest." Coco laughed.

"How *could* you measure the volume of your mouth?" I pondered.

We both lifted our heads at the same time.

"You drink!" he said.

"Right—and measure how much."

"You fill your mouth as much as you can and then spit it out into a measuring cup."

We both wrinkled our noses.

"If you had a set amount, you could fill your mouth and then subtract what was left over," I said.

"I'm doing it tonight," he said eagerly. "You, too?"

"Okay."

"I'll bet you six marshmallows that mine's bigger," he said.

"But mine's greater," I replied. *Stupid.* But Coco just laughed.

Lena's head popped up into the window of Ms. Lawson's room, then disappeared.

Next she leaned in from the side. Her black hair fell down like the sheets of snow that slid off the roof and crashed to the ground during class.

Next it was just her fingers: the blue-, black-, and purple-polished tips were flittering bees around a flower.

"Someone is trying to get your attention," Coco said.

"Someone is," I said.

"It's Lena."

"I know. We're working on a project."

"The Africa project?"

"What? No. That's a solo project, remember? And, anyway, it hasn't started yet."

"You seemed like maybe you worked ahead," he said with a shrug.

Lena popped up and pressed her lips against the glass in a big pucker-up smooch.

I am going to kill you, Lena.

"I wonder if she knows how dirty that glass is. I saw Toby do a fish face in that exact same spot during homeroom," Coco told me.

I wrinkled my nose, and that made Coco laugh, which was too much for Lena. She threw the door open.

"I've got the answer!" she cried.

"It can wait until after school."

Lena stepped farther into the classroom. "So you really do study words in here? That's it?"

"Yep." Coco nodded. He looked at me sideways. "And talk a little, too."

Lena managed not to react in an exaggerated way. "About what?"

"Oh, you know, the problems that have plagued our world for generations," he said breezily.

I snorted.

Lena looked from me to him and back again. She grinned. "Try a word on me," she said.

Coco picked up a card. "'Shrieval,'" he said.

"Shrieval," she repeated. "Like an evil shrew."

"Um, more like related to a sheriff."

"Oh, well, then, that's easy. *S-H-E-R-R-I-F-A-L*."

"Ruth?" he prompted.

"*Bzzz*. No. Shrieval. *S-H-R-I-E-V-A-L*. Shrieval."

"Exactly," Coco said.

"You really have a chance," Lena said. "My BFF could be the spelling champion of the school."

"So what's your project?" Coco asked.

Lena opened her mouth, but I said, "It's not really a project—"

"More like a game," Lena interrupted.

"It's just a silly thing we're doing. Girl thing."

"Oh." Coco's voice was dipped and hollow. But I didn't want the whole world in on it. Even Lena was maybe more than I wanted.

"Right," she said. "Anyway, I found out the thing we need and we can go after school. My mom says you can stay for dinner again if you need to."

"I can just meet my mom at the library."

"Dude. Don't subject us to full-bellied clams. Give us another night. I saw ravioli in the freezer."

"We'll see," I told her. "There's something I need to do at home tonight."

Lena shrugged at Coco. "I guess our Ruthy is a woman of mystery."

I pictured myself shrouded in a black coat, stalking the streets of Promise, led on by vague clues. Smoke would drift off the street like it did in movies—where does that smoke come from, anyway?—and then Coco and Lena would emerge, but I would disappear before they could catch me.

"I guess so," he agreed.

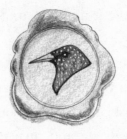

SIXTEEN

Chagrin

W hy don't you want to tell Coco?" Lena asked. "I bet
he'd be great at these riddles. He would have known
who wrote 'The Raven' and we wouldn't have needed to get
my sister involved."

She was right. He would be great at it. And I bet he would
like it, too: digging into the clues was kind of like uncover-
ing the mysteries of the bones. I shoved my hands into my
coat pockets. "I just don't want it to be a big thing."

"You don't want anything to be a big thing."

Lena walked with her left foot pointing out and her
right foot pointing in to leave strange tracks in the snow.
"Anyway, I talked to Adam. He about fell out of his chair
when I told him I had a Dungeons and Dragons question.

He grabbed me and dragged me down like he didn't want anyone to know. How stupid is that? So he likes a game. So what?"

"Adam?" I demanded. "You told Adam?"

"Yeah. I just told you: he's a big gamer."

"But you can't just go blabbing about it all over the place."

Lena stopped walking and turned to look at me. "You wanted to know the answer, didn't you?" Her voice was flat, but I could hear a bit of an edge underneath it. I nodded. "What else was I supposed to do?"

I kicked at a chunk of ice stuck to the sidewalk. "I don't know. Just ask him without telling him about the clues."

"Just go up and say, 'Oh, hey, Adam, can you tell me what "natural twenty" means? And "level seven"? And "flying high"? No reason, just because.' Like he wouldn't smell that out."

"But Adam? Of all people?"

"We can't all be hanging out with Coco, can we? Oh, wait, you don't want to tell him, either, for some weird, secret reason."

"It's not a weird, secret reason. I just don't—"

"Don't want it to be a thing—I know."

We stood there in the cold, our breaths filling up the space between us with puffy white clouds. But not the nice type of puffy white clouds that might have leprechauns floating upon them. The mean kind, blown out by an angry wind.

It had never been this hard with Charlotte.

The clock tower in town hall chimed off four rings.

"We should go," Lena said.

But then, Charlotte had left.

"It's just that . . . ," I began. "It's just that I'm not used to having all these . . . all these"—I spread my hands wide—"people around, you know?"

She cocked her head to the side. "My life is full of people, remember?"

"I just don't know if we can trust him."

"Sometimes you don't know, Ruthy. I didn't know with you. I just saw someone who stood up to Melinda, and I liked that."

"I don't stand up to Melinda. I cower in front of Melinda."

"Well, you didn't that day in the locker room."

"You're the one who's brave," I said.

"I know," she agreed. "And smart. And gregarious." She linked her elbow around mine and we started walking again. "Do you know that word? It's one of Lucia's vocabulary words, and I thought I would use it to stump you."

"It means 'outgoing and friendly.' Which you are. And I am not."

"You could be," she said. "Or not. I like you just the same. Now, let's go find this clue."

"Did he at least tell you what it meant?"

"Sort of. He said we were right, that rolling a die is how you get your power and the power of spells. It was all kinds of confusing, but a natural twenty is the best roll you can get. And then each character has levels that they go through, and I think that maxes out at twenty. He's a level-seven dwarf, by the way, and I think you should be very proud of me for not calling him a level-seven dork. Not because of the game, but because of everything else."

"And the clue?"

"He didn't really have any insight."

"Perfect." So another person knew about the clue, and he didn't even have anything valuable to add.

"But we should just go into the post office, I think. Maybe there will be something there that makes it clear."

The post office was an old, stately building at the corner of Main and Congress Streets. The steps were slabs of granite that were slick with water and salt. We held tightly to the railings as we climbed. When we opened the door, we saw a counter with three windows, each surrounded by a filigreed archway.

"Charlotte's dad Alan, he's an architect, and he said those archways used to have gates—bars, you know, because people used to send so much money through the post office and they didn't want to get robbed."

"Bang-bang," Lena said. "If I'd been born in a different time, I could have been a bank robber."

Now there was just one old postmistress sitting behind the middle window. She glanced at us when we came in and narrowed her eyes.

There was a display of Valentine's Day cards and stamps, and, beyond that, a shelf of shipping materials.

"Boxes?" Lena whispered. Then she shook her head. She knew that hiding a clue in those boxes could only result in its being found accidentally, maybe after it was mailed halfway across the world. Then she tugged on my arm. "Boxes!" she said again, with just a little more volume. The far right wall was covered with small boxes, each with a tiny window and a keyhole.

"Post office boxes," I said. "That has to be it!"

We walked closer and saw that each one had a number. "Twenty and seven," I said. "Twenty-seven?"

We followed the numbers, but we couldn't find one with a twenty-seven on it. They seemed to start at one hundred.

"Count the columns," Lena said.

We counted over twenty rows.

"And then up seven," I said. We started at the bottom and whispered the numbers together: *one, two, three, four, five, six, seven.*

The window on the box was painted orange.

"This is it," she hissed.

I pressed on the door. I guess I expected it to pop open, but nothing happened. Lena tried to pry it open with her fingernails. It stayed firmly shut.

"This is it," she said. "It has to be it. The orange paint. All of it lines up."

"But there's no key."

We stood there and stared at the bronze box with the orange window. Just stared and stared and stared.

"I guess I'll go back to the library," I told her, admitting defeat.

"Yeah," she said. "I guess I'll go back to clams."

Outside, it was snowing again. Light flakes fell slowly as if they were stuck in honey.

---<o>---

That night I took out the glass measuring cup, the one that measured in milliliters, since a milliliter is the same as a cubic centimeter. I filled it up to 250. Mom came into the kitchen, glanced at the measuring cup, and arched her eyebrows. "What do you think the volume of your mouth is?" I asked her.

"The volume? Like length times width times height?" She opened her mouth wide and put her fingers in as if she had a tiny ruler.

"Volume as in the amount it can hold. Then we can convert it into centimeters."

She nodded and crossed the kitchen over to me. "Is this for science?"

I shook my head. "It's just a thing we were talking about. We're going to pour as much as we can into our mouths and then subtract it from 250 milliliters. Then we will know the volumes of our mouths."

"We?"

"Me and Coco."

"Coco who is helping you to study for the spelling bee?"

I wanted to say, "No, the other Coco." But I said, "Don't start. Just watch me and make sure I don't spill any."

I tipped my head back and poured the water in slowly. I had to move my tongue out of the way to keep the water from shooting back out like a waterslide. The water got stuck at the back of my throat and I thought maybe I would gasp like a drowning person, but I closed my eyes and waited until the water was at my lips. Mom took the cup from my hand, and I spit into the sink.

"Two hundred five milliliters are left in the cup."

"So that means forty-five milliliters in my mouth."

"My turn," Mom said.

"Really?"

She dumped the cup and filled it up again. "Did you ever find out about the snow?" she asked. "Why it's so quiet?"

"Not definitively," I said.

Outside, the moon lit the yard: white, white, and more white. This must be how astronauts feel in their little space capsules, staring out at the cold vastness. "Do you think it's warm when you're in space? I mean in the shuttle or the space station or whatever?"

"Well, they do show them wearing T-shirts and stuff," she told me. "You know that gravity changes their muscles. Their legs get small and their torsos get bigger. They have to exercise their legs so they don't get atrophied."

"Because there's no gravity?"

"I think so," she said. "We had an astronaut come and talk to us at med school. He was pretty cute."

"Mom!" I said.

"This was before I met your mum, of course."

I shook my head. She picked up the measuring cup. "Ready?"

She closed her eyes as she poured it in. Her mouth was cupped like one of those fish pitchers that were so popular in the tourist shops this summer. Singing fish pitchers. They were supposed to make a lovely sound when they were being poured, but to me they just looked like a fish was about to kiss another fish and got frozen.

Mom pounded the counter, and I took the measuring cup from her. "Fifty-five milliliters."

She leaned over and let the water out of her mouth in a smooth stream. "Really?" she said. "That big?"

I nodded.

"We never built that snow fort."

"I thought we were waiting for Mum," I told her. It was a lie. I had never thought we were ever going to build the fort.

I wrote down our numbers.

Outside, big clumps of fluffy flakes fell down. "Mum's never coming home," I said as I watched them cling to the glass of the kitchen windows.

"Don't say that," Mom said, her face tight.

"Not until springtime," I said. "It's like we're frozen in here and she has to wait for the ice to melt to get back."

"Thankfully this isn't a fairy tale. She'll be back next week."

"If you say so."

"I do."

But Mother Nature had different plans.

SEVENTEEN

Purga

It snowed all night, but they kept school open. There were just four of us in homeroom: Lucas, Melinda, Charlotte, and me. None of the island kids were there, because the ferries weren't running. And the people who lived out farther, in the smaller towns or right on the coast, like Mitchell and even Lena, they didn't make it in, either. I'd looked for Coco before school, so we could compare the results of our water-in-the-mouth experiments, but his bus had swerved off the road and stuck itself in a snowbank before the driver had even picked up any kids.

Melinda and Charlotte were all twisted up together like usual, and Lucas was working on the Rubik's Cube, so I sat at a table as far from them as possible and read my book.

When Ms. Broadcheck came in, late again, she told us that they only needed to feed us for it to count as a day, then they could send us home and we wouldn't have to make it up in the summer. I felt like all the other kids owed us one for making it in.

Since there were so few of us—and so few teachers, too— they sent us to the gym. Ms. Wickersham set up stations like basketball free throws and the mini-trampoline. Ms. Lawson tried to teach some girls how to knit. Mr. Wynne, the art teacher, rolled out a huge piece of paper and let kids write and draw all over it with markers. That was where Melinda and Charlotte went, drawing pictures of flowers and hearts and unicorns and writing "Melinda and Char"—that's what Melinda had started calling Charlotte—"BFFs forever."

I went over by Mrs. Abernathy, the librarian, to read. A seventh-grade girl sat against the wall and wrote poetry in her journal in large block letters.

Dev was there, too, with Adam, playing chess on a fabric board. Lucas crouched down next to them with his hands wrapped around his legs. I watched Adam move his knight.

Mrs. Abernathy slid a book over to me. The cover was plain with no picture. *The Hobbit* by J. R. R. Tolkien. People were always trying to get me to read J. R. R. Tolkien.

"It's fantasy," she said. "You love fantasy."

"I love the Taryn Greenbottom books. Not the same."

"You should give it a try. Every reading diet needs a little variety."

I wondered if this was true, or if it was just the type of thing librarians said to keep themselves in business. "No, thanks. I'm fine with my reading diet."

"You've read Andromeda Rex," Dev said. "That's variety."

"Exactly," I said to Mrs. Abernathy, though I was loath to admit reading the rival of Harriet Wexler. "I've read Andromeda Rex."

"Only the first two," Adam reminded us.

"Give it a rest," Dev muttered.

Lucas bounced up and down. "Your move, Dev," he said.

"It's slight variety," Mrs. Abernathy said. "I've already checked this out to you. Why don't you just take it?"

"It is a pretty good book," Dev said without looking up from the chessboard. "You might like it, Ruth."

I held up *The Riddled Cottage*. "I'm reading an advance copy of Harriet Wexler's new book. I don't have time."

Dev moved a bishop. "No skin off my nose."

Lucas slapped his forehead in an exaggerated way. "Dev," he moaned. "I can't believe you did that."

"Did what?"

"That!" Lucas said. He gestured with both hands at the board. "I'm not going to say it out loud, because it's possible that Adam hasn't picked up on the horrible, horrible move you just made."

Adam's gaze scanned the board, zigzagging wildly from corner to corner.

"He doesn't see it!" Lucas said gleefully.

I didn't see it, either, but that was no surprise. I searched the room. Melinda and Charlotte were still drawing on the rolled-out paper. They were stuck together at shoulder, hip, ankle.

Mitchell was shooting free throws with some seventh- and eighth-grade boys.

Ms. Wickersham looked about ready to collapse.

"You know that it's against the rules of chess for you to harass me like this," Adam told Lucas.

"True," Dev agreed.

Adam moved one of his rooks and captured one of Dev's pawns.

Lucas shook his head but kept quiet. Still, Adam demanded: "You wanna play? You think I'm doing such a bad job?"

"I've got next game," he said. "Remember? Unless you wanna play, Ruth? I could see if I could beat you in even fewer moves than I did last time."

I shook my head. "I don't think that's possible."

"I liked it, too, by the way," he said.

"Liked what?" I asked.

"*The Hobbit.* I liked the dragon."

I did like it when there were dragons in books, but I remained unconvinced. "I'm not going to read *The Hobbit.* I'm only halfway through this, and I still have almost two hundred pages to go." I shook the book at them.

"I thought it was only so-so," Adam said. "The Lord of the Rings trilogy was way better, and *The Hitchhiker's Guide to the Galaxy* was even better than that."

Dev rolled his eyes. "What does *The Hitchhiker's Guide* have to do with *The Hobbit?*"

Dr. Dawes came into the gym. I thought maybe she was going to tell us that we were having lunch, even though it was only nine forty-seven, according to the clock that hung behind a cage above the basketball hoop. Like, do they think that someone is going to steal it? Or that it might break free on its own and run around the court?

"They're both classics," Adam said, his voice rising in pitch.

Dr. Dawes didn't stop in the middle of the floor or call the teachers over to her. Instead, she marched straight to Charlotte.

"One is science fiction and the other is fantasy," Dev said. "Totally different."

"Totally different," Lucas agreed.

"Sure you'd side with him," Adam said.

"Your move, Adam," Dev said, his voice soft.

Dr. Dawes crouched down low and put her hand on Charlotte's shoulder as she spoke. Charlotte's body went tense and still, and even though I had no idea what Dr. Dawes told Charlotte, I knew it wasn't good. Principals just don't talk to you like that when they have good news, or even neutral news. Dr. Dawes helped Charlotte to her feet and led her out of the gym, arm still over her shoulder.

—◁◦▷—

Melinda tried to lord it over everybody, but she wasn't the only one who had heard Dr. Dawes, so by the time we were dismissed—after a lunch of peanut butter and jelly sandwiches and premature Valentine's Day cookies—everyone knew what had happened. Or at least part of the story.

Mom picked me up. Without me having to ask, she drove us right into town. You couldn't get too close because of the fire trucks and police tape, but it was near enough to see what wasn't there.

Melinda told everyone that the library had been damaged by the storm, and that there was something wrong with Charlotte's condo. That was what Dr. Dawes had said, according to one of the other girls: "Charlotte, all this snow has done some damage to the library and your home. Your dads want to see you."

It wasn't damaged, though. It was destroyed.

The roof of the library building had collapsed. Charlotte's home dropped right down into the second floor of the library, everything crashed together like a black hole opening up and then folding in on itself. I half expected to see little astronauts or aliens emerging from the rubble.

We got out of the car and walked closer. There were

books in the snow, dotting it red and blue and green and purple. They were sprinkled over the snow like the Christmas decorations that had just come down. They didn't even look like books there, jostled and out of order. But then the wind picked up and a few of them had pages that fluttered in the breeze. The snow blew around them as if the whole world—my whole world—had been turned into a snow globe.

Mom talked to a police officer. I didn't hear what she said. *What books are lost?* I wondered. *Were any saved? Is Harry Potter completely gone, all seven volumes? And Andromeda Rex?* I couldn't take any comfort in his destruction. And *Tuck Everlasting* and *A Wrinkle in Time* and *The Westing Game?* Was someone able to save poor old *Harriet the Spy* in her red sweatshirt?

They were my friends. My friends are gone.

And the notes. If there were any more clues in the library, I would never find them.

Mom walked back toward me now. She had her arm around Charlotte, whose eyes were red and who wore her father's goofy earflap hat, not caring who might see. "Charlotte's going to stay with us for tonight. Maybe a day or two."

"Okay," I said.

I let her have the front seat.

◄◊►

Mom made cream of mushroom soup from a can. It was one of Charlotte's favorites, and mine. She found some frozen

French bread and started reheating that. Then she pulled out the old countertop mixer and searched the pantry for ingredients to make chocolate chip cookies. "We don't have any brown sugar," we heard her muttering as we slurped our soup. "Why don't we have any brown sugar?"

"It's okay, Theresa," Charlotte said. "I don't need cookies."

Mom emerged from the pantry. She was crying.

"I'm sorry, Charlotte. I'm just so sorry."

"It's okay," Charlotte said.

"You know you can stay here as long as you need to. Your dads, too."

I didn't know where her dads were, but I didn't think it was a good time to ask.

Charlotte nodded.

Mom sat at the table with us. She drew one knee up to her chest and started tearing the bread apart and dipping it in the soup. She shook her head.

"We had Valentine's cookies for lunch today," I told Charlotte.

"Really?" she asked.

"Ruth—" Mom began.

"Yep. I guess they were just clearing out the freezer. Do you think they were meant to be for this year or left over from last year?"

"Maybe the year before that," Charlotte said, cracking a hint of a smile.

"Like maybe the cafeteria workers went back there and

were like, 'Hey, what's this? Valentine's Day 1987? Perfect!
There are only fifty-seven kids here today, anyway.' And then
they watched them while they were baking to make sure they
didn't mutate into Killer Cookies from Outer Space or anything."

"You'd better not let them know you're on to them. They
already have it out for you."

"Why do the cafeteria workers have it out for you?" Mom
asked.

Charlotte glanced at me. I shrugged, and she said, "I was
just playing along."

Mom looked from Charlotte to me and back again. I knew
she knew Charlotte was lying, that there was something we
were hiding, but she almost looked grateful that Charlotte
would still lie for me.

After we cleared our dishes, we went into the TV room
and tried to find something good to watch. When we couldn't,
I said, "We could study for the spelling bee."

She twisted her fingers together. "Are you sure?"

I wasn't. I mean, what if our studying gave her the one
word she needed to beat me? But I couldn't take it back.
"Sure."

We took out our lists and started quizzing each other
back and forth. Charlotte didn't ask any clarifying questions,
and I didn't tell her why Coco said you should. "'Ingrate,'"
she said to me.

"Ingrate. *I-N-G-R-A-T-E*. Ingrate."

"Yep."

"'Longitude,'" I said to her.

She spelled it perfectly.

We went back and forth like that until we got all the way through the seventh-grade challenge words. She missed four. I didn't miss any.

"I'm really tired," she said. "Do you think we could just go to bed?"

I gave her some of my pajamas. Mom took her clothes to wash them. "Mix and match with some things from Ruth, and no one will know you're rewearing them."

If Mom knew that rewearing clothes was such a sin, she could have dropped me a hint.

Charlotte and I didn't talk until the lights were off, like the darkness was a switch.

"I don't know where we're going to go. Where we're going to live," she said, her voice hitching.

"Mom said you can stay here for as long as you need."

"But after. After that, then what?"

"Your dads will figure it out. They'll get a new house. It will be okay."

"Do you think it will still be in Promise? I don't want to go to a new school."

"It will be in Promise," I assured her.

She was crying now, just a little, but I could hear her. I didn't know if I should get up and go to her, give her a hug.

"All our stuff," she said. "I don't even know what I have and what I don't have."

"I'm sorry," I said. It was stupid—so very stupid and small in the face of all that had happened—but I didn't know what else to say.

"And all the books," she said.

"I know," I said. "It was awful seeing them out in the snow like that, like someone dumped out the world's biggest backpack and didn't even care."

"The pages just looked so sad," Charlotte said.

"And the notes. The notes are all gone, too."

I heard her roll over in bed and tug the covers up over herself. "Why do you have to be like that?"

"Like what?"

"Like you're still nine years old." She whispered the words. "Mystery games and secret coded messages. It's all dumb."

And it was, I realized. Compared to her house, it was nothing. "I'm sorry," I told her.

"I never liked any of it," she went on, as if I hadn't apologized. "Those drawings you had me do—those kinds of stories. Those weren't the stories I liked. Fairies and elves and all that. Baby stuff. And the 'experiments' in the blender. Gross. I always just did it for you."

"Charlotte," I said.

Her voice was rising in pitch, the words coming faster and faster like she was running toward the edge of a cliff and she couldn't quite stop herself. And then she went over. "That's the problem with you, you know? You act like the whole world revolves around you, and you don't even realize it. I mean my house—*my house*—is gone, and all you can think about are those stupid clues."

"I said I was sorry."

"Whatever," she said. "G'night."

"Good night."

She was still crying, but I stayed right in my bed.

EIGHTEEN

Knavery

In the morning, we dug out the snow in front of the garage while Mom made us breakfast. I ate alone, though, because Charlotte wanted to take a shower. She said she sweated and that she smelled bad, which I knew wasn't true.

Mom wrapped her hands around her coffee and watched me eat my pancakes. "You girls seem to be doing okay," she said.

"Definitely," I agreed. I wondered if I should start keeping track of all the lies I told her.

"It's a tragedy, of course, but sometimes tragedies bring people together."

I jammed my mouth full of pancakes, one bite right after

another until it was a big sweet and sticky blob inside my mouth. Mom sipped her coffee.

"Since you can't go to the library after school, I was thinking you two girls could come back here together."

I swallowed, then swallowed again. "You never let me stay home alone."

"You wouldn't be alone. You'd be with Charlotte."

"So now she's my babysitter?"

Mom frowned at her coffee. "You would look out for each other. But no using the blender." She grinned.

My stomach lurched as I remembered Charlotte's words the night before.

"Charlotte's dads are still figuring out what they're going to do. Insurance will put them up in a hotel, but I said they were welcome to stay here. We'll see."

Charlotte came into the kitchen then. Her hair was wet and leaving a spot on her T-shirt—my shirt, actually, the one she'd slept in. She was holding her lightly padded bra by a strap. "It's still wet."

Mom stood up. "Come on. I'll get you one of Ruth's. They're clean and she's never even worn them. Not quite as fancy as that one, but it will do for one day."

They left together, Mom's hand on Charlotte's back.

◄O►

"You should have stayed with me!" Melinda declared as she enveloped Charlotte. "You didn't have to stay with her."

"It was fine," Charlotte lied.

They were both acting like I wasn't even there, so I sat down with Lucas. He was studying for the map quiz in humanities. "I thought you memorized everything right away," I said.

"I do. This is the first time I'm looking at it."

Of course.

"I couldn't believe it when Dr. Dawes came in and then I actually saw the pictures on the news," Melinda gushed.

"It was on the news?" Charlotte asked.

"Oh, yeah. All over the news. They even had the helicopter shot and that cute news reporter, the one on channel eight. He was there."

"Oh."

"You didn't see it?"

"We didn't watch the news," Charlotte told her.

"If you'd been at my house, you could've watched it." She rubbed Charlotte's arm. "Anyway, maybe that cute reporter will want to interview you."

"Maybe," Charlotte said.

"Mozambique!" Lucas called out.

Charlotte dropped her head. "I didn't study," she said. She glanced at me. I hadn't studied the night before, either, but I had studied earlier that day with Lena.

"It'll be okay. Ms. Lawson will give you a break," Melinda told her.

"We've known about the quiz for a week," Charlotte said.

Mitchell said, "Just sit next to Lucas."

"Ha!" Lucas said. "Good idea, but I have my patented no-cheater stance." He demonstrated how he blocked his paper from view. "You lower-level life-forms don't stand a chance."

Lena came in then, followed closely behind by Ms. Broadcheck, who flashed a soft smile at Charlotte and then said, "On a day like today, I think we need doughnuts." With a flourish, she pulled out a box of doughnut holes.

"Those aren't doughnuts. They're doughnut holes," Lucas said.

"Then don't have any," Melinda said. "I'll have yours."

Ms. Broadcheck gave us each three, saying, "So I hope you'll understand why I was late today. You would not believe the line at the drive-through!"

The bell rang as we were still eating. I held my last doughnut hole as we filed out, navigating so I was near Charlotte. "You can sit near me," I whispered.

She raised her eyebrows at me as if she hadn't quite heard me, or didn't understand.

"In humanities. Sit near me."

She nodded.

My stomach dropped as I realized what I'd just agreed to—what I'd just proposed. On the way out the door, I threw the doughnut hole in the trash.

◅◦▻

Instead of my usual seat in Ms. Lawson's room, I sat in the back. Lucas took the seat to the left of me, so I put my bag on the one to the right.

Charlotte entered soon after that. She saw me, saw my bag, and stopped. Her eyes were shiny and sad, like ice cubes in a cup of tea. Melinda was right behind her. "Okay?" Melinda asked.

Charlotte nodded. She started walking toward the seat I had saved for her.

Dev dropped his books on the desk in front of me, and I jumped. I didn't even notice him coming in.

Ms. Lawson wasn't in the room yet. Maybe she was absent. Maybe there would be no map quiz.

Charlotte stopped at the desk in front of the one I'd saved. She bent over and adjusted her sock in her boot. Melinda sighed and grabbed another desk.

I could hear everything. The incessant ticking of the clock. Lucas cracking his knuckles. Charlotte's shallow breaths. It was like I was wearing headphones turned up high. I could even hear my blood pumping. I looked at my wrist. I expected my veins to be pulsing, huge.

Charlotte stood still. She wouldn't look at me, but she took the seat next to me, dropping my bag to the floor as she did.

Usually Ms. Lawson looked all happy on map quiz day, but today she glanced over at Charlotte and gave a sad smile. This could be it. She could say that Charlotte didn't have to take the test, and I wouldn't have to make this decision.

She didn't.

Instead, she passed out the maps.

It was the whole continent of Africa. Some parts were filled in already, and we had to fill in the parts that were not.

It all swam in front of me. The map on the paper and the map in my head wouldn't come together. I coughed. Closed my eyes.

When I opened them, the world was steadier, and I began. Ivory Coast. That was easy because that's where Mom was in the Peace Corps. The equator. Which is on top: Tropic of Cancer or Tropic of Capricorn? Capricorn is the longer word, so it's like it's the base. It goes below.

The Congo. The Niger. The Nile.

I blocked out everything and just wrote.

Lesotho, Burkina Faso, Tunisia.

Maybe I would even finish before Coco today.

Could Charlotte keep up with me? Maybe I should slow down.

Indian Ocean, Red Sea, Mediterranean Sea.

It was perfect. Perfect. Usually I made one mistake or two, but not this time. I knew it.

Maybe I should make a mistake. Maybe Charlotte should.

Neither of us had ever cheated before. At least, I didn't think she had. We didn't know how to do it.

Chad, Zambia, South Sudan.

It wasn't really cheating, though. She would know it

under normal circumstances. She would learn it. Wouldn't she? Yes, she would.

Mount Kilimanjaro. Lake Victoria.

"Ms. Lawson?"

"Yes, Charlotte?"

"I'm not feeling so well. Can I go to the nurse?"

Ms. Lawson hesitated. "Let's step into the hall, Charlotte. Bring your map."

She knew! Ms. Lawson knew! Otherwise she wouldn't make Charlotte take her map, right?

Charlotte picked up her map. She hadn't written anything on it.

They stood just outside the window. Charlotte was crying. Big, fat tears that I could see all the way from the back of the room. Ms. Lawson looked into the classroom. Maybe she was just checking to make sure that everything was okay. Or maybe Charlotte had told her our plan. My plan. I flicked my gaze back to my map.

All that was left was the big country right in the middle of the continent. I knew it was the Democratic Republic of the Congo, but I didn't write it in. Instead, I started erasing my answers.

NINETEEN

Mootable

Here," Charlotte said. She handed me a shoe box. It looked like it had been walked all over. The top was dented and the sides were twisted. "My dads brought this by. It's one of the only things that made it through. They thought I would want to have it, but it's actually for you."

I started to open the box. It was after school, and I was waiting in Ms. Lawson's room for Coco, so we could study some more. He wanted to make up for the day he'd lost because of the school bus accident.

"Ruth," she said.

It was our things. Us.

There was a picture of us at the Topsham Fair two summers ago. A snow globe from a trip we took to New York

City. There were several drawings she did of my stories. I held up one that showed an old man lying back and looking at the clouds. His hand was extended out toward the sun, and on the tip of his index finger was a spider that seemed to be staring up at the sky, too. I remembered that day. It was the summer before last. Our moms and dads rented a place on a lake in the center of the state, and it turned out to be infested with spiders. I said it was because the original owner left it to his kids, and they were all hermits (the cranky kind, not the literary kind) who hated each other and hated the sun and hated the lake; it was the only reason I could think of to put a place like that up for rent and not spend the whole summer there. I said the old man cursed the place with spiders, so she drew him setting the first one free. The cabin was in the background, just the edge of it. We had shared a room with bunk beds, but we slept together on the bottom one under a mosquito net my moms had picked up at Renys.

I wanted to put the lid back on, but I couldn't help staring.

And as I stared, I noticed something else: two envelopes made from origami paper. "The notes!"

She winced.

She had only told me about one, but there were two, each a different color of origami paper. Now I had six clues!

"They're just a game."

I pulled them out and placed them on the desk in front of me. *Which shall I open first?*

"What do you even expect to find?" she asked, and I realized I'd never thought about the clues leading someplace, of there being an end to them.

"Something." I suppose I had thought they would lead me to her. I lifted my eyes. "I've found more. That's what I was doing in the gym that day when you and Melinda found me. It's a scavenger hunt, I think, it's—"

"There's no pot of gold or prince at the end. This isn't a fairy-tale quest."

But it could be, couldn't it? Mum told me a story she'd read in an in-flight magazine. This guy buried a whole bunch of money or maybe gold out west—she couldn't quite remember—and then he wrote a novel that had the clues with where to find it. Maybe these clues were something like that, and somewhere in Promise was a treasure waiting to be found.

"Ruth," she said. "Let's not talk at school anymore."

I held the envelopes in my hand: purple and red. The red one had tiny dragons printed on it. I imagined them breathing fire, it coming out and enveloping us both, me and Charlotte. She could draw that, the flames dancing out and surrounding us, pushing us together in a smaller and smaller circle. She could. She would have. Once.

"Okay," I said.

And then she was gone.

I had the two notes still in front of me, and I put my finger on the one with the pale purple envelope dotted with tiny gray elephants.

Through the door's window, I could see Charlotte talking to Melinda. And Coco. Melinda had her head tucked in toward Coco's like they were old friends.

Maybe they were.

"Sorry I'm late. What's that?" Coco asked as he burst through the door.

"Nothing," I told him. "I'm ready to start."

"Good, because these last two weeks are going to go fast. Stand up."

I stood at the front of the room. He had his Merriam-Webster dictionary in front of him. We were going off-list. "'Gusset,'" he said.

"Definition?"

"'A usually diamond-shaped or triangular insert in a seam—as of a sleeve, pocketbook, or shoe upper—to provide expansion or reinforcement.'"

I knew this one, but I had to play by Coco's rules. "Country of origin?"

He ran his finger across the page. "Middle English from the Anglo-French."

Anglo-French. Maybe I wasn't so sure, after all. "Can you use it in a sentence."

He frowned. "Um. That shirt has a nice gusset."

I said the word, then started spelling: "*G-U-S-S-E-T-T-E.* Gusset."

"Sorry. *Bzzz.* Wrong. It's *G-U-S-S-E-T.*"

"But you said it was French."

"Anglo-French. Anyway, you can't assume it's *E-T-T-E* just because it's French. That depends on whether it's masculine or feminine."

Out the window, the snow swirled around. I couldn't tell if it was snowing again or just the wind picking up the same old flakes and throwing them into the air like day-old confetti.

"You could have asked if there were alternate pronunciations."

"Are there?"

"Well, the dictionary gives the Anglo-French original, which would be *gous-say*, but truthfully I don't know if the judges would let you hear that. It's worth a shot, though."

"Sure, okay."

"Is everything all right?"

I nodded. "I'm fine. Let's keep going."

He flipped back and forth through the dictionary, quizzing me on word after word. It was enough to get my mind off Charlotte and the box and her house and the map quiz—just barely.

<hr/>

Of course my mom was late, so I ended up sitting in the vestibule between the school and outside. The heat was blowing down from a vent above my head as if it were connected to a portal to the Tropics. I could've just climbed up on the bench, removed the cover of the vent, shimmied through, and before I knew it there'd be white beaches and blue oceans. I wish I had. Then I wouldn't have heard what came next.

From the seat, I could peek into the office. Mrs. Lambert, the secretary, was on the phone, but her gaze kept going up to the clock. I didn't blame her. I hoped she wasn't waiting for me. Like maybe she had Ruth-duty, stuck waiting here until my mom came to get me.

Silly. There was still basketball practice going on, and, anyway, there was someone else in the office. A man. He stood just outside of Dr. Dawes's office. He had dark brown hair that he wore slicked back, and his cheeks—at least the one I could see—had a streak of red on it as if drawn with crayon by an angry child. He was gesticulating with his hands as he spoke, but I couldn't hear him.

Digging around in my backpack, I found my Harriet Wexler book. Taryn was out of immediate danger and she wandered through the woods singing elf songs to herself. She'd need to find food and shelter, but for now she was so relieved at her narrow escape from the river that she was perfectly content to meander and think about the leaves and the moss and the tiny berries that grew as perfect as moonlit pearls.

There was a whooshing sound as the glass door to the main office opened. It was the angry man striding through, and behind him was Coco. Coco's eyes were glassy, and his cheeks were streaked red, though more like watercolors than his father's crayon marks. I rocked back on the bench and pulled my knees to my chest. "Dad," Coco said. "Dad."

"I'm sorry, kiddo. We'll keep working on it."

"Don't, Dad."

"Can't give up now." He ran his hand over his smoothed hair, and I wondered if it came off greasy. "If they can have a spelling bee, they can have a geography bee."

"I don't want to do a geography bee."

"Why not?" his dad asked while looking at the trophy case. "That's just the type of thing that Harvard camp would love to see on your application."

Coco shook his head.

"Coco, this is the final stretch here. They're throwing obstacles in our way, but we can't let them beat us."

"I don't care about a stupid geography bee or a stupid spelling bee or a stupid anything bee."

"You're helping that girl study." He turned his eyes away from the gleaming trophies to look at Coco. "Emma told me."

Coco traced the toe of his winter boot around the outline of a chessboard tile. "It's not—"

His dad waved his hand, and Coco stopped talking.

Not what? my brain demanded.

"I'm not concerned about that. I just don't understand why you want to take a backseat. This geography bee thing—I took a look at the website, and let me tell you, you'd be a shoo-in."

"I could have been a shoo-in for the spelling bee, too. But not everything needs to be a competition. It's just dumb memorization, anyway."

His dad cocked his head to the side. "What do you mean, could have been?"

"Nothing, Dad."

"No, Christopher. What do you mean?"

"I don't even care who wins the bee, if it's Emma or Ruth or Dev or someone else entirely. I'm only helping her because—" His voice dropped off. "Let's just go."

Because why?

"Are you saying that you purposely didn't make the bee?"

A phone rang the melody of a popular song, maybe even one of those April Showers songs that Charlotte liked so much. I wasn't sure. Coco's dad pulled his phone from his pocket and answered it, all the while watching Coco, who studied the floor. I didn't know what to do, where to look. I picked up my book, but wasn't that like I was trying to ignore him?

I *was* trying to ignore him. But maybe I should have caught his eye.

Only.

Only I wished he would answer his father's questions. What did he mean, he could have been a shoo-in for the spelling bee?

But I knew. I knew. Dev said it himself. He said there was no way he could have done better on that test than Coco. And Ms. Lawson had told him right in front of me. Coco should have been in the spelling bee. He messed up the test. On purpose. Because he thought the bee was dumb. Dumb like me.

I grabbed my book and lifted it in front of my eyes.

Taryn's elf songs seemed awfully stupid themselves right about then.

I couldn't help but lift my eyes, though, when they walked through the vestibule. His dad came first, staring straight ahead and still talking on the phone. Coco, who gave me a quick glance through wet lashes, came next.

We didn't say anything.

———◄○►———

I laid the clues out on my bed. They were all still folded so the red seal with the little bird looked up at me. One at a time I unfolded them, so now I was looking at the words. Each was written in a different pen, but the handwriting was all the same: small letters that were so uniform, they almost seemed like they had been typed. The illustrations were beautiful, too. They looked like they were drawn with the same fancy kind of colored pencils that Charlotte used— not the kind my moms got me at the grocery store. Instead, these were richly colored. But the style was totally different. Charlotte's drawings were light, bright, and airy, both curvy and elongated. These were darker, with harder edges, but no less gorgeous. They looked like the drawings on the covers of the fantasy books people were always trying to push on me.

I picked up the first of the two that Charlotte had given me.

Under cover there is stored
Meanings, sometimes three or four.
"See also" takes you for a ride,
Until I have you locked inside.
My base may look fixed and strong,
But you can lift me. If I'm wrong,
Your next clue remains locked below.
So flex those muscles, off to school you go.

This was the one Charlotte remembered: *something about meanings.* The border was a chain of metal links that was held by a strong man at the top of the card. The man's face was strained with effort, as if he was trying to rip the chain apart.

As I read the clue, I pictured Coco with his dictionary. So, the next one was hidden in a dictionary, then. I started to fold the card when the final phrase caught my eye: "off to school you go." School. Not the public library, but school. She had gone looking for—and found—the next clue in a dictionary at school. That meant Charlotte had been intrigued, too, and had tried to follow the clues, only she had gotten stuck and hadn't been able to solve the next clue.

I smoothed out the card. It was one of the longer clues, and the picture up top was smaller. The image was of a girl with pale white skin, red lips, and dark hair: Snow White. Her border was leaves with little woodland animals peeking out. This one read:

Add Snow White and her seven dwarfs,
2 droids for Luke Skywalker, of course.
1 true ring to rule them all.
A decimal is a place to stall.
Snow White's gone, the dwarfs alone.
This system your next clue has shown.

Now you might ask, this little key,
Just what does it mean for me?
Hold on tight and you will see,
Someday it will set clues free.

⁕⁕⁕

It seemed like a math problem. Snow White plus her seven dwarfs, well, that made eight people. Then two, then one, then a decimal, and then just the seven dwarfs: 821.7. "This system has your next clue shown." It was a Dewey number on a book! And that made sense because I had found the clue about King Ferdinand in the J. Samuel Samuelson book of poetry in the 821 section of the library.

Looking at them in a jumble on my bed wasn't helping. I rearranged them so they were in the order I found them.

First the one telling me to look up—so simple and plain compared with the others.

Next came King Ferdinand, and after that I found the flag clue in the gym. I picked up the page torn from the phone book, a sickly yellow. Then I had the two from Charlotte: the strong man and the maiden Snow White.

Six clues in total. What would Charlotte think if she knew we had found so many? And how many were there to find? There could be little clues all over this town, just waiting to be discovered.

As I stared at the cards, I noticed the asterisks on the bottom, each a different number. I rearranged them from least asterisks to most: the strong-man clue had two asterisks, then Snow White had three. Then came King Ferdinand with four, the British flag had seven, the phone book had eight; and the look-up one, the first one I had found, had twelve.

The stars were the order!

The strong man led Charlotte to Snow White, and

Lena and I had found the phone book note by following the flag clue.

But wait. I found the flag clue following the moves on the chessboard the way they were described on the King Ferdinand clue. So either I was wrong about the numbering system or I did something wrong with the chess moves.

I looked over the clues again. Those asterisks, why else would there be a different number of them on each card? What else could it possibly represent? It had to be the order. That meant we were missing at least three: the first one, the fifth one that should have come after King Ferdinand, and then there had to be one in the post office box, one that would lead to another clue, unless the post office box itself was the end.

Coco would be good at this. All the books he read, and the way he thought about things in such an orderly way. But no. I could still hear him in the hallway talking with his dad. *I don't care about a stupid geography bee or a stupid spelling bee or a stupid anything bee.* He didn't care. I wasn't sure why he'd been going through the whole ruse of studying with me if he didn't care about the bee, but in the end it didn't really matter. The outcome was the same.

Anyway, I could do this myself. I just needed to think a little harder. I had never relied on anyone in the past except for Charlotte. And look what happened both times: I'd thought he was my friend, but he wasn't. Just like Charlotte. Just like everyone, probably, in the end.

I blinked my dry eyes. I needed to go to bed. I swept all the clues into the box, which I'd emptied of everything else except for one small key. It was bigger than a diary key, but much smaller than a house or car key.

The Summer of Lost Keys.

Two summers ago, we kept finding lost keys. We found one buried in the sand at the beach, silver and warm when we pulled it out. It was just a regular house key. Then, in the library, we found an old-fashioned key with a filigree on one end, and what looked like three uneven teeth to go in the door. We found a key with a key chain that said RAYMOND on it, and we puzzled over whether it was the name of a person or a place. We also found two tiny keys. This had to be one of them. One had been next to a potted plant by the ice-cream place down on the piers, and the other had been sitting on the end of the ferry dock. We kept them all, telling ourselves that these keys meant something, and someday we would be called upon to use them.

I guess she'd given that up as silly, too.

My computer dinged to let me know I had a chat message. It was Lena. Or so I assumed. The screen name was Cooler-ThanYou2.

Can't chat. Wanted to let you know that you need to do the Wonder Woman pose. Supposed to be in bed. Talk tomorrow.

Lena had already logged off, and I decided that maybe I didn't want to know what the Wonder Woman pose was, anyway.

After I closed the chat window, I opened up a browser and searched for the camp at the Harvard Museum of Natural History. It was run in conjunction with their Peabody Museum of American Archaeology and Ethnology. The page was filled with glowing, smiling kids alongside photos of artifacts. It said they would get to handle real bones and other ancient objects and learn the stories behind them. They would even get to look at unidentified items and try to date and figure out where they came from.

Coco would love it.

I clicked on APPLY and read what they were looking for: *academic excellence.* Not a problem. Lucas might be the smartest kid in school, but Coco was definitely the most successful. *Cooperative spirit.* Perfect. *Leadership.* I hesitated. He was a leader for sure, but not of any club or team. He just was. But that would be hard to prove, I thought. *Each candidate should have a record of achievements, honors, and accomplishments.* Like winning a geography bee. Or a spelling bee.

What about quiet leaders? I wondered. What about guys who would be willing to take a backseat in order to help someone else? It didn't seem fair. It wasn't my problem, though, and I didn't know why I even cared. Coco was as good as dead to me.

I picked up old King Ferdinand. Lena had her special sources, and I had mine. If I'd messed up the chess clue, then I needed to speak to some chess experts. Taryn sought out help when she needed it; it didn't mean she was tied to those people forever. In fact, there were only a few characters who appeared in more than one of her books. The next day I would talk to Dev and Lucas, and they would help me solve the King Ferdinand riddle.

TWENTY

Discipline

Hoping to catch Lucas before he went into homeroom, I shoved my coat and bag into my locker, slammed the door, turned, and started striding purposefully. I felt like Taryn Greenbottom heading toward a foe. Rounding the corner, I saw Ms. Lawson coming down the hall, waving. I checked over my shoulder, but, no, she wanted me. "Ruth," she said as she came up to me. "Let's talk."

Instead of going into her room, where her homeroom was gathered in the corner on the couch and beanbag chairs, she guided me to the teachers' room. Ms. Broadcheck was in there and chose a coffee pod from the decaffeinated box and put it into one of those one-cup machines that Mom says are going to be the actual downfall of our environment. "Morning, Ruth!" she said. "Just getting my morning buzz."

"It's decaf," I said.

"My mind is easily tricked," she said as she left the room.

Ms. Lawson sat down at a small table and pulled out a stack of maps from her bag. Mine was on top. My stomach plummeted like an elevator cut loose from its line in a cartoon, the wire snapping out above me and hitching in my throat.

"I need you to explain this to me."

I didn't say anything. What could I say?

"You had everything right. Everything. And then you erased it all. Why?"

"I guess I just wasn't so sure of myself."

"About every identification?"

"Yes."

She frowned. "I can't give you credit for erased answers."

"I know."

She ran her fingers through her short hair. "Most students would probably put up a fight here. Let me play your part. 'But, Ms. Lawson, you said yourself you can read them, and if they are right, can't I at least get partial credit?'"

"You don't give partial credit. That's your rule."

"I am not one hundred percent rigid," she said. "I'm trying to help you out here."

"I know."

"The test was the day after the library collapse," she said, as if I could have possibly forgotten. "I know that place was important to you and that Charlotte—"

"Charlotte has nothing to do with this," I said quickly. Too quickly.

"Charlotte took a makeup."

I lowered my eyes. So Charlotte had not sold me out. She had just walked away. Again. It was stupid to be mad at her for not cheating, but I was.

"I think you should take a makeup, too. I'll average the grades."

"So the best I can get is a fifty?"

"Actually, this test warrants a thirty since you did follow the directions for shading and such. You could get a sixty-five and still walk away with a semester grade in the high eighties or low nineties without any extra credit work."

"And if I don't do the makeup?"

She hesitated. "Your map test goes in as a thirty, which will sink your grade, and your lack of initiative will disincline me from giving extra credit."

She was frowning hard now, her lips pressed so hard together that they were white and wrinkled around the edges.

"Okay," I said.

"Okay," she agreed. "Today during study hall."

"But—" I began to say that I had plans to study with Coco, but realized this would give me an excuse not to have to see him.

She arched her eyebrows.

"Can you just tell Coco when he comes that I can't study?"

"Of course," she said.

We stood together and walked out of the room.

When I finally got to Ms. Broadcheck's class, homeroom was nearly over, and Lucas was hunched over one of his graphic novels.

———◄◦►———

"Is this some kind of alliance?" Lucas asked. "I'm not manipulating the outcome of the spelling bee, if that's what you're after." We were sitting at a table in the library during independent reading time. Lucas had a graphic novel version of *Beowulf* and Dev had a book with a dragon on the cover. I had my Harriet Wexler book. We were holding them up in front of us, but none of us were reading.

"That's not what I'm after. I need some chess help."

"So what do you need Dev for?" Lucas asked.

"Two heads are better than one," I told him.

"Three heads are better than my one head. Maybe."

"Do you need coaching or something?" Dev asked. He glanced toward Ms. Lawson and Mrs. Abernathy, who shared a table by the circulation desk. "I have a chess coach who is quite good. I can get his e-mail address, and your mom can get in contact with him."

"Not exactly. Can you keep a secret?"

The two boys let their books drop and leaned their

heads in. I hesitated for a moment. Once I told them, I couldn't take it back. But that didn't mean I had to bring them along for the rest of the clues, did it? No. The clues were mine. I would get the boys' help and then I'd be back on my own. I'd solve the whole thing, and then wouldn't Charlotte be surprised.

I spilled.

"That. Is. So. Cool," Lucas exhaled. "Let me see all the clues."

"I just have the one with me." I pulled out the envelope, which I'd tucked into my book like a bookmark. Lucas sighed, but I handed it to Dev.

He nodded. "Chess moves, sure."

"I thought I figured it out. I stood at the sculpture of King Ferdinand and I followed the floor tiles like a chessboard, and I found a clue. But it's not in the right order with the other ones I found."

"Which knight were you?" Dev asked.

"Black or white, you mean?"

"No," Lucas said, snatching the note. "He means were you king side or queen side."

"Oh. I guess I was king side."

"So let's try queen side," Dev said.

There was no way we could all excuse ourselves and go out in the hall during the whole school reading period. Just getting them to sit at a table with me—without Coco or Lena or anyone else—had been hard enough and we were pushing

it with all our whispering. "Can you meet me after school?"
I asked.

Dev said, "Sure. My brother has basketball practice. I'm
stuck here, anyway."

"I'll call home. My mom will probably show up with
cookies, she'll be so excited I have after-school plans. She
keeps asking when I want to have you back over."

"My mom said once the snow melts," Dev told him.

"Not you, Ruth. I told her you probably didn't want to
come suck at chess again."

"Gee, thanks," I said.

"You do suck at chess."

"And you suck at playdates." Dev laughed, and Lucas
didn't even look put off by it. Still, I added, "But I would
come again. I've decided on some names for your insects."

"You don't name them. They are not pets," he told me.

"Willy the wasp."

"No names. Anyway, how could you tell which one is
Willy?"

"Rutherford the dragonfly."

"It's a girl."

I giggled. I could see Coco looking over at us from his
table. His lips twitched into a smile, but his deep eyes were
soft and he gave me a sort of head tilt and shrug as if to say,
What is going on over there?

I picked up my book. I'd managed to avoid him all day,
which had taken some quick moves on my part—ducking

into the girls' bathroom, sneaking lunch into the library. But I couldn't stand to look into his deep brown eyes and realize that they weren't actually windows to his soul. It had all been a sham—he didn't care about the spelling bee or me or any of it. There was no way I was going to let him in on the clues.

"And who can forget," I said to Lucas, "Bedelia the queen of the honeybees."

Lucas dropped his book and threw his hands up with disgust.

"Lucas, Ruth, Dev." Ms. Lawson's voice was sharp from her perch over by the circulation desk.

I started reading. Taryn was finally about to find shelter: a small abandoned cottage in the woods.

I glanced back up, though, before I dove into the story. "After school," I mouthed.

Lucas and Dev nodded.

———◄o►———

Lucas placed himself on the crosshairs of the four tiles that made the square for the knight on the left side of the Ferdinand statue. "So forward two, over one," he said.

"Why not over two, up one?" Dev asked.

"Duh. If this were the start of a chess game and the knight tried to do that, he'd land on one of his own pawns."

I glanced over at Dev, who admitted, "He's right."

Lucas took giant steps from block to block, then paused.

I said, "If you go left, you just go outside. I stopped in the office, but there was nothing there. If you go right, you end up in the gym. There was a clue there, but it wasn't the right one."

"How do you know?" Dev asked.

I pointed at the asterisks on the bottom of the clue he was holding. "Those stars. I think that's how they numbered the clues."

"Who's 'they'?" Lucas asked, mimicking Ms. Lawson's voice. She had declared a war on imprecise pronouns. But he had a point. Who had hidden all these clues?

"So I guess I go straight," Lucas said. "That would be a lousy move. Why would anyone play that?"

"We're talking about an imaginary chess world where knights transform into rooks," Dev said.

Lucas didn't look convinced, but he took Mother, May I giant steps across the hallway. We could all see the doorway as he headed to it: MAINTENANCE.

Before Dev or I could say anything, he knocked.

Silence.

So he twisted the knob, and the door opened with a click.

"Lucas!" Dev cried out, but we both hurried in after him. I was expecting mops and brooms and shelves of cleaning supplies, but instead there were mechanical workings: pipes, tubes, circuit-breaker boxes. "What next?" Lucas asked.

"That's all it says," I said.

"Read the whole thing again," Lucas replied.

Dev lifted the paper and read:

Our <u>Great King Ferdinand</u> joined the warring masses,
And to honor him we pass him as we run to all our classes.
But if you stop and listen to the marble man,
He will tell you where to look, ye miners with a pan.

"My <u>knight</u> in dingy armor
Move as by your plan
Then by crook or <u>rook</u>
Straight as you can."

* * *

"'Miners with a pan,'" Lucas murmured.

"That's the only part that we haven't used," Dev said.

"Gold miners would shake river sand through a screen to see if there was any gold," I told them, thinking of our fifth-grade unit on the gold rush.

We all looked around. There was no screen. No pan. Certainly no gold.

Lucas got down on his hands and knees and peered

behind the pipes. "Wait," he said. Crawling on his belly, he slid forward. His head disappeared as his toes pushed him forward. "Yow!!!" he cried out as he jerked back. He was holding his arm.

"What happened?"

"One of the pipes, it was burning hot."

His skin was turning pink. Dev and I exchanged a look, but before we could say anything, the door was thrown open and there was Dr. Dawes. Her face went from concerned to confused, as if she couldn't imagine three people more unlikely to be together in the maintenance closet. "What exactly is going on here?" she demanded.

I should've said something. This was my quest. But my tongue was swollen in my mouth as if Dr. Dawes were actually a witch who had cast a spell on me—not a bad ability for a school principal, if you think about it. Dev, though, Dev was confident and a good speaker, and polite, too. He'd say something smart. When I turned, though, he looked as tongue-tied as me. Finally, it was Lucas who spoke. "We were looking for a chessboard."

"A chessboard?" she asked.

"Mr. Noonan plays. We play against each other sometimes, when he's off the clock, of course, and I thought he said this is where he keeps his board. But I guess I was wrong."

"And your arm?" Dr. Dawes asked. Lucas was still cradling his right arm in his left.

"I jostled up against one of the pipes."

"Jostled?" she asked.

"To push up against one another. It derives from 'joust.'"

"Really?" I asked.

"Really." He nodded.

"Interesting, but not relevant," Dr. Dawes said.

I began to explain how it was relevant, but Dev grabbed my arm.

"Let's get you to the nurse," Dr. Dawes said to Lucas. "I think she's still here. If not, we'll go to the athletic trainer."

"I bet that would be the first time someone went to the trainer with a chess injury, huh?" Lucas asked.

Dr. Dawes put her hand on his shoulder and guided him down the hall. "The three of you should know better than to go into the maintenance closet. Didn't you see all those mechanical systems? That's the heart of the school, the lifeblood."

"I thought the library was the heart of the school," I said.

"The library is the intellectual hub of the school," Dr. Dawes said, and then added without missing a beat, "And where you can go to borrow a chessboard. Dev and Ruth, go ahead there now. I'll take care of Lucas."

I glanced at Lucas. He nodded. And then, when Dr. Dawes's back was turned, he flicked up his left hand. In it was a tiny orange envelope: a seventh clue.

TWENTY-ONE

Flense

Homeroom. Lucas could give me the clue in homeroom. With any luck he'd have some subtlety about the situation. *No. This is Lucas. Wait for him by the door.*

I shoved my coat into my locker.

That he'd had the note all weekend without my even seeing it was almost too much to bear. I had developed numerous plots for how I could get it from him: snowshoe through the woods into town and then out to his house (I looked online and we lived thirteen miles apart—so twenty-six miles round-trip, but maybe his mother would drive me home), track him down on the Internet and send him repeated messages, or, the most desperate, tell my mom I wanted to have another playdate with him.

In the end, I just stewed. I stewed about the clue and whether it was really the missing fifth clue in the series. I stewed about Mum not being home, and I stewed about Coco. I just couldn't figure out what he wanted. Why had he pretended to be so nice to me, when really he thought I was just a foolish girl with a stupid pursuit? My imagination could conjure no reasonable explanation—though, of course, plenty of unreasonable ones. My personal favorite was that he was a golem, a figure made of clay that has life breathed into it. In Jewish legend, the golem was a savior, so this meant he was some kind of inverse golem. But who had sent him? The person with the most motivation, of course, was Melinda. Mean, sneaky Melinda. But I didn't think she had the patience or the intellect for the dark arts.

When my mind spiraled that way, it was better to get back to thinking about Lucas. He could have solved the next riddle and already found the next clue. This was why you didn't bring people into your own private sagas. They took them over. I should have just kept it to myself—no Dev and Lucas, no Adam, and maybe even no Lena.

"Hey, Ruth." I knew the voice. It was Coco, still sounding warm and friendly even though he was a big betrayer. Sure, I knew there was no golem, but I had seen him talking so chummily to Melinda that same day. I couldn't shake the idea that she was in on this: some elaborate plan to make me crash and burn at the bee so that Charlotte could win.

I pretended to be looking for something in my locker.

This was a mistake, because it gave him a chance to come over and stand next to me. I could smell the brown sugar oatmeal he must have had for breakfast.

"I was just checking on studying for today. We have a lot to do since we missed Friday."

"I was taking a test."

"Right," he said. Ms. Lawson had turned him away at the door just as she had promised. "What about today?"

I still had my head in my locker. Way in the back, there was a squished-up granola bar. *Gross.* "I have to get something in the library." This wasn't exactly a lie. When I had finished the map test—100 percent correct again—I had gone to the library and worked with Mrs. Abernathy to try to figure out why the world seemed so quiet after a snow. We couldn't find anything, and she'd suggested we e-mail a professor at UMaine. She'd promised she would get some names for me.

"We could meet in the library and once you get what you need, we could study."

"Um, I don't think so. Mrs. Abernathy and I are working on something."

He shifted his feet in the brown puddle of dirty snow that had melted off his boots. "We're getting close to the bee," he said.

"I know."

"So we still have work to do."

"I guess so."

"What are you even looking for in there?"

I pulled out the granola bar. He wrinkled up his nose, and his freckles seemed to hop around like popcorn kernels in a pan. "I just need to throw this away," I told him. I remembered now. Mom had packed it even though we weren't allowed to have nuts in school, and so I'd taken it out of my bag and forgotten about it. "It's contraband," I told him. And then I left him right by my locker as I dropped the old, ruined granola bar into a trash bin and went on my way to homeroom.

I felt a little bit bad about it, thinking of him there in the puddle with his hat on crooked and not realizing what he had done wrong. But I knew. He was messing around with me. I wasn't sure why, but he was. Maybe he was working for Melinda. Or maybe he was part of some mad cabal set on overthrowing the tyranny of the Scripps National Spelling Bee. "Cabal" wasn't a spelling bee word, but Mum liked it because she found conspiracy theories fascinating. Anyway, I decided not to feel bad anymore, and instead pushed open the door to Ms. Broadcheck's room.

Lucas was waiting just inside the door, shifting his weight from foot to foot. "Finally," he exclaimed, and thrust the envelope at me. I snatched it from him. It was warm and slightly damp from being in his hand.

"It's a doozy," he said.

So he hadn't figured it out!

When I turned my head, I saw Charlotte watching us,

but she snapped her gaze in the other direction as quickly as I grabbed the envelope from Lucas.

———◦———

I kept the envelope in my hand until science class, where I pulled it out. The little bird seemed to be winking at me. Unfolding it, I saw that a dusty-looking path wound its way around the outside edges of the card and finished up at the top, in a graveyard, the headstones crooked and moss-covered. It read:

The Planeswalkers know
You take the card from the library
And bury it when you're done.
On the path, you face history.
Walk the path, do the math:

Start with the prime numbers under 100
Whose digits give you 10.
Choose the happy median.
Add it to: The square root of
The cube of five divided by
The sum of 3 and 2.

✳✳✳✳

At the bottom were five asterisks. My theory was right! The asterisks indicated the number of the clue, which meant this one would lead me to the sixth clue, filling in the gap before the Union Jack clue I had found in the gym. If I solved the riddle and found the next clue, I would have numbers two through eight. That still left the problem of the post office box, but I could deal with that later. One thing at a time.

"Everyone, the mnemonic for taxonomy," Mr. Sneed directed.

"Kings play chess on fine grain sand," we all sang back to him, just as we had every day since we'd started studying species classification.

"And that means?"

"Kingdom, phylum, class, order, family, genus, species."

Truthfully, I would probably never forget. Also, "mnemonic" was a great spelling bee word with that silent *M* at the beginning.

Mr. Sneed droned on at the front of the room. He'd been teaching science forever. Legend was that he had been a teacher at the high school, and when they moved the high school to a new building and the middle school into the old high school, well, Mr. Sneed had stayed behind, still teaching the same stuff in the same way. He passed out typewritten handouts with a purple hue, and everything he said in class was the same as what was on the sheet, so you didn't really have to pay attention.

I reread the clue. The first half made no sense, but I thought I could do the math problem. Lucas probably had started there, too.

So, the prime numbers under 100. I listed them out as best I could: 2, 3, 5, 7, 11, 13, 17, 23, 29, 31, 37, 43, 47, 53, 59, 61, 71, 73, 79, 83, 89, 97.

"Today we are going to examine Cetacea," Mr. Sneed said. "What class do Cetacea fall under?"

"Mammals," we all said back. It seemed like we'd been studying mammals forever, even though Mr. Sneed had said we'd just be hitting a few of the highlights. When he'd said that at the beginning of the unit, his creepy corners-of-the-mouth-only smile made me realize it would be a slog, like Taryn trying to get through the Swamp of Memoriam.

So, the primes that added up to 10 were 37 and 73. That made the happy median the average? No, wait. I'd missed one—19. Okay, so that made 37 the median. Now what? The cube of 5.

"Correct. Cetacea are marine mammals. Examples include whales and porpoises."

This was exactly what was written on the handout.

"What's that?" Coco whispered to me.

I stared down at the clue. Mr. Sneed couldn't stand people whispering in his class. Supposedly he'd once heard a girl whispering, even though she was sitting way back in the room. He'd stopped class and given her such a dressing down that she'd started bawling. She had cried so hard, her nose started to bleed.

"Is that for math?" he asked.

I narrowed my eyes and refocused.

The square root of the cube of 5. The cube of 5 was 125, but I had no idea what the square root of 125 was. There was no way I could get a calculator out of my backpack.

In front of me, Lucas raised his hand. "Yes, Mr. Hosgrove?"

"Whales get earwax just like people."

I tried writing out the equation:

$$\frac{\sqrt{5^3}}{3+2}$$

That didn't help me much. I could do 3 plus 2, of course, but I was still stuck with that square root of 5 cubed.

"Thank you, Mr. Hosgrove."

"But," Lucas went on, "they never clean it out. I mean, it's not like whales have Q-tips, right? So it stays in their ears their whole lives, and when scientists pull it out, it can be up to a foot long."

Melinda said, "Eww," and we all shuddered at the thought of a foot-long tube of earwax.

"But it's really cool because the wax tracks everything they've gone through. Everything from the salt levels of the water to the pollutants they come in contact with."

"Interesting, but not relevant."

Lucas's shoulders slumped. Had the teachers all agreed that this would be their line for him?

I raised my hand, and Mr. Sneed called on me without any enthusiasm. "I disagree," I said. "I think it's very relevant."

"Miss Mudd-O'Flanahan, things either are relevant or they are not. There's no such thing as very relevant."

"Fine. But it *is* relevant. We're studying the whole classification system, which is like the web of life, right? And the whales and their earwax, that shows all the pollutants in our ocean and what's going to damage that web. And it's not just science class stuff. It's real life."

"Science class is facts, Miss Mudd-O'Flanahan. It is real life."

"Right, but also, I mean like the fishing industry and tourism—our oceans are vital to the peninsula. And what Lucas is saying is that whale earwax is like the key that tells us what's going on and then maybe we can try to fight the pollution and the trash and the climate change and everything else that is ruining the web of life."

"A very impassioned speech. Perhaps you and your mother ought to write an e-mail about it."

Everyone laughed, except Lucas and Lena. Even Coco laughed.

"Maybe we will," I said.

Some people just shouldn't be teachers.

◄◦►

"Forty-two," Lucas said when we got out to recess. He, Dev, and I stood near the building, stomping our feet to try to keep warm.

"But forty-two what?" I asked. "The first part of the clue makes no sense."

"We should ask Coco," Dev said. "He'd be really good at this."

"No," I said.

"Why not?" Dev asked.

The snow looked like a field of jagged diamonds. "We don't need any help. Anyway, he'd just think it was dumb."

I could see Coco across the field. He had a black plastic sled and was getting ready to slide down the hill.

"It's better with a small group anyway," Lucas said. "More loot to go around."

"We don't know that there's any loot," I told him. "We don't know that there's anything."

"I'm not saying to invite the whole world. I just think Coco would be really helpful."

"No," I said. "Anyway, I haven't had a chance to show it to Lena. She might have some ideas."

Coco held the sled in two hands, sprinted forward, and then dove onto it like those crazy skeleton riders at the Olympics.

"Planeswalkers," Dev said. "I can't put my finger on it, but it sounds familiar. Maybe I could ask Coco without explaining the whole thing?"

I rolled my eyes.

"It's just that he's been my best friend forever. We do everything together."

"Things change. And maybe you don't know him as well as you think you do."

"You were wrong in science class," Lucas said to me.

"What?"

A chunk of snow slipped off the roof of the building, bringing with it a cluster of long, sharp icicles.

"You know an icicle can kill you if it hits you at just the right angle," Lucas said. "I saw it on *MythBusters.*"

"What was I wrong about in science?"

"The web of life and all that. The wax just tells you what *was* there. It can't tell you what pollution is coming next or how to stop it."

*De*scriptive, not *pre*scriptive. Like baseball statistics and Coco's family in the spelling bees. Great. Now I had Coco memories haunting me along with Charlotte memories. Maybe they could hang out—throw a boy-girl party to celebrate my misery.

Lone wolf. I was meant to be a lone wolf, and now here I was surrounded by a pack of hyenas. We'd once visited this zoo and amusement park in the southern part of the state. It was just about the saddest thing you'd ever want to see. All the animals had threadbare patches on their fur and wandered from one side of their cage to another without any life in their eyes. That was what was going to happen to me.

"I've gotta go," I said. I needed to get back inside to think. Back with Taryn Greenbottom on her own solo quest. Sure, Taryn usually traveled with her group, but those fellows were different. They were smart and loyal and brave, and they never, ever, ever let Taryn down. She was always the one leaving them. As usual, I realized, Taryn had the right idea.

TWENTY-TWO

Nemesis

Because my week couldn't get any better, on Tuesday we started volleyball in gym class.

Lena and I changed in the supply closet and I noticed that the bin of basketballs was sitting right where the volleyballs used to be—and the volleyballs were gone. I hoped this was the work of a flock of volleyball-loving penguins called to play snow volleyball out on the field, but I knew the truth. "Oh, no," I moaned.

"Did you forget your gym clothes?" Lena asked.

I shook my head. "Volleyball. Game of death."

"Really? I kind of like it. I'll help you out."

But of course Ms. Wickersham split us up. And it wasn't just that Lena was on another team. No, her team was playing on a completely different court. And who was on my team? Why, Melinda, Charlotte, and Coco, of course, plus Lucas, which would have been fine, only he was even worse at volleyball than me, so it wasn't like he could help me out and cover for me.

It didn't take long for the other team to figure out that we were the weak points, and soon they were firing every serve and spike our way. "It's like the balls are magnetically attracted to us," I complained to him.

"At least something is," Melinda said.

Charlotte looked at me, then looked away. She had just about perfected the move. It almost would have been better if she'd laughed along with the girls on the other side of the net.

On the next serve, though, Dev smacked it so it nearly hit Melinda in the face. That was like flipping a switch. She went from regular, mean Melinda to mean Melinda with a super-competitive streak.

"Come on, Ruth! Could you even try a little?" she yelled when I flinched away from yet another ball.

We were losing three to six. If the game would just end, we'd rotate and our team would be going up against Lena and a bunch of other relatively sane people. Lucas served. The ball flopped into our side of the net.

Melinda threw her hands into the air.

"It's just a game," Coco said. Big phony. He was only pretending to be nice to me, so they could finish up their diabolical plan.

Melinda sniffed in hard. "What do you know about it?" she demanded.

He blinked his eyes quickly, as if no one had ever snapped at him before. It almost made me think they weren't in cahoots.

Melinda picked up the ball and threw it hard at Lucas, who caught it with an "oof."

"Take your makeup serve," she said. "And get it over the net this time."

Lucas held the ball out with one hand, then used his other hand to send it over the net. It slipped over and fell down so close to the net that the other team didn't have a chance to get it.

"Yeah!" Melinda punched the air.

Lucas had to serve again. This time they were ready for him, with Ashley, one of Melinda's basketball friends, way up by the net. The serve veered to the left, and Dev popped it back up. Ashley jumped and tried to spike it, but ended up smashing it into her own toe.

She rolled the ball to Melinda, who tossed it to Lucas. "I have to serve again?" he asked.

"You keep serving until we lose the point. And don't even think of losing the point on purpose."

So Lucas served again and got it over. This time they returned it easily. Coco bumped it up, then Charlotte pushed it over toward me. I took a deep breath and slapped at the ball. By some miracle it made its way over and landed in a hole among the other team.

"Awesome, Ruth!" Charlotte called out.

"Dumb luck," Melinda said.

She was right, but whatever.

"Good play," Coco said to me softly.

"I don't care about stupid volleyball," I said back to him.

Lucas's wrist was turning pink where it smacked the ball when he served. He tossed it in his hands.

"All tied up," Melinda said.

"I just want to let you know that, even with the marked improvement I'm showing, statistically I am unlikely to get another serve over," Lucas said. "I've never done more than one before."

"Just serve the ball." Melinda leaned forward on her toes. She blew her hair out of her eyes.

Lucas tried again and sent it sailing over the net and beyond. It was about to go out, but then Dev did a heroic dive and popped it back in. "Dev!" Ashley cried out. "Let that go!"

Another girl on her team managed to control the ball and get it back into play, and Ashley spiked it over. Straight to me, of course.

Melinda jumped in front of me, her elbow catching me in the ribs. I toppled to the ground and she fell on top of

me. Her knee hit my stomach. "Ruth!" she cried as she dis-
entangled herself. "You're useless."

"You ran into me!" I cried out.

"I did not. And, anyway, I called it. It was between us
and I called it and you should have stepped aside."

"I didn't hear you call it," Lucas said.

"Me, neither," Coco said.

Ms. Wickersham trotted over. "What's going on here,
kiddos?"

Melinda pointed at me. "It was between us. She should
have moved. She practically tripped me." She rubbed her
elbow, and then her ankle.

"You okay?" Ms. Wickersham asked. "You hurt your ankle
again?"

Of course. Ms. Wickersham coached the girls' basketball
team, and Melinda was her star player.

"I don't know. Maybe."

"Why don't you go get some ice."

"If I'm sidelined, it's all Ruth's fault. There should be
two gym classes. One for athletes, and one for idiots."

"Did you trip her?" Ms. Wickersham asked. She tried to
make her face look soft and caring.

"No," I said.

"She didn't," Coco said. "Really."

"I don't need your help," I said to him. He recoiled. It
was like watching one of those sensitive plants that collapsed
in on itself when you touched it. I didn't care. I turned to

Ms. Wickersham. "Either you believe me or you don't, Ms. Wickersham. She crashed into me because she didn't think I would hit the ball. And I probably wouldn't have. So I guess she was right. Because Melinda's always right, isn't she?"

"Ruth—" Ms. Wickersham said. Her voice had a sheen of calm over a layer of panic, like when there's a thaw that just melts the snow enough so it turns to ice, and then it snows again on top. "No one is accusing you of anything."

I shook my head and pressed my lips together. No one was? Melinda was. Melinda had.

"Put some ice on that, Melinda." Ms. Wickersham's voice edged closer to anger. Melinda heaved a sigh and limped over toward the first aid box, where she grabbed one of those ice packs that you smash and some sort of chemical process gets going to make it cold. When she smacked it, she glared right at me. "Volleyball is a tough game to get the hang of," Ms. Wickersham told me.

"Ms. Wickersham," Charlotte said, barely above a whisper. "It's true."

"Ruth really tripped Melinda?" Ms. Wickersham asked.

"No." She stepped closer and leaned her head right into Ms. Wickersham, with her back to Melinda. "Melinda ran into Ruth. She didn't call the ball. I know it was an accident. She's probably embarrassed."

"It wasn't an accident," I said.

Charlotte looked up at me with her sad eyes—the sad

eyes she'd worn ever since the library collapsed—and I shut my mouth. I shouldn't ruin her gesture. It just might be the last favor she ever did for me.

◄◦►

During study hall I asked Ms. Lawson if I could go to the library, and then hurried there as fast as I could so Coco wouldn't find me.

Mrs. Abernathy beckoned me over. "No word yet from the professor," she said. "Sorry about that."

"It doesn't matter," I said. "It's just the way things go."

She pushed her glasses up into her hair, where there was already another pair of reading glasses. "It's a good question. You have me curious now, too."

"My mom was the one who asked," I told her. "I just said I would try to find out. I think I'm going to go read now."

"I still have *The Hobbit* if you want it."

I shook my head and held up *The Riddled Cottage*.

"Harriet Wexler. Got it."

As I walked back to my spot, I thought I saw Coco at the library door. I tucked my head down and tightened my shoulders. He wasn't an idiot. If he saw me, he would know what my body language meant.

I dropped to the floor under the stairs and pulled my knees up to make myself as small as possible, like a roly-poly bug curling up into a spiral. I knew I should still be studying for the bee, even on my own. When Mum came back, I wanted to be able to wow her, leave no doubt in her mind that I would win. But instead I opened up *The Riddled Cottage.*

When I'd left Taryn, she'd been in trouble. She'd found the cottage in the woods. Tired, cold, and soaked through from a rainstorm, she'd stumbled inside, and there, sleeping on the floor, she'd found a troll.

Now Taryn stared at the troll. He stood up, stretched his arms above his head, and belched the stinkiest, loudest belch that Taryn had ever experienced. It knocked her right onto the floor. The troll marched over to her and loomed above her. She was sure it was the end of her days. He scooped up a club and held it above him, ready to thrash her. But there was something in his eyes—fear, remorse, panic—and Taryn yelled out, "Wait!"

"Wait?" the troll croaked back.

"I am Taryn Greenbottom, squire to Sir Laudholm the Brave. Who are you?"

"I am Charlak Rapshidir, Troll of the Forest. You have come upon my cottage and, as is my cursed duty, I shall kill you."

"Cursed duty?" Taryn asked. "Is there no way around this fate?"

"Solve my riddle, and we shall be free."

Then he told her the riddle:

My visage high above your city,
Shines like gold, but half as pretty.

Arms I've none, but hands I've two:
Mondo, mini, black not blue.
Climb my stairs and have no fears,
All that threatens are my gears.

I stuck my finger in the book to mark my place. Visage.
What was a visage? The dictionary was on the other side of
the room on a huge stand. If I came out, Coco might still be
there waiting for me, so I moved on to the next part: "Shines
like gold, but half as pretty." Silver, maybe.

Arms I've none, but hands I've two:
Mondo, mini, black not blue.

What has hands but no arms? It sounded like something
out of one of those old joke books from elementary school.
When is a door not a door? When it's ajar! Mondo, mini—that
was like big and small. Big and small hands? A clock!
    I didn't worry about Coco. I scampered across to the
dictionary and flipped to the *V*s. "Visage" was a face. A clock
has a face and hands but no arms, and, yes, gears!
    I sprinted back to my nook and flipped back to the page
with the riddle. Taryn pondered it for much less time than I
had. "A clock," she said simply.
    And then a magical thing happened, as magical things
are wont to do in Harriet Wexler books.
    The troll collapsed in on itself. I've won! *Taryn thought.*

I've defeated the troll! *But it was stranger still than that. For in the place of the troll, a man seemed to grow up out of the ground. The troll's clothes were far too big for him and hung off him like bedsheets. "Lord Charlesmoore!" Taryn called out,* for that was who the man was: a noble knight who had been missing for years. He had entered the Forest of Westbegotten and never returned, presumed dead.

"Taryn Greenbottom!" he exclaimed. "I knew it would be you who answered my call." And then he kissed her.

And I threw the book against the stairs.

TWENTY-THREE

Freebooter

My luck—as little of it as I had—ran out on Wednesday. Coco caught me on my way to the library.

"Ruth," he said, just as I was reaching for the door. He had a stack of word cards in his hand.

I wished for one of Taryn's vials of invisibility juice.

I turned. "Oh," I said. "Studying. I forgot."

"You didn't forget."

"We don't have to do this," I said.

"Do what?"

"Study. I'm really prepared."

"You are. But you can be more prepared."

Outside, the snow was shiny and hard across the playing

fields, reflecting back the dull, flat sunlight. "I can study on my own."

He hitched his backpack up onto his shoulders. It was blue and perfectly clean, unlike mine, or anyone else's, for that matter. My red one had a black stain all up one side from where a pen had broken.

"You heard. The other day, you heard me and my dad."

I nodded.

"I didn't mean it."

"You do," I told him. "You said you don't even care who wins. You and Melinda are just—"

"Melinda?"

"I saw you talking to her outside the room that day. With Charlotte."

He turned red. Not slowly like normal, but instantly, brightly. "She thought," he began. Then again: "She said—" He shook his head. "I'm not working with Melinda on anything, and I tried to tell you before—"

"Well, even if you're not working with Melinda, you still think spelling bees are stupid. So stupid you purposely messed up on the test so you wouldn't have to be a part of it."

"I don't think spelling bees are stupid. I was angry with my dad."

"What was that thing about the geography bee?"

"Some schools do them. It's a lot like the spelling bee, I guess, but through *National Geographic*. And he was trying

to convince the school to do one. I guess he thought that I
could win."

None of this sounded especially awful to me. "So?"

"So, I don't care about winning."

"Then why are you helping me beat Emma? I mean, if
you think it's so stupid, why not just help your sister win
again?"

"It's *all* my dad cares about. Winning."

His voice had that foghorn quality to it again, so loud yet
forlorn, and I realized that even if I didn't understand exactly
what was bothering him, it pulled as heavy as an anchor. I
didn't know what to do with my hands. They felt like they
were hanging off my body, weighing a million pounds. I didn't
know what to do at all. Mom would reach over and pat his
forearm, maybe even give it a squeeze, but I was not my mom
and he was not my son. He was my friend. Maybe. "Oh."

"I'm better than Emma. A lot better. I would've beaten
her. And so my dad would've backed me. He would've cheered
for me, not her. He wouldn't care about her at all."

"That still doesn't explain why you wanted to help me
instead."

"I know it doesn't make sense," he conceded. "In my
mind, it did. Sort of." He shook his head. "My dad was a
great athlete. Soccer, basketball, baseball. He went to college on a scholarship. He won and won and won. And then
along came us kids, and none of us are very good at sports.
But we're good at spelling. And geography. And math. My

brother is the top scorer on the math team, and he's only in tenth grade. And for my dad, it's like, well, he can't be the dad cheering in the stands at the big game, but he can still be on the winning team."

I nodded.

"I just wanted him to see that sometimes you do things just because, you know. Just because it's fun. Like when you are spelling, figuring it out, it's fun."

I wasn't sure if "fun" was the right word. "I guess it's more satisfying if it's not a word I have memorized, and I figure it out from the roots and origin and all that."

"Exactly," he said. Then again: "Exactly. Sometimes I wonder if my dad even liked playing those sports. He doesn't play them anymore, not at all. He doesn't even watch them on television unless he's going to someone's house for a Super Bowl party or whatever."

"So how was my beating Emma supposed to help with that?"

"I don't know." He shook his head. "It was never a clear plan. I just wanted him to see—this is what I tried to tell you before—*he's* the reason they flubbed. The pressure and the enthusiasm. But it would have been so much worse for Emma if he didn't care, you know?"

"And worse for you," I said.

"I thought that if he saw me helping you, and if you won, he'd get so mad that we'd have to talk. He'd have to stop and look and see what he was doing, and we could actually talk about it." He held the cards in his hands up to his chest as if he were hugging them, and himself. The one on top said *OUGHT/AUGHT,* and I guessed we were supposed to be working on homonyms again. "Ought," as in should, an obligation, versus "aught," or everything, the opposite of naught. He sighed. "I'm sorry, Ruth. I really am. I was using you, I guess, but I thought it was okay because I was also helping you. And now we're friends, and—" As he spoke, his face got redder and redder, so his cheeks were taking on a purple hue.

"He was right, though. It would help you with your Harvard camp application."

Coco shrugged, but it was more like his head sinking down into his chest than his shoulders coming up to reach his ears. "It was stupid."

"It wasn't so stupid," I told him. "Sometimes you can want and want something so much from a person, and you just can't get them to do it."

He lifted his brown eyes. "Like what?"

I could have told him about Mum, how she was never home. Or about how Mom always talked big but never followed through—or worse, would decide to do something and make a big mess for me, so now I was stuck changing in the supply closet. Instead, I reached into my bag and pulled out two origami-paper envelopes.

◄○►

"To the buses!" Coco cried when we met after school. He'd managed to rally everyone, and get calls made home so we could all take the bus to the library. Even Dev, whose mother never liked to let him do anything without properly evaluating the situation first. Coco had actually gotten on the phone with her and charmed her into letting Dev go by promising to keep an eye on Dev at all times. He also had to promise that Dev would wear his boots, hat, and gloves, and that he wouldn't eat any food unless it came from Coco or Adam.

We took up four seats on the school bus. Me with Lena, Coco with Dev, and then Adam and Lucas sat separately. But we all leaned over into the aisle. "So we're just going to walk from the library to the cemetery?" Dev asked. "That doesn't sound like much of a plan." He tugged his hat down so it nearly touched his gold-flecked eyes. In Taryn Greenbottom's world, people with gold-flecked eyes were always exceptionally trustworthy.

Adam had told us that the clue referred to Magic—not like magic tricks, but the game: Magic: The Gathering. He said the players were called Planeswalkers, and that you took cards from the library and put them in the graveyard. So we decided we'd walk from the library to the graveyard in the hopes that something would come of it.

"It will come to us," Lena assured him. "That's how Ruthy and I found the British phone booth. Did you know there was one of those on Sea Street? Bright red British phone booth?"

"Next to Pledge Allegiance Comics," Adam said.

I was beginning to think we should have brought Adam along earlier.

Dev glanced over at me and Coco. We were sort of sitting next to each other, me and Coco, with just the seat back between us. "So you two have been studying a lot, huh?" he asked.

"A bit," I said, while Coco said, "Yeah."

"I think I'm ready," Dev said.

"You're ready," Adam replied, sounding a little exasperated.

"I'm totally ready," Lucas said.

"We know," Lena said. "Born ready, right?"

Dev scratched at some paint on the fake leather of his seat. "Do you sometimes worry that you'll know a word and then just muff it?"

"No," Lucas answered.

"Modesty. Respect. Humility," Lena told him.

"Humility," Lucas said. "The state of being humble. Humble, Middle English, derived from Latin, '*humilis*,' low, and '*humus*,' the earth. Low on the earth."

"Like a bug," I said.

"An insect," he corrected.

"It's not like I think my mind will go blank, but that I'll confuse myself," Dev said. "Like it'll be 'sultan,' and I'll think, oh, that's easy. *S-U-L-T-A-N.* But then I have this second track of my brain, like left speaker–right speaker, and the second track is saying, 'Wait, no, that's too easy. It must be *E-N*, or maybe even *I-N*.' And I talk myself out of the right answer."

I wish I could tell him that I felt the same way, but this had never happened to me.

"Squash it," Adam told him.

"I can't," Dev said. "It's loud."

"It's like in tennis. You have all this time when the ball is coming to you. So it's like, 'Okay. Here comes the ball. It is going to land to the left of the center court line. But wait. Maybe there is spin on it. Or maybe it will have a funny bounce.' And you can't let those thoughts get in. You just have to squash them. That's what they mean when they say 'Keep your eye on the ball.' It means don't think, just hit."

"You don't hit a spelling word," Dev said.

But maybe you sort of did. Maybe when you're at the top of the game, and your mind is dialed in, the words are just there. I wondered if that's how it was for Lucas.

"We'll work on it," Adam promised. "Maybe at our next practice I can throw tennis balls at you while you spell."

"You'd like that, wouldn't you?" Dev asked.

"Yes," Adam said. "Yes, I would."

The bus rolled to a stop in front of the library. It was still all collapsed. The salvageable books had been moved into storage units while the town tried to figure out what they were going to do next. I had heard Mom talking on the phone with Mum. The insurance company didn't want to

pay until they did a full evaluation of the design and recon-
struction history. "Alan's afraid they'll want to pin it on
him," she'd said.

We all just stood there in front of the wreckage. The building was folded in upon itself, like a speller at the national
bee who misses an easy word.

I wished I could close my eyes as we walked by.

"That's just so crazy, isn't it?" Lena asked.

"It's not crazy. It's not insane or cool. It's awful."

"Hey, I didn't say it was cool," Lena replied. "I meant
awful. I meant it was there one day, and now the whole thing
is gone."

"It's Charlotte's house, too."

"I know," Lena said.

Coco was a few steps ahead of us. Glancing over his
shoulder, he asked, "Forty-two, right? The answer to the
math problem on the last clue?"

"Forty-two," I said back. "That's what Lucas got."

Coco nodded and smiled and nodded again. Then he
nearly tripped over a pile of snow. He stumbled into Adam,
who made an "oof" sort of noise. Red crept over Coco's face,
and he stared straight ahead as we rounded the corner and
kept going up the hill toward the cemetery. Lena grabbed my
arm and made a kissy face. I think it was a kissy face. I threw
snow in it.

We walked past the historical society, which was housed
in an old lighthouse that had been decommissioned. "If I was

going to hide a clue, I'd hide it in there," Adam said. "It's the coolest building with this awesome spiral staircase, and they built bookshelves that go all around the walls in a big circle."

Like the Seattle Public Library, I thought, thinking of what my mum had told me.

"You just hang out at the historical society?" Lena asked.

Adam shrugged. "My mom said that we used to own waterfront property up here, like, generations ago, but somehow it was swindled out of my great-great-great-grandfather's hands. When I figure out where the land is, and who took it, we're gonna take it back, and I'll be rich and happy."

"Quite the plan," Lena replied.

"Hey!" Lucas said. He was stopped in front of a plaque next to a statue of the fisherman's wife. It wasn't any specific fisherman's wife, just one in general, staring out toward the ocean, holding a basket of apples while her skirt twisted around her legs. "Did you know that there is a fish hidden in the skirts somewhere? I bet I can find it first."

I came up beside him and looked at the plaque. It was part of the town's History Path. There were locations throughout the town with historical significance, and you could walk from one to the other and learn all about them. In the summer you'd see tourists doing it, though mostly the older ones. We'd walked part of it in third grade, but all I remembered was that Charlotte had stumbled and scraped her knee and spent the whole rest of the trip limping along beside me.

I read the plaque by the statue:

Museum on the Street
The Fisherman's Wife
39

This sculpture was created by Arnold Aaron Lophanger. The model was his niece, Lucinda Lophanger, who was a fisherwoman herself and died a widow. Mr. Lophanger felt that she had a naturally sad and pensive face, hence his choice of her as a model.

The sculpture was first placed closer to the town square in 1897. In the 1920s, suffragettes took umbrage at the implication that women simply stayed home, watching and waiting for their men. They hung placards on the statue saying "Votes for Women." In the 1960s, the statue was once again the target of women's rights activists, who decorated it with their undergarments and placed real fish in the basket, implying that women, too, could fish, much like Ms. Lucy Lophanger herself.

In 1972, the sculpture was moved to make room for the new town hall. Here she has enjoyed quieter days. Perhaps as a nod to her profession, Lophanger hid a fish inside the folds of the woman's skirt. Can you find it?

"I've got it!" I exclaimed.

"What? No way! Where?" Lucas replied.

"Not the fish," I said. "The clue!"

Everyone turned to look at me. I put my finger on the

number 39 on the plaque. "'On the path, you face history. Walk the path, do the math.' It's the History Path! We need to find number forty-two!"

"Let's go!" Coco said.

"I haven't found the fish yet," Lucas said.

"Come on," Dev cajoled.

"Not yet."

"We can leave you here," Adam told him.

"No, we can't," I said. "We go together. We can look for the fish on the way back."

"The fish?" Lena asked. "It's right there."

She pointed and it was like the fish appeared right on Lucy Lophanger's hip.

"How'd you know?" Lucas demanded.

"Where would you put a fish?" she replied. "So come on, let's go."

We all started walking, faster now.

"Tell the truth," Lucas said to Lena. "You knew beforehand."

"I didn't," she replied, but she was smiling like a cat who had caught that very same fish, so maybe she wasn't quite telling the truth.

Outside of the cemetery was another plaque. "Forty!" we cried out.

Inside the gate, paths went off in three directions. "Which one?" Dev asked.

I shook my head.

"Counterclockwise," Lucas said. "These sorts of things always go counterclockwise."

I didn't know if that was true or not, but it seemed reasonable. We set off on the right-most path.

"I've been thinking about the clues," Lena said.

"What about them?"

"Well, who put them here, for starters?" she asked.

"I don't know."

"And why?" Adam asked. "Seems like an awful lot of work."

"And are they leading someplace?" Lena asked.

What do you even expect to find? That was what Charlotte had asked me. *There's no pot of gold or prince at the end. This isn't a fairy-tale quest.*

It felt like a quest, though, all of us together, this motley crew. That's what Harriet Wexler always called it when Taryn got together with a band of friends and foes on a quest. She usually did wind up with a group around her—other squires, magicians, sometimes even thieves. Everyone always had a special role, and the quest couldn't be completed without each one of them. *The Riddled Cottage* was different. She was all alone. Well, all alone until that stupid Lord Charlesmoore kissed her. Maybe I did like it better when she was with the others, after all; there was more laughter and excitement, even if they did sometimes slow you down.

"The purpose of any quest is glory," Lucas said.

Adam shook his head. "The purpose of any good quest is treasure, preferably gold."

"That could be," Lena said. "It doesn't really matter so much what it is, as where it leads. One quest leads to the next, doesn't it, Ruthy?"

"For Taryn Greenbottom it always does," I agreed.

"And one of those quests will lead me right out of this town."

"You want to leave Promise?" Coco asked with some surprise.

Lena shook her head. "The two of you are supposed to be smart."

"But don't you want to leave?" I asked Coco. "I mean, if you're going to be a forensic anthropologist, you can't just wait for more old graveyards to be discovered around here."

"Well, sure, I'll probably travel all over the place, but I guess I always figured I'd come back here."

"Not me," Dev said. "I'm with Lena."

"Really?" Lena and I said simultaneously

"Why is that such a surprise?"

"You seem like a stay-putter to me," Lena said in a way that managed to not sound mean.

Dev pulled his hat off and tucked it into his pocket. "I have a twenty-year plan. Finish Frontenac Consolidated Middle School and then attend the Maine School of Science and Mathematics."

"Your parents will never let you go there," Adam said.

The Maine School of Science and Mathematics was a public boarding school for exceptional math and science students. It was also so far north, it was practically in Canada.

"And then I will attend an Ivy League university, or MIT or Stanford. And then I will get a Rhodes Scholarship and go to Oxford. I will eventually get my doctorate and secure a position at either Cambridge or Oxford, or possibly the Sorbonne. That's in France. What matters is that it's a city with a lot of smart people."

"Wow," I said. "That's long-range."

"There!" Coco called out. We all followed as he ran to the next plaque. Number forty-one. It was all about the trees in the cemetery. One of them had been planted by Frontenac himself.

"Boring," Lucas said.

"Keep going," Coco said. "At least we know we're going in the right direction."

So we walked on. Adam started whistling a camp marching song, and Dev joined in. Soon we were all whistling and marching.

"It feels like we stepped into a different time," Lucas said.

"Time travel is impossible," Dev told him.

"It's theoretically possible," Adam countered. "Just not physically possible yet."

"But if it were ever *going* to be possible, then someone would have come back and—" Dev began.

"That's not what he means," Coco interrupted. "He means it feels like a real, old-fashioned adventure."

"A quest," I said.

"A quest," Lucas repeated. "Exactly. And you know how quests end? Victory!"

"There it is!" Lena said.

We ran up the slippery path. Lena stumbled and grabbed my arm, so we practically fell on top of the plaque.

Museum on the Street
Lord Whitcomb Vertrand
42

In front of you is the grave of Lord Whitcomb Vertrand, a wealthy gentleman who came to Promise in his later years. He built a grand mansion overlooking the bay, where he entertained guests from all over the world. He claimed he made his fortune in importing and exporting from his native England, where he alleged aristocratic status. It wasn't long after his arrival, though, that another story of his past began to emerge. Lord Whitcomb Vertrand, it was rumored, was actually the dreaded pirate Greenbottom. Greenbottom had stalked the seas between Canada and North Carolina. He earned his name for the vivid green satin breeches that he wore. Legend holds that he buried gold on the coast of the peninsula, but that claim has never been substantiated.

"Huh," I said.

"What?" Coco asked.

"Nothing," I said, shaking my head. "Just in the Harriet Wexler books, the character's last name is Greenbottom, too."

"It's a good name," Coco said.

"But where's the clue?" Lucas asked.

"It's got to be hidden on the plaque or stand somewhere."

Lucas crouched down behind the stand, while Lena ran her hand around the edge, trying to find an opening. The base was iron, while the top was a single, solid piece of wood.

"Maybe the clue is in the words?" Adam said. "Like the gold! The buried gold!"

"I don't think so," Coco said.

"There was gold in another clue, wasn't there?" Adam pressed. "We *are* on a treasure hunt!"

"No," I said. "They've all been written down." We were right. We'd solved the riddle and we were in the right place, I knew it. So where was that sixth clue?

"Look at this," Coco said. "It says that this was placed here in 2013." He read, "'Generous funds from the Promise Historical Society and a grant from the Maine Humanities Council allowed us to replace aging markers on the History Path.'"

"Oh, no," I moaned. "It's gone."

"A total dead end," Lucas said.

"So no gold, and my shoes are going to have salt stains?" Adam asked.

"That's why you should wear boots, nimrod," Dev said as he pulled his hat back onto his head.

"A nimrod, traditionally, is a skilled hunter," Lucas told him.

"Ha!" Adam said. "I am Adam the Nimrod, great and skillful hunter."

"I'm sorry," Coco said to me. "It's not over yet. We could keep going, follow the later clues you found."

"If only we had that key," Lena said.

"What key?" Adam asked.

"The one it talks about in the clue with the maiden on it. The Snow White one. 'Now you might ask, this little key . . .' Ruthy and I found the post office box, thanks to Adam. And if we had that key, we could get in, and then this day wouldn't be a total bust."

I felt myself growing hot. How had I not put that together? "Actually," I said in a soft voice. "Actually, we do have the key."

———◄◦►———

We raced back down the hill toward town, slipping and sliding on the icy paths. When we made it to Main Street, we slowed to a walk, but only because we were getting some dirty looks.

The clock tower bells started chiming. One, two, three, four. "Come on!" Lena cried. "Before they close!"

"What time do they close?" Coco asked.

"I don't know. Post offices keep the wackiest hours. Let's go." She grabbed my arm and tugged.

We all stumbled up the stairs, across the marble floor, and over to the boxes.

Lena hopped from foot to foot and blew on her hands while I dug in the pocket of my jeans for my key.

"I still don't understand what we're doing here," Adam said.

"That clue you helped me with. The one with the natural twenty, it was actually a code about a post office box, and Ruthy and I found it, but we didn't have the key."

"But when Charlotte gave me the box with the clues and our—with everything, it had a tiny key in it. I thought it was . . . I thought it was for something else."

"Charlotte?" Adam asked.

I yanked the key from my pocket. I'd been carrying it with me, wondering if I should give it back to her so all the keys would be together. "Yes, Charlotte."

"Charlotte Diamond? Popular Charlotte?" he asked.

"Beautiful Charlotte," Dev teased.

I groaned. Everyone loved Charlotte. Even my own motley crew. "She found some in the library. No big deal. Well, actually . . ." I started to explain my theory that she had sought out one of the clues and found it in the school library.

"Ruthy! The key!"

I passed it over to her. "It has to be the right key, doesn't it?"

"A post office box." Dev sighed. "What do you think might be in it? People keep all sorts of treasures in a post office box, don't they?"

"That's a safe-deposit box," Adam replied. I think he was a little happy to be able to get back at Dev for teasing him about Charlotte. Did Adam really like her? I imagined boys all over Frontenac Consolidated swooning over her, dreaming of her at night.

Lena jiggled the key. I bit my lip. It was the wrong key. But then, no, it slipped in. It was like we had all been holding our breath, and let it out in one big whoosh of a sigh.

Lena turned the key.

The box was jammed full of flyers and circulars—the kind of stuff addressed to Current Resident. She pulled everything out and let it fall right onto the floor.

"Lena!" Coco said. We both crouched down and began picking up the fallen mail.

"There!" Lucas said. His hand shot into the box and pulled out a tiny envelope. It was green with silver stars like nighttime on some foreign planet. He handed it to me. The paper rustled as I opened the flap and pulled out the note.

There was the red seal with the bird staring at me. I

unfolded it to find a picture of a science-class-type flask bubbling over with a greenish-brown liquid. The border looked like an old picture frame, and in each corner was a tiny insect. Before I started reading, I noted the nine little stars on the bottom of the clue.

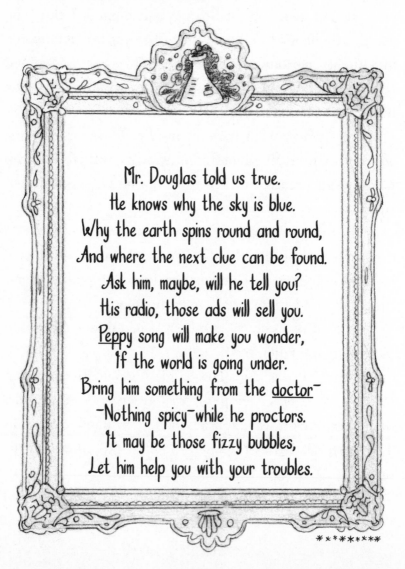

Mr. Douglas told us true.
He knows why the sky is blue.
Why the earth spins round and round,
And where the next clue can be found.
Ask him, maybe, will he tell you?
His radio, those ads will sell you.
<u>Peppy</u> song will make you wonder,
    If the world is going under.
Bring him something from the <u>doctor</u>‾
    ‾Nothing spicy‾while he proctors.
It may be those fizzy bubbles,
Let him help you with your troubles.

＊✶＊✻＊✶＊✷

"Who's Mr. Douglas?" Lucas asked. We all looked at each other, but no one had the answer.

"I guess that's our next mystery to solve," I said.

"The quest continues!" Adam cried out.

"The quest!" Coco agreed.

And then, as if we had planned it, we all yelled in unison, "The quest!"

The old postmistress narrowed her eyes at us and shook her head, but as we ran giggling out of the post office, we yelled it again, over and over: "The quest! The quest! The quest!"

TWENTY-FOUR

Fidelity

Lena wanted to make me a special dinner and dessert to get ready for the bee. She asked to do it the night before, but Mom swore Mum would be home by then—it was still almost a week away. So, after we burst out of the post office yelling about the quest, the boys were picked up by their parents, and Lena and I walked down to her house. I sat at the kitchen table while Lena worked, chopping mushrooms and peppers.

I had the clues laid out in front of me, all in order. There were seven of them. We were still missing the very first clue and the sixth one—the one that should have been on the History Path. "Do you think they found it when they took down the old sign?" I asked.

"The clue? Maybe. It depends on who took it down. A lot of the grounds guys come to the shack. If they work like they eat, most of them wouldn't notice. I saw Burt Wildwood take down a full-belly clam sandwich in two bites once. He washed it all down with Mountain Dew. It was the most disgusting and impressive thing I have ever seen in my life."

"They probably wouldn't have realized how important it was, anyway."

Lena started peeling potatoes. "Do you want some help?" I asked.

"Nope. This is your special meal."

"Speaking of special meals, my mum told me to pick a restaurant in Portland for us for my birthday dinner."

"Really? Man, there are so many places I would like to try. Fore Street, Salt Exchange, Duckfat."

"But I was thinking maybe, I don't know, maybe I do want a party, after all."

"Yeah?" she asked. She didn't sound disappointed. "Like what kind of a party?"

"A boy-girl party, I guess."

"Sure, of course. We'll invite the guys. But what kind of a party?"

"Like a theme?"

She laughed as she tossed the potatoes in salt. "No, no. Unless, of course, you want to do a pirate theme and we can all talk like pirates. *Yo ho ho and a bottle of rum!* That would be cool."

"I don't think so."

"I mean, like, will it be at night or in the daytime? Are we going to play games or watch a movie or stuff our faces with pizza or what?"

"I hadn't really thought that far. I haven't even talked to my moms about it yet."

"Don't you think you should soon? Your birthday's a week from Saturday, right?"

I picked up the last clue. Maybe dinner was the best idea, after all. I read the clue again to myself, then said, "Mr. Douglas, Mr. Douglas, Mr. Douglas."

"Ugh, why are you talking about him?" It was Lucia, passing through the kitchen and trying to steal Lena's peppers.

"You know him?"

"Sure. He's a science teacher at the high school. In between classes, he stands out in the hall and just glares at all of us like we are all up to no good."

"You probably are up to no good," Lena said.

"Not me," Lucia said. She snagged another pepper and said, "Lucky me, I had Ms. Hensworth for ninth grade. Maybe you'll get stuck with him."

"What's so bad about him?" I asked.

"Besides the glare? Well, he's tough, especially on kids that usually do well in school. Margaret Nixon got transferred out of his class because her parents thought he would ruin her GPA. And you can hear him yelling at his class from halfway down the hall. And his classroom is full of dead animals. I mean full."

Lena and I exchanged a look. "Does he like to listen to the radio?" I asked.

"All the time," she said. "He has a little one playing in his back room. Classic rock. That was a weird question."

"You're weird," Lena said.

Lucia responded by taking another pepper and biting her thumb.

"Do you bite your thumb at me?" Lena asked.

"I do bite my thumb, sir," Lucia responded.

"Do you bite your thumb at us, sir?"

"No, sir, I do not bite my thumb at you, sir, but I do bite my thumb."

They were laughing now, and it seemed like they were speaking another language. Lucia still smiled as she left the room.

"*Romeo and Juliet*," Lena explained. "My parents are a little Shakespeare-obsessed. I'm named after Rosaline, who, by the way, is the girl Romeo supposedly liked before Juliet came along and swept him off his feet. Who names a girl that? That's why I go by Lena."

"I like Lena better," I said.

"Good. Me, too."

"It must be nice to have your sisters, all of you in this house all cozy."

"Ha!" she half laughed. "You mean all up in your business? Oh, hey, I never told you about Wonder Woman!"

I remembered the chat message she had sent me ages ago. "What about her?"

"Lucia was telling us that, according to her gym teacher, when you need a confidence boost, you should stand like Wonder Woman. You know, with your fists on your hips and your chest puffed out. Like this." She put down the knife and stood with her legs shoulder-width apart, hands on hips, elbows back a bit. She shook her head, and the red streak peeked out like a stream of lava. "I feel more powerful already. You need to do this before the spelling bee."

"Okay," I said, but without much enthusiasm.

"Promise," she said.

"Promise?"

"Do it now," she demanded.

I stood up and put my hands on my hips.

"That's not it at all!" she exclaimed. She strode over to me and pulled my elbows out so they pointed like wings. "Now lift your chin," she said.

"I feel silly," I said.

"But strong, too, right? So promise?"

"I promise," I agreed.

"Good." She turned and went back to the counter. "Now, listen. Mr. Douglas. It has to be him, right? 'He knows why the sky is blue,' and what's the rest of it?"

"'Why the earth spins round and round, and where the next clue can be found.'"

"So we have to go see him."

"And bring him something from the doctor," I said.

"Doctor Who again?"

"There was never any Doctor Who. Just England. But, anyway, it's not capitalized. It's underlined. And so is the 'Pep' in 'Peppy.'"

She shook her head. "How are we going to get to the high school?"

I balled my hands into fists and pushed them onto my forehead. "With this and the spelling bee, I'm too wound up to even think."

"You will do awesome. Know why?"

"Because I've been studying and Coco has prepared me and I rock and yadda-yadda-pump-me-up speech?"

"No," Lena said. "Well, yes, all of that is true. But you will win because you will be the only one to have Lena's world-famous mushroom medley frittata!" She dumped all the vegetables into a pie plate and then poured beaten eggs on top of them. "Not to mention molten-chocolate devil cakes with honey!"

"Honey? Because of the bees?"

"Yes! But even better, bees and honey are symbols of language and speaking well. It's perfect!"

"Where'd you learn that?"

"Lucas told me."

"Of course."

"Of course."

"You know what else he told me?"

"What?"

"That he is going to crush you. Maybe."

"He said maybe?"

"He said maybe."

It was the best piece of news I'd heard all day.

TWENTY-FIVE

Cynosure

In the summer, you can barely walk across the street without getting hit by a trolley, but in the winter, the trolleys
only run once an hour. Lucas, Lena, and I waited at the
stop, stomping our feet to keep warm and seeing who could
puff out the biggest cloud of white air.

"I'm a fire-breathing lizard," Lena said.

"There are no lizards that can breathe fire," Lucas said.

"Really?" Lena asked. "Isn't that where the idea of dragons came from?"

The snow in the road was nearly black and a car drove
through a mound of it, sluicing it up toward us. I jumped
back, but Lucas got splattered. I don't think he even noticed.
"No," he said.

"I thought the idea of dragons came from dinosaur fossils," I said.

"Sure," Lena said. "But the fire breathing had to come from somewhere, right?"

"What time is it?" Lucas asked.

Lena checked the time on her phone. "It's three twenty-seven."

The trolley was scheduled for three fifteen. We all peered down the street for the telltale green-and-red vehicle.

This trip was not entirely sanctioned, not for Lena and me, anyway. Lucas told his mom he wanted to go meet a science teacher at the high school, and since that was perfectly in character for him, she hadn't flinched. I had told Mom I was going to Lena's, and Lena told hers that we were going to hang around in town. My mom was going to pick me up at five thirty. The timing was tight. And if we got caught, we couldn't even claim innocence on a technicality, since the high school was over in Port Stewart.

Coco had piano practice, which he had begged to get out of, but his dad said no way since he thought Coco had been acting strangely overall and wouldn't let him avoid another one of his passions. "I don't even like the piano," Coco had told me. "I'd rather play the drums. My piano teacher does give me these butterscotch candies, though, from Switzerland, where he's from. I'll see if I can get you one." Adam had an orthodontist appointment. "I think my parents are going to have heart attacks if it turns out I need braces. They're already talking about raiding my savings account, but they don't know I have a secret stash." And Dev, well, without Coco or Adam, there was no way his mom was going to let him come, even if Lena did seem like a nice girl.

Just then the trolley rolled up. It almost didn't stop, as if the driver wasn't expecting passengers, but then it swerved over to us. We each handed our dollar to the Santa-esque gentleman behind the wheel. The only other person on the trolley was an older woman, who sat right up front and held on to the pole with her hand encased in a knit mitten.

We went to the very back of the trolley. "Lucia says his classroom is on the first floor, third on the left. He's always there."

"Always? Like overnight?" Lucas asked.

"Of course not," I said, but Lena said, "Who knows?"

The trolley wound its way out of Promise and into Port Stewart. The closest stop was about a quarter mile away. As we approached, I noticed we were racing by other trolley stops. "How do we let him know we want to stop?" I asked. I had never actually ridden the trolleys before. They were mostly for tourists, and I hadn't even realized they ran year-round until we'd started searching for a way to get to the high school.

"Pull the cord," Lucas said.

"What cord?" I asked.

He looked up, and so did Lena and I, and there was a

thin, plastic cord. Lena stood and tugged on it. The driver glanced up in surprise. "You need a stop?" he asked.

"At the corner of Allagash Street and Frontenac Road," Lena said.

The driver nodded but didn't say anything else. A few minutes later, he pulled over. "The trolley will be back here at five oh five, right?" I asked at the top of the stairs. "To go back to Promise?"

"That's Nelly's route. She's not always on schedule. Early sometimes. Late sometimes."

"You were thirteen minutes late," Lucas told him.

"Lucas," I hissed. I turned back to the driver. "But she'll wait, right? If she's early, she can't leave until five oh five, can she?"

The driver shrugged. "Nelly does what Nelly does."

I glanced at Lena and Lucas. "Maybe we should just—"

"No!" Lena grabbed my sleeve and tugged me down the stairs. "Thank you!" she called to the driver as he shut the folding doors. "It just means we have to be quick."

———◄○►———

The window of Mr. Douglas's door was covered with cartoons and photographs: a supernova, a *New Yorker* comic about wormholes, a picture of a bee's eye in extreme closeup. I didn't recognize that last one; Lucas did, of course, and we practically had to peel him off it to get inside. We knocked, but no one answered, so we pulled open the door.

I had never seen a classroom like this.

On the back wall were three large aquariums. One had a bright red snake in it, another a lizard, and the third appeared to be empty, but it had a light shining on it. Shelves on a side wall were full of animal skeletons and taxidermied specimens: possums, river otters, raccoons, all local animals. There was even a weasel about to eat a mouse. Hanging from the ceiling were bee and wasp nests of all different sizes. Lucas identified them in a reverent whisper. "Paper wasp, bumblebee, hornet."

Just to the left of the door was a bookcase, but it didn't have any science books on it. It was all fiction, and all different kinds: fantasy, realistic, classics. There was even a Harriet Wexler book.

The front lab table was covered with papers, and the whole room smelled a bit like a pet store.

There was no Mr. Douglas. There was, however, faint music playing from a connected room. "'His radio, those ads will sell you. Peppy song will make you wonder, if the world is going under,'" Lena whispered to me. And then, louder, "Mr. Douglas?"

There was a crashing sound, and then a man emerged from the room. He was bald on top of his head, with a ring of blaring white hair around the lower half. His eyes were pale blue, sharp as diamonds, and narrowing down on me and my friends. "Who are you?" he demanded.

None of us spoke. Lena stepped closer to me.

Mr. Douglas strode farther into the room and put his hands on the lab table at the front. Picking up a Bunsen burner, he said again, "Who are you?"

"We are questers," I heard myself say. "We have come to ask you where the next clue may be found."

His eyes flashed and his face softened. "Are you, now? And what makes you think I would have that information?"

I pulled out the clue. "We found this," I said. "We've been following all the clues and they led us here."

He reached across the table in a swift motion and grabbed the clue from my hand. "It says here you are to bring me something."

We had hoped we could breeze past that part. We hadn't figured out what he wanted. "I—" I began. "We—"

"I, we, what?" he demanded. "This paper is very clear. You are to bring me something from the doctor. Don't touch that!"

I swiveled my head to see Lucas leaning very close to a football-shaped nest that was sitting on a table in the back room. "It's buzzing," he said.

"It seems it was not as abandoned as I had been led to believe."

"Vespula are tricky like that," Lucas said as he backed away. He slipped his backpack off and unzipped it. Then he pulled out a bottle of Dr Pepper and handed it to Mr. Douglas, who smiled for half a second. He dropped the bottle in the trash. "Charlie and Storm and the boys would be shocked, but I don't drink the stuff anymore. I guess you're still entitled to your clue. Wait here."

We stood by the lab table. "How did you know?" I asked.

"What do you mean?" Lucas asked. "'Doctor,' 'peppy,' 'fizzy bubbles.' They might as well have spelled it out."

Mr. Douglas returned holding a small origami envelope. My heart raced in the familiar way. He handed it to me. "Thank you!" I said. "We won't bother you anymore."

"Wait," he said.

According to Mr. Douglas's clock, it was four thirty. Plenty of time if Nelly came on schedule, but if she was early, we could miss the last ride back into town. "We really ought to be going," I said.

He ignored me and walked around the lab table over to the small bookshelf of fiction. From the top right, he pulled out an old, worn book. Another clue? He held out the book to me. "Take this."

The Fellowship of the Ring by J. R. R. Tolkien.

Why were people always trying to get me to read Tolkien? "Um, I already have a copy. Two, actually."

"Not this one."

No, I certainly did not have an old, smelly version.

"What grade are you in?" he asked.

"Sixth," I said.

He nodded. "Then you should have plenty of time to read it by the time you get to me. Get wise."

I swear I could hear the clock ticking behind me. I took

the book from him and shoved it into my backpack. It seemed lighter than it looked. Maybe it was printed on that old, thin paper. "We really do need to go," I said.

"We need to catch the trolley," Lena explained.

He shook his head. "We'll see if I'm still around by then, of course. Students, teachers. I don't know half of them half as well as I would like, and I like less than half of them as well as they deserve."

"Okay," I said.

"You'll have enough time to forget, at least," he said.

"Forget what?" I asked.

"Everything you've learned so far." He checked his watch. "You'd better hurry. Nelly is early more often than she's late, and late more often than she's on time."

He pushed open the door for us and watched us as we ran down the hallway for the door. I had the eerie feeling he was watching us the whole way home.

———◦———

We arrived at the trolley stop just as Nelly was approaching. We crashed into our seats at the back of the car, and the book Mr. Douglas had given me dug into my side. I unzipped my backpack, pulled the book out, then slid it back in between two of my binders.

"That looks like an old copy," Lucas said. "You should be careful with it."

"It's just another copy of *The Fellowship of the Ring*,"

I told him. "He's as bad as Mrs. Abernathy, trying to get me to read Tolkien."

"Maybe if you just read some, everyone would leave you alone."

"Guys! The clue! The clue!" Lena reached for my bag, but the clue was in my pocket. I slipped it out, then pulled the clue from its orange envelope. "Ohh," Lena breathed when she saw the card. Ten asterisks danced along the bottom. A set of stairs looped around the edge of the card in an impossible circuit, like something out of an M. C. Escher drawing. Ms. Tudor, our math teacher, had them all over her classroom, and sometimes I got lost in their illusions during class.

My visage high above your city,
Shines like gold, but half as pretty.
Arms I've none, but hands I've two:
Mondo, mini, black not blue.
Climb my stairs and have no fears,
All that threatens are my gears.
Tucked beneath the mighty wheel,
An envelope shall truth reveal.

٭٭٭٭٭٭٭٭

"Clock," I said. "It's the clock tower."

"How'd you get that so fast?" Lucas demanded. He flipped the clue over as if maybe it was written there.

"I've read it before." And I had. In Harriet Wexler's book. It was the clue that turned the troll into nobility, and ruined the whole stinking series. It was a weird coincidence, but fortunately there were no troll-disguised noblemen around. Only Lucas.

"Well, then," Lena said. "I guess I know what we're doing tomorrow."

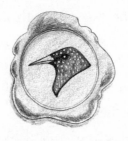

TWENTY-SIX

Synchronous

The clock tower sat on top of town hall. It was white clapboard on top of the brick building, and the chimes rang out so loud that some days I could even hear it miles away at our house.

We had planned feverishly during lunch, with Dev writing everything down and Coco making sure we stayed on task. It was Friday, so if we didn't get into town hall that day, we'd have to wait until the next week—spelling bee week. The only way into the clock tower was through a door at the end of a hall on the third floor of the building—the floor with all the public town offices on it like the Recreation Department and the tax collector. We had all been there at one time or another with our parents, whether to sign up for a rec program or to wait while they registered their cars. It always seemed to be buzzing with people, and we hoped that would help to mask our activity.

We chose to go through the door on the side of the building rather than the grand one out front. It seemed less showy, I guess. Coco held the door open for an older woman clutching envelopes. She thanked him in a clipped voice. "Headed up to pay the taxes," she said. She pushed the button on the elevator.

"Let me go with you," Adam said. He tilted his head a little toward her.

We all turned to him. Helping little old ladies wasn't exactly in his wheelhouse.

"In fact, we will all go in the elevator with you," Adam went on.

So we all climbed into the small space. The woman chattered as the elevator went up. "I've lived in Promise for all my life. That's eighty-nine years. You'd think after a certain amount of time they'd say, 'Yep. Good and done. Consider your tax bill paid in full from here on out.' But it doesn't work that way."

"The only two things that are sure in life are death and taxes," Adam said. Lena elbowed him hard in the stomach.

"Death, taxes, and arthritis," the woman replied.

"My grandmother has arthritis," Lucas told her. "She soaks her hands in warm water to keep them loose."

"I'll think on that," the woman told us. "What are you all here for?" she asked. She looked each of us in the eye, hers wizened and yellow on the white part. "I was a teacher for thirty-nine years and I can smell when something is up."

"We're working on a project," Adam said. "Maybe you can help us."

"This isn't one of those interview-an-old-person projects, is it? I can't stand to tell another story to another kid angling for a good grade."

"No," Adam said. "It is a school project, though. Sort of."

"It is or it isn't?"

"Extra credit."

"Grade grubbers. I knew it."

"Not me," Lucas said. "I just get good grades naturally."

"Worst of all," she told him, which made Lena laugh.

"You, I like," the woman said. I thought she was talking to Lena, but she stared right at me. "You look earnest. Earnest is good. Are you earnest?"

"Sure? I guess so?"

"You don't sound so sure. Maybe I was wrong."

Dev slid his foot against mine. "I have the courage of my convictions, if that's what you mean," I said.

She smiled. "And what are those convictions?"

"They're a bit complicated to get into on an elevator ride."

"I see. The best convictions are complicated. Like stories."

"The truth is, we need to get into the clock tower."

She didn't ask why. She said, "You know where the door is?"

"End of the corridor," Dev told her. He'd studied the floor plan on the town's website. "You have to go right by the tax collector's office to get to it."

"I see," she said. "I don't suppose there's any harm in you helping a woman to the office."

The door to the elevator opened, and we all emerged. Adam put his hand under her elbow. She shook it off, but then let him take it again. "For show," she whispered. "I certainly don't need your help. Don't think for a minute that I do."

"No, ma'am," he said.

"And don't *ma'am* me. No one in Maine says 'ma'am' to you unless you're dying or mean."

We all shuffled down the hall with her. When we got to the tax collector's room, she looked over her shoulder. "None of you fall off," she warned. We nodded. She turned back to the office. "Alfred!" she called. "You take a seat, young man. We have some talking to do about this tax bill. And let me tell you, mister, that this is going to be worse than learning the states and capitals."

"Mrs. Valentine," we heard from inside the office. "Lovely to see you as—"

"North Dakota!" she called. Behind her back, she gestured us to keep going.

"Dakota City," the man said.

"Bismarck," Lucas said, probably too loudly. But it didn't matter. We were clear.

———◄○►———

You don't realize how big the insides of a public clock can be until you are right up beside them. The main gear was nearly as tall as me, the cogs slipping into place with three other gears. Long, heavy chains hung down and down and down into the dark below.

Outside, we could see the whole town. In the distance was our school, its flat roof covered in snow. And there was the Salt and Sea Shack. A ferry boat puffed along in the water. Closer, we could see the library: a messy, muddy gray smudge across the white snow.

The sun was setting. "Hurry up," Dev said. "Someone might have seen us."

"Hurry up who?" I asked.

"You," he replied. "Find the clue."

Lucas started to giggle.

"It's not funny just because it rhymes," I reminded him. "Anyway, why do I need to find it? Any of us can find it."

Dev frowned. "Isn't that why we're here? To help you with your quest?"

"It's not just my quest, is it?" Was I as alone as Taryn in the Forest of Westbegotten, after all?

Lena put her arm on mine. "The quest!" she called out.

"The quest!" the others replied, and our voices echoed around the chamber of the clock tower.

"Now, what did the clue say?" Lena asked.

Coco read from the paper: "'Climb my stairs and have no fears, all that threatens are my gears. Tucked beneath the mighty wheel, an envelope shall truth reveal.'"

"The mighty wheel," I said, looking at the gears. I didn't see an envelope. "Maybe this is another one that's gone missing. I mean, I'm sure this has been cleaned."

Lucas shimmied around behind the gears. His feet were on the window ledge, his hands above the gears.

"What are you doing?" Coco reached out to grab him, the clue from his hand fluttering to the ground. Dev bent over to pick it up.

"I'm looking for the next one," Lucas said. "That's why we're up here, right?"

Lena dropped down to her hands and knees and crawled under the mechanism. She sat up on the other side. "It looks the same from over here. Just gears, gears, gears."

"Beneath," I said. "How far beneath?"

We all looked down.

I was the first one down the stairs. Adam stumbled behind me. I caught him by the arm. "I'm okay," he said. "I'm okay."

We kept going down and down and down past the door to the town hall, and lower still. The only light came from the top of the tower, and it was growing scanter by the minute. "Go, go, go!" Lucas called.

We made it to the bottom of the stairs. A small chamber that the chains from the clock dangled into. There was nearly no light. Dev had a tiny flashlight on the pull of his coat's zipper, just in case he was ever caught in a cold, dark space, I guess. He held it out and scanned every corner, every inch.

Even though we'd stopped descending, it was like we were still sinking down.

"Another miss," Coco said.

"It's okay," I said. "I mean, we have a later one. The one about looking up in the library."

"But you wanted them all," Lena said. "Right?"

I kicked at the ground. "It would be nice to see how all the pieces went together."

"Go back!" Lucas called.

Dev swung the tiny beam of light back, and I saw a glint. "There!" I said.

"Where?"

"There!" I said again.

Lucas, too: "There, there, there!"

It was a tiny metal box, like the kind you might get mints in, leaning up against one of the wall boards. It was cold in my hands when I picked it up, and I had to really force it to get the rusted hinges to open. But inside, there it was. One yellow envelope.

———◦———

Back up the stairs and down the corridor, we tried to walk, but it was like the race walking we had to do in gym class.

In the tax collector's office, we heard Mrs. Valentine. "Really, Alfred, how can you be a civic employee if you don't know basic civics? The Preamble to the Constitution. Again."

We crammed into the elevator.

"'We the People of the United States,'" Lucas murmured, "'in Order to form a more perfect Union, establish Justice, insure domestic Tranquility, provide for the common defence, promote the general Welfare, and secure the Blessings of Liberty—'"

"You can't help it, can you?" I interrupted.

"What?"

"Answering the questions?"

He shook his head. "'To ourselves and our Posterity, do ordain and establish this Constitution for the United States of America.'"

"Read the note," Adam said. He clapped his hands together in anticipation, his leather gloves muffling the sound. "It's going to lead us to the treasure!"

"To victory!" Lena added.

"Outside," I told them. I turned back to Lucas. "You could write it down," I said. "The things you want to say. The answers and the things you think of. Maybe if you wrote it down, you wouldn't need to say it, and people wouldn't be so mean about it."

"Maybe people just shouldn't be so mean." It was Coco who said it. His cheeks were flushing like maybe he was afraid he'd embarrassed me.

"You're right," I said. "People shouldn't be." But what I meant was, *I* shouldn't be. I'd been as annoyed by Lucas as anyone, and it turned out he was one of the people who had helped me the most—helped *us* the most.

The elevator doors slid open, and I handed the envelope to Lucas. "Your turn," I said.

Dev pushed open the door and we stumbled out into the cold air. The temperature had dropped and our breath seemed to freeze as soon as it came past our lips and noses. The envelope shook in Lucas's hand. "I've never been a part of anything like this before."

"None of us have," Coco told him.

"No, I mean a team like this. At my last school, the food was good, and none of the kids were really mean, but I never found a group to be a part of."

"You don't say," Adam said, and Dev elbowed him hard in the side.

"I feel the same way," I told him, then I glanced at Lena.

"When I first found the clue in the library, I wanted to do it myself. Or maybe with Charlotte—"

"Charlotte Diamond?" Adam asked.

"Yes," I sighed. "She found some, too. And I thought maybe it would, you know, bring us back together. It was stupid. Anyway, I didn't want to tell anyone about it, but I told Lena, and she told—"

"Everyone!" Lena said.

"Right," I agreed. "So now here we all are."

"Here we all are," Lena echoed.

We all looked around the circle, our puffy breaths making a cloud between us. "It matters," I said. "This quest, it matters to me. That's all I'm trying to say."

"It matters to me, too," Coco said.

"And me."

"And me."

"And me."

We all turned to Adam, the only one of us who hadn't spoken yet.

"Jeez!" he said, throwing his hands up in the air. "It matters! It matters! So let's read the clue before we freeze and they make us a sculpture like that fish lady."

I peered over Lucas's shoulder as he read. This card had a Celtic knot at its top center that had tails that reached down to encircle the card. Along the bottom edge of the card were eleven asterisks.

Circle back, you're nearly through.
The next one, then just one more clue.
Summer's coming, dark and drear,
Soon those tourists will appear.

In the word hoard you will find
Books with numbers on their spines.
A 2 a 9 a 2 again⁻
Not too easy for Athena's friend.

****

"It fits!" I cried out. "I found the clue in the mythology section."

"The two ninety-twos," Lucas said. "Greek and Roman religion."

"You memorized the Dewey decimal system?" Adam asked him.

"Just the things I care about. Five ninety-two, invertebrates. Seven ninety-two, stage presentations. That's usually where you can find books about magic."

"And you looked up?" Dev asked me.

"Yeah," I said, and the truth of it came crushing down on me: we'd been all over this town chasing clues, and they led me right back to where I had started all by myself. "Nothing."

"What do you mean, 'nothing'?" Lucas asked.

"I mean I looked up at the ceiling, I looked all around the shelf it was on. There was nothing there. And now the library is gone."

In the fading light I could see all their faces looking tired and pulled down. This was my fault. I had gotten them all involved, and really, hadn't I known from the start that it wouldn't lead anywhere? I just didn't realize it would be over so soon. "I'm sorry," I said.

"You don't need to be sorry," Coco said, but his voice had that low and hollow foghorn quality.

"Yeah," Lena said. "It was fun while it lasted, wasn't it, guys?"

No one answered.

Lena patted me on the back.

"We were so close," I said. "Just two more—that's what it says."

"Come on," Coco said. "We need to get back to Lena's house. Our parents will be waiting for us."

"Sure," I said. And everyone agreed.

"It was fun," Dev said to me as we walked along. "Isn't that the point of a quest?"

I thought of Taryn Greenbottom. Fun wasn't what she

was after. Satisfaction. Completion. I shook my head. "No. The point of a quest is finishing it."

"There will be other quests," Coco said.

Which was easy for him to say since he had a whole life planned around adventures digging up bones.

"But not this quest," I said. "Not these clues. I just wanted to see it through. I wanted to see where it led and I wanted—" I had already told them so much—too much, maybe. "I wanted those answers."

"What was the question?" Lucas asked.

"I guess I wanted to know that, too."

We came around the corner to Lena's warm house, all lit up from inside.

No finish. No prize. No nothing. Without those last two clues, the rest were just slips of paper.

TWENTY-SEVEN

Graupel

Mum's plane was delayed again, until Monday, the day before the bee. "Big bummer, I know," she said over the computer. "But the snow is coming down in pellets, is what I heard."

I looked out the window, but it was hard to tell if the snow was any different. "You've been gone over a month," I told her.

"Don't I know it!"

I'd been counting on her to distract me from the stupid, pointless circle I had made with the clues. I'd led my friends all over town when there was no way we could have solved the final riddle. Some quest; Taryn Greenbottom never would've gotten caught up in something so foolish.

"What did you do for underwear?" I asked her.

"Underwear?" She laughed. "You can drop off your laundry at the hotel."

"Laundry. Room service. It's no wonder you don't want to come back."

The screen flickered and when it un-pixelated, Mum's face seemed to have been cast in shadow. "Ruth, you know that isn't true, don't you?"

"Sure," I said. "Of course. I'm just suffering from angst. *A-N-G-S-T.* Angst."

She didn't smile, not even a little at the corners of her lips. "It'll be different when I get home. You'll see. I'm working on some changes and—"

The screen froze with her face contorted like a Halloween mask: eyes looking up, eyebrows to the sky, her lips pressed forward like she was chewing something really tough.

"Mum," I said. "Mum? Can you hear me? You're frozen."

Her goofy-twisted face stayed on the screen. "Well, if you can hear me, I love you. See you soon."

I waited another moment, and when she made no noise, I clicked on the red button to send her back into cyberspace.

———◦———

Mum and Mom made plans for me to go to Lena's after school on Monday while Mom went to the airport, but when Mom came to pick me up, she was alone. The spelling bee was the next day and Mum's flight had been delayed again. My mind started jittering on the car ride home from Lena's house. It was like I had a whole bunch of letter tiles in my head and they were all bouncing around. "She'll be here," Mom said. "In the morning, when you wake up. She'll be here."

"Sure," I said.

"She's at the airport. They haven't canceled the flight yet."

"Sure," I said again, and watched the snow fall onto our windshield.

We talked to her on the computer again when we got home. She sat on the floor in the airport in front of the big windows that looked out on the tarmac, so it looked like she was floating in space.

"I will be there," she insisted.

"It's supposed to snow again," I told her.

"I will be there," she promised. "If I have to commandeer a pack of sled dogs, I will be there."

Mom sat next to me, her knees drawn up toward her chest with a cup of tea resting on them. She was wearing a purple robe that was made of fleece at least three inches thick. On her feet she had bunny slippers that Mum gave her as a joke, but which she had worn so much, the bottoms were nearly gone and the bunnies' pink noses had turned a grayish brown. "And I will definitely be there. I have the day off of work, and Margie knows not to even think of calling me."

"Tenet," Mum said.

"Tenet?" I repeated back to her. A tenet was a belief or principle. Was she trying to tell me it was a matter of principle that she would be back? Beliefs can't control the weather.

"It's on the Words You Must Know list, not to be confused with 'tenant.'"

"*T-E-N-E-T*," I said. "Tenet." I had studied the word with Coco—the whole list, actually. "I'm all set, Mum. I've been studying like crazy."

"With Coco," Mom said. "I can't wait to meet Coco. I could stay awake at night wondering what type of parents named their child Coco."

"It's not his real name. That's Christopher."

"Oh. That's a bit of a disappointment."

"Well, I'll have to thank Christopher for filling in for me. Tomorrow. When I meet him. Because I will be there."

The snow in the backyard weighed the boughs of the pine tree down so far, they touched the ground. Could someone make a home under there? "A tree fort," I said. "We should make a tree fort when you get home. Instead of a snow fort. A snow tree fort."

"Okay," Mum said. Her eyes flicked over to Mom's face.

"Something we talked about," Mom said.

"Let's talk about your birthday," Mum said. "If this friend of yours is really a foodie, we ought to go down to Portland. The airline magazine had a whole feature on the restaurants of Portland. I had no idea! It's a real food paradise."

"Sure," I said, as if that hadn't been the plan all along. Mum was too far away to know what was going on anymore.

"I'll send you a link to the article, and you pick one. We'll go Saturday."

"Okay," I said again. I still thought it would be fun to have a party with everyone—Lena, Coco, Dev, Adam, and Lucas—but didn't feel much like celebrating. Anyway, I didn't want to start the inevitable discussion broaching such an idea would bring. Their joy would be just a little too much to bear.

"'Nauseous,'" Mum said.

Coco and I had wondered why this was on the commonly confused word list. It was the definitions that were the problems. Most people say they feel nauseous when they are feeling sick, but really "nauseous" means "*causing* nausea." "Nauseated" is the word you should use. Maybe Mum would find this interesting. Maybe she already knew. "Nauseous. *N-A-U-S-E-O-U-S*. Nauseous."

"Perfect!" she said. "I'm trying to keep you on your toes. I imagine up there on the stage under the hot lights, it would be easy to get distracted, to lose your flow."

"I'll be okay."

"You'll be more than okay. And I will be there. And Mom. I promise."

Sometimes the more someone promises, the less you believe them.

TWENTY-EIGHT

Quell

The twelve chairs were in a semicircle on the stage. Our names were printed on paper and taped to them so we knew where to sit. We were all jumbled up. My seat was between Coco's sister, Emma, and a seventh-grade boy. Charlotte's seat was across from mine. We were standing off to the side of the stage, in the wings, because Dr. Dawes was going to announce our names the way Ms. Wickersham did at pep rallies.

I stood in Wonder Woman stance, just like Lena had made me promise.

Mum had made it back in the night, after all, well after I'd gone to sleep. She'd driven me to school that morning.

We didn't talk, just practiced words. She and Mom sat in the front row with Alan and Eliot. Mum had a piece of paper, ready to write down all the words so we could study them for the county bee. She was so sure I would be one of the top two to make it.

Lucas stood next to me. He bounced from foot to foot. Charlotte stood off to the side, all by herself. Her eyes blinked slowly like a toy doll's.

"Look at this," Lucas said. He pulled something golden from his pocket. He held it up right in front of my nose so I could see it in the scant light: a bee encased in amber. "It's my good-luck charm."

"I thought you didn't need luck."

"Coco told me I didn't have it in the bag, after all."

Coco. He sat out in the audience, too, with Adam and Lena. Behind them was Melinda. She had written *CD* for "Charlotte Diamond" on her cheeks with blue marker and wore a blue ribbon in her ponytail. All the girls in that group did. They had pom-poms, too. Were pom-poms even allowed at a spelling bee?

Dr. Dawes snaked her way through the crowd of spellers, then turned to look back at us. "You all ready?" she asked.

We nodded and mumbled yes. Because what else could we do? Run screaming for a dictionary?

She raised her fist in the air and then flipped it into a thumbs-up before striding across the stage in her red suit. The podium was on the far side. When she reached it, she held up

"Vendetta," Charlotte said. She traced the letters on her hand. She hesitated. "Can I please have a definition?"

"Go, Char!" Melinda called.

"Quiet from the audience, please," Dr. Dawes said. "Vendetta: 'a very long and violent fight between two families or groups.' A secondary definition is 'a series of acts done by someone over a long period of time to cause harm to a disliked person or group.'"

I couldn't be sure, but I thought her gaze flicked over to me. I wanted her to get this word wrong. This word.

"*V*," she said. I watched her trace the letter on her hand. "*E-N-D*." She took a deep breath. "Vendetta, *V-E-N-D-E-T-T-A*." Melinda started cheering even before she knew Charlotte got it right, and the crowd around her joined in. Dr. Dawes seemed uncertain about what to do with this newfound enthusiasm for the spelling bee.

Lucas's turn was next. "Lucas, your word is 'dugong.'"

Lucas grinned.

"Do you need a definition?" Dr. Dawes asked.

I was pretty sure she wasn't supposed to do that. But Lucas said, "A dugong is like a manatee. You can find them in Asia, Africa, and Australia. When I go to Australia, I'm going to go scuba diving and I hope to see one. Also a cuttlefish. That's 'cuttle' with *T*s, not 'cuddle' with *D*s. They are definitely not cuddly."

"That's interesting, Lucas. But not relevant. Are you ready to spell 'dugong'?"

one hand, and everyone in the audience did the same as they quieted down. Lucas, too. "Pavlov," he mumbled.

"Welcome to the Frontenac Consolidated Middle School Spelling Bee."

Then she explained the rules. The most important rule, the one most people don't understand, is that even if you miss a word, you might not be out. You have to wait until the whole round is done. If everyone else misses their words, too, then the round starts over. That's not very likely in round one or two, but when you're down to three or four spellers, it can happen. When you get down to the final round, the rules change again, but Dr. Dawes waited to explain that.

And then we began.

◦◆◦

My first word was "alligator." Easy. Still, I asked for the country of origin just so Coco didn't blow a gasket.

"Spanish," Dr. Dawes told me. *Who knew?*

While I spelled, Ms. Lawson and Ms. Wickersham compared my answers to the official spelling lists in special binders they held on their laps. They sat in the first row right in front of the microphone so they wouldn't miss a single letter. Ms. Lawson was the head judge, and she gave a quick nod to Dr. Dawes who said, "Correct."

Charlotte got an even easier word: "unity." She didn't ask any questions, only traced out each letter on her hand as she said it. She didn't hesitate after each letter like some of the kids I've seen on television; still, I was surprised she had a strategy.

When Dr. Dawes nodded that she got it right, the crowd around Melinda cheered. Not just the sixth graders, but the popular kids in all the grades. It was like they decided they were going to take over the spelling bee along with everything else in the school. Then Lucas got "pretzel," and when he asked for a definition, everyone laughed. Even Dr. Dawes chuckled.

The seventh grader next to me got out on "access." He forgot the second *c*.

And then there were eleven.

It kept going like that for four more rounds. The words weren't too hard. Some people made mistakes. Charlotte didn't. Lucas didn't. I didn't. Emma got the hardest word of the round: "banzai." She bit her lip and tugged at her blond hair. I tried to see something of Coco in her. She was all round cheeks and an upturned nose. The only thing the same was the way they turned red, starting at the neck and working up to their cheeks. "Can I get the country of origin?" she asked in a soft voice.

"Japanese," Dr. Dawes told her.

She looked up to the ceiling. I looked up, too. I couldn't help myself. In the audience, I saw their dad. He leaned forward. Coco examined his hands in his lap.

It's Japanese, I wanted to tell her. The tree. *B-O-N-S-A-I.*

"Can I please have the definition?"

"'A Japanese cheer or war cry.'"

Oh. Not the tree.

"Banzai. *B*," she began, then hesitated. I could feel t[he] audience waiting, waiting for her to fail. "*A-N-Z-A-I*," sh[e] said all in a rush. "Banzai."

"Yes!" Dr. Dawes exclaimed.

I felt lucky that my word was "magnolia." If I'd ha[d] "banzai," I'd be right out.

Dev came right after her. He was doing well. He spoke co[n]fidently into the microphone and even joked with Dr. Dawe[s].

"'Periphery,'" Dr. Dawes told him.

"Periphery. *P-E-R-I-P-E—*" He stopped, catching his mi[s]take. It wasn't his brain confusing him: just a simple mistak[e,] a slip of the tongue. "No," he said, but he shook his head. Onc[e] you start, you have to keep going. You can go back and sta[rt] over again, but you can't change anything. "*R-Y*," he finishe[d]. He was out. When he went to sit in the audience, Adam ga[ve] him a hearty clap on the shoulder, which I figured might [be] the closest Adam ever came to hugging someone. The fif[th] round was over and we were down to six: Charlotte, Luc[as,] Emma, an eighth grader named Chloe, a seventh grad[er] named Max, and me.

Across the circle Charlotte scuffed her feet along [the] floor and twirled her hair.

In the audience, Mum gave me a thumbs-up.

Charlotte stepped up to the microphone.

"Charlotte, your word is 'vendetta,'" Dr. Dawes [told] her.

"Yes. Dugong. *D-U-G-O-N-G.* Dugong."

"Correct."

Max was given the word "flotilla." You could tell right away he wasn't sure of himself. He rocked back and sucked in his cheeks. But he didn't ask any questions. "Flotilla. *F-L-O-A-T-I-L-L-A.*"

I shook my head as Dr. Dawes said, "I'm sorry, Max. That's not it."

He sat back in his seat and waited for the round to end.

Chloe got the word "robot."

Country of origin: Slavic, from "*robota,*" meaning compulsory labor. I looked down at Coco, who smiled back at me. Charlotte was looking at me, too. I could feel her eyes boring into me, and when I checked, she was indeed glaring.

He likes you.

Well, she might feel jealous, but she shouldn't blame me about stupid Mitchell. She could have him if she wanted to. I was still pretty sure that he'd loved her forever.

My turn was next. "Ruth, your word is 'keelhaul.'"

I think they would have kicked me out of town if I didn't know this nautical word. Still, I asked for the definition because of Coco, and because I just like it.

"This isn't a pleasant one," Dr. Dawes said. "'To haul under the keel of a ship as punishment or torture.' Thus, also, 'to rebuke severely.'"

I didn't know that secondary definition. I wished I could use it in a sentence. *Hey, Charlotte, thanks for keelhauling me.*

"Country of origin?"

Mum nodded in the front row.

"Dutch," Dr. Dawes said.

"Keelhaul. *K-E-E-L-H-A-U-L.* Keelhaul."

"That is correct. Emma, you're the final speller for this round."

When Emma and I passed, she gave me the smallest of smiles. I wondered what it meant.

"Emma, your word is 'mizzle.'"

Emma giggled. "Mizzle?"

"Yes, mizzle."

"Are there any alternate pronunciations?" She was still smiling. I watched Coco. He was biting his lip. Did he really want her to lose? I didn't think so. And I didn't want him to.

"No, just mizzle."

She nodded. "May I please have a definition?"

"Mizzle, 'to rain in very fine drops.' Now *that* is a useful word."

"Mizzle. *M-I-Z-Z-L-E.* Mizzle."

"Very good! That ends round six."

She should have told Max to return to his seat, but she didn't, and he didn't move. She called Charlotte to the microphone. Charlotte glanced over her shoulder at Max. "Dr. Dawes, I think you—" She was not near enough to the microphone for it to pick up her voice, but we could hear her on the stage. "I mean I think Max—"

"Oh!" Dr. Dawes called out. "I'm so sorry. Max, please take a seat in the audience. A round of applause for Max."

He scowled at Charlotte as he walked by and whispered something under his breath, something that unsettled her. I saw it in the flash of pink on her cheeks and the way she rubbed her hands on her skirt.

"Charlotte, your word is 'oolong.'"

Charlotte sucked in her lower lip. I didn't want her to go out this way, thrown off by whatever Max said. But then again, she'd done far better than I thought she would, and she was making me a little nervous.

"Country of origin?"

"Chinese," Dr. Dawes said merrily.

"You've got this, Char!" Melinda called out, as if Charlotte had somehow absorbed the entire Chinese language in the month she'd spent in an orphanage there.

"Oolong," Charlotte said. "*O-O-L-O-N-G.* Oolong."

Correct.

Lucas got "linseed," Chloe spelled "boysenberry," I got "genre," and Emma spelled "honcho." And so, another round began. And another, and another. We were up to round eleven when Chloe finally went out on "fennec," an Arabic word for "a small pale-fawn fox."

Four remained.

———◄○►———

Dr. Dawes announced that there would be a break. I practically ran from the stage to the bathroom. I didn't realize how badly I had to go until she announced it.

When I stepped out of the stall, Melinda bumped up against me. Hard. I stumbled back against the metal frame of the door and shook the whole thing. "Whoa," I said. I didn't mean to talk. It was like the force of her blow pushed the air from me.

"What are you doing up there?" she demanded. She was so close to me, I could smell the baby-powder-scented deodorant she used and the peanut butter she must have had with breakfast.

"Spelling," I said, and resisted adding: "Duh."

"I thought you were her friend. She said you were her friend."

"Charlotte?"

"Yes, Charlotte, you idiot. Charlotte your friend who lost her house and they're going to blame it on her dad. And this is how you treat her?"

I didn't care what Melinda said, not one bit. But Charlotte, she had said that all I cared about was myself and my stupid games. And here I was doing it again.

I wished Melinda would ram me against the stall again, maybe sucker punch me to the belly. It would hurt about as much.

◄○►

The chairs were rearranged while we had our break. Emma, Lucas, me, Charlotte. She was already sitting there when I sat down, looking down at her shoes. Real shoes—ballet flats— not the stupid, useless boots she had been wearing since she met Melinda, even when it was still seventy degrees in the fall. Her hands were folded in her lap and her hair fell down like a curtain between us.

I could let her win.

Except I couldn't control Lucas or Emma.

Wait and see. I had to wait and see, and if it got down to just me and Charlotte, then I'd do what I had to do.

Dr. Dawes returned to the podium as Lucas and Emma sat down. She shook a piece of paper. "As we go into the final rounds, the rules change ever so slightly. If everyone in the round gets their words wrong, they all stay and a new round begins. To win the bee, you must win by two words. That is to say, if three of the spellers in the round spell the word incorrectly, and the fourth speller spells his or her word correctly—"

"His," Lucas whispered, but he was not speaking to me or Emma. He was speaking to himself—or perhaps to Dr. Dawes, correcting her.

"—then that speller must spell a final word in order to win the bee. If he or she misspells that championship word, then each of the spellers from the previous round return. Let's begin. Emma."

Emma's face was fully red now, all the way down to the

collar of her shirt, and probably beyond. In the audience, Coco watched her with his hands clasped together.

"'Pachyderm,'" Dr. Dawes said.

"Can I please have the definition?" Her voice cracked.

"'A type of animal that has hooves and thick skin.'"

"Could you use it in a sentence?"

"Ruby the elephant is a pachyderm."

"Pachyderm," Emma said. And then, more clearly, "*P-A-C-H-Y-D-E-R-M*. Pachyderm."

Coco made a little "Yes!" gesture, but I was thinking, *No, no, no, it's* I-D-E-R-M.

Dr. Dawes nodded and my stomach sank. Wrong. I was wrong. Would all the words in this round be so hard? Maybe I wouldn't need to let Charlotte win, after all. I'd lose without intending to.

Emma sat and Lucas stood. Dr. Dawes smiled down at him from the podium. "'Infinitesimal.'"

"*I-N-F-I-N-I-T-E-S-I-M-A-L*," he said, while I was still picturing the word in my head.

I shook as I walked to the microphone. I was wrong to think I could do this. Wrong, plain wrong. And Coco would be disappointed, and Mum, too. She sat next to Mom, leaning so far forward, she was practically bent in half.

"Ruth, your word is 'dip-thong.'" That was what she said, anyway, but I could picture the word in my head.

I knew this one. I knew it.

I glanced down at Coco, who had drilled it with me.

"Diphthong. *D-I-P-H-T-H-O-N-G*. Diphthong."

"Very good!"

Coco shook his head, though, because I went too fast and didn't ask any questions.

When Charlotte went to the microphone, the whole crowd of popular kids rose to their feet and started hooting and hollering. It took Dr. Dawes two full minutes to get them calmed down, and even then it meant that teachers moved over and sat with them. Mom and Mum and even Alan and Eliot craned their heads around to see what all the fuss was. Mum gave me a shrug and another thumbs-up.

"Charlotte, your word is 'apartheid.'"

Her whole body relaxed. We had studied apartheid in humanities.

Still, she wrote the letters on her hand as she said them. "*A-P-A-R-T-H-E-I-D*."

And so we started again. When Lucas went up for his turn, Coco, Dev, Adam, and Lena beat their hands together, and when it was my turn, they yelled out "Ruth," low and deep like when Red Sox fans used to cheer for Kevin Youki-lis: "Yooooouuuukkkk," but for me it was "Ruuuuttthhhhhh!" And Charlotte's fans waved their pom-poms but didn't get all wild again.

We did three more rounds, then four. On the sixth round, Emma got a word that sounded just like "Nana," like your grandmother or the last part of "banana." She froze. Her cheeks got redder and redder, and I could even see her scalp under her hair burning.

She repeated the word, and Dr. Dawes repeated it back to her.

"Can I have the definition?" she asked.

"'Knowledge,'" Dr. Dawes told her.

"Origin?" she asked.

"It's a Sanskrit word."

"Nana," she pronounced. "Nana, nana, nana. Could you use it in a sentence?"

"He practices nana yoga," she said.

"Are there any alternate pronunciations?"

"Yes. Gyana."

I shook my head. I had no idea. Emma cleared her throat. "*G-Y-A-N-N-A.*"

"I'm sorry, no. It's *J-N-A-N-A.*"

Coco had both his hands over his mouth while Emma went and slumped back into her chair. In the audience, I looked for her father to be scowling. Maybe he would even stand up and walk out. Instead he gave her a smile. I tried to see if she smiled back, but Lucas was in the way as he walked back up to the microphone.

He spelled "gingham," I spelled "ersatz," and Charlotte spelled "sassafras"—another one I probably would have gotten wrong, adding an extra *s* to the end. But still, I felt like I was in that zone Adam had talked about.

Unfortunately, so were Charlotte and Lucas. We went nine more rounds.

And then it happened.

"Lucas, your word is 'aviary.'"

As the grin spread across Lucas's face, I knew what was happening. I wanted to leap out of my chair and tell him, *No, no, no! Ask for the definition!* But he started spelling. "*A-P-I-A-R-Y.*"

"I'm sorry, that's wrong."

"What?"

"It's wrong."

"No, you see, I'm a beekeeper, or I was. I know how to spell 'apiary.'"

Dr. Dawes's face softened as she understood what had happened. The judges in the front row exchanged glances, but we all knew the rules. "Your word was 'aviary,' Lucas, not 'apiary.'"

His eyes widened, but he returned to his seat on the stage. He knew the rules, too.

I tried to catch his gaze as I made my way up to the microphone, but he kept looking at the pocked boards of the stage.

"Ruth, your word is 'shrieval.'"

Lena made a whooping sound. I wanted to smile, but my stomach was all roiled up because of what had happened to Lucas. And because if Charlotte and I both got our words right, it would just be me and her, but if I got mine wrong, and she got hers right, then she would only need to spell one more to win.

I could give her that. I could give her that small thing.

"Ruth?" Dr. Dawes prompted.

But she might get her word wrong. Or her championship word. There was no telling.

"Shrieval," I said. "Can I get a definition?"

Lena raised her hands in a *what are you doing?* gesture.

" 'Of or relating to a sheriff.' "

I saw Ms. Lawson in the first row, and I thought of the map test.

Melinda glared at me. If she could, I knew she would have sent blasts of ice from her eyeballs to freeze me to my spot.

You don't know her, I thought. *You might be her best friend, but you don't know her at all.*

"Shrieval. *S-H-R-I-E-V-A-L.* Shrieval."

"That is correct!"

Charlotte walked to the microphone. Melinda beat her hands together until Ms. Broadcheck put a hand on her shoulder.

"Charlotte, your word is 'detente.' "

"Detente," she said. She looked over her shoulder at me. We just stared at each other. She gave a tiny smile. Maybe. Then she turned around and said, clear and confident, *"D-A-Y-T-A-N-T."*

Dr. Dawes tilted her head to the side and made her eyes look soft. "That's incorrect."

"Okay," Charlotte said.

So it came down to this. Get the word correct, and I was the champion.

"Choke!" I heard someone yell. Not Melinda. Ms. Broadcheck would be right on her. She was sitting there, though, smiling like a cat on a mouse.

Again, louder. "Choke!"

Lena leaped to her feet and spun around. "This is a spelling bee, not a basketball game, you classless hooligans!" she yelled.

Dr. Dawes rapped at the podium like a judge calling for order. "The enthusiasm for this year's spelling bee is remarkable, but Lena is correct. This is not a sporting event, and at any rate, Frontenac Beavers always practice good sportsmanship. Please refrain from heckling." She took a deep breath. "Ruth, your championship word is 'perfidy.'"

Perfidy. I knew the word. How to spell it, what it meant, that it was Latin in origin, but I asked, "May I please have the definition?"

"'The quality or state of being faithless or disloyal.'"

Behind me, Charlotte scuffed her foot across the floor. In front of me, my friends held hands.

Faithless or disloyal.

What would it mean, in this instance, to lose faith in Charlotte? To be disloyal to her?

What had it meant to her?

Because she knew that *D-A-Y-T-A-N-T* was wrong. Really wrong. Hadn't she?

Was that perfidy toward me? Throwing the bee and giving it to me. Had she lost faith in my ability to win? Or was it loyalty?

My hip and shoulder still stung from being slammed into the stall.

I knew this much: Melinda knew nothing of either loyalty or faith.

"Perfidy," I said. *"P-E-R-F-I-D-Y.* Perfidy."

"Correct!"

TWENTY-NINE

Alchemy

That night I sat in my room and looked at the certificate I had earned. Maybe earned. I couldn't shake the idea that Charlotte had muffed on purpose.

Either way it would be the two of us headed to the Knox County Spelling Bee. Only one of us could go on to the state bee, though.

My stomach was full of the strawberry shortcake we'd had to celebrate. Mom had made the biscuits the night before. When I asked her what would have happened if I had lost, she'd said, "Not a possibility."

I had downloaded a chess app onto my tablet, and I was thinking of doing some practicing—I wanted to get better so I could play with Lucas, Dev, and Adam—but then I noticed

my backpack. The book Mr. Douglas had given me stuck out
of it. It looked a little off. Like it wasn't quite holding its shape
as a book. Taryn would think it was a book with a spell on it.

I wasn't sure how I felt about Taryn now that she was off
kissing royalty who had spent some time being trolls. Everyone changes, I guess, even old, familiar characters in books.
And, anyway, maybe Lucas was right, and if I just read some
Tolkien, people would stop insisting that I needed to. So I
pulled the book out and flipped it open.

I blinked.

The pages had been cut out carefully so that a space
about the size of two decks of cards was left. In that space
was a pewter figurine of a dragon, a die with twenty sides,
and two folded-up packs of paper.

The first was graph paper, and when I unfolded it, I saw
a map. It was drawn carefully with pencil, busier at the middle but spanning out to the edges of the page. It seemed to
be of a town, but an older town, or a fantasy town. The
map's key promised that the town held places like the Word
Hoard, the Hill of the Dead, and the *Cursus Publicus*, perhaps a place for publicly cursing others? A mermaid was
drawn in the water.

The second was actually several pieces of paper, and it
was a story.

In Middle Earth a motley crew assembles to save the
world as we know it. Four hobbits, two men, a dwarf, an elf,

and a wizard, too. They rambled to destroy the ring in the mountains of Mordor.

Now it is your time. Dare you join this fellowship?

The rules are simple.

Twelve more clues will be hidden. One for each month. You have a month to solve each riddle. Plenty of time. On the full moon of each month, the next clue will be hidden. Seek it. Leave each where you found it for the next traveler. Where does this quest lead? What is the endgame? Follow and you shall find out. You must be wise, learned, disciplined, and above all, not a FROG.

If you agree to join this fellowship, proceed with your first clue:

My WORDS are legend.

Legends are HISTORY,

My field of study.

ONE BOOK only in your shire.

*

It was the story of a quest. Our quest. It took the adventurers from place to place, and in each place they needed to find a clue. Our clues.

With your strength, the book has been found, and now you must climb the hill to the Scholar's Shrine. Four travelers begin this tale: Half Elf, Troll, Halfling, and Thief. To make it to the end, you will need to build a motley crew. Find a wizard to see you through.

There were small drawings alongside the story, almost like sketches. First a small crowd of figures setting off along the path. It grew as the story went on.

You walk a long and winding path to find your next clue. Shall the Half Elf teach you his songs to pass the time? Perhaps that will draw an elf lord into your presence. The road is long, and the leaves do change color.

You have demonstrated your strength, and your intelligence: now you must go boldly into battle. Be wise with your strategy: though it may seem like a game, there is more to the story.

As I read, I held the map in my other hand, and I realized that the places on the map matched up to the clues. Our clues. Our town.

And then I realized I had missed the biggest piece of the puzzle, even though it had collapsed at my feet.

THIRTY

Pandit

Pledge Allegiance Comics was in an old brick building with the word "Carnegie" over its door. When you stepped inside, it was alive with color. Rack upon rack of comic books, each neatly organized by publisher, genre, date. There were shelves full of action figures. Some I recognized—Superman, the Green Lantern, the Flea—others I did not.

A man stood behind a glass counter filled with what I assumed were the best of the best, the things for the real collectors. He glanced up at me when I came in but didn't say anything, just pushed his geek-chic glasses back up his nose and returned to his conversation with a teenage boy. "It's not about winning, dude," he said.

"Then it's not a game," the boy replied. He wore a black T-shirt with a huge dragon on it.

Here was what I had forgotten: the library hadn't always been the library. First it was the department store. Charlotte's dad had renovated it less than ten years earlier. Before that, the library was much smaller, a little brick building paid for by some wealthy steel magnate in the early 1900s. Carnegie. When the library moved out, the comic shop moved in.

For the answers you seek, look up.

I looked up, but the ceiling was covered with posters. Comic posters, movie posters, game posters overlaid one another. There was not one empty spot.

Those couldn't be the answer, because whoever put the clues down, when they did it, this was still the library.

"Can I help you?" the man asked. The teenage boy had moved on to a shelf of graphic novels. Violent-looking ones, from the covers.

I shook my head.

"Admiring my posters?" he asked. "Up there?"

"Sure," I said. "Yeah."

"I just noticed you were spending a lot of time staring at them. As if you thought you might find some sort of answer there."

No way. No way, no way, no way.

"I do seek answers," I said.

"Rider," he said. "Out."

"What?" the boy asked.

"We're closing early. I have some business to take care of."

My eyes widened. What had I done?

"Dude, it's three thirty," Rider said.

"Closing."

"I haven't made my choice yet."

"Dude, you come here every day. You never buy anything."

"Maybe this was going to be my day."

"My loss. Out."

The boy gave me a funny look as he left the store, the bells above the door chiming like fairy bells. The man turned the sign to CLOSED but didn't, I was glad to see, lock the door.

"What do you know?" he asked me.

"What?"

"What clues have you found?"

"All of them," I said. "Well, except for the one that was supposed to be on the History Path. That was gone."

"Yeah." He settled back onto the stool by his cash register. "I tried to get that one but wasn't quick enough."

"So," I said.

"So?" he replied.

"Do you have the answer?" I asked.

"That depends on the question." He shook his head and laughed. "Man, I've been waiting twenty years for this. For someone else to follow the clues. To find it. Kept that post office box."

"Bought this place," I said.

"That was just good luck. I used to have a much smaller place—I took over an old gaming store there."

"Wizards and Warcraft," I said, the name of the store whose phone book ad we'd found the clue on.

"Yeah, that's right. I knew the owner, Liam, 'cause—well, he was a friend of Mr. Douglas's, my favorite teacher. And he needed some illustrations done for his advertisements, and Mr. Douglas suggested me. Then, when Liam was selling, he asked if I wanted it. It was over by the Chinese restaurant. I was hungry all the time." He patted his belly. He didn't have much of one.

"So you did all of this?" I asked. "This was your game?"

"Mine and Harriet's. She really came up with most of it. I just made up the clues and put them around town while she was in New York."

"Harriet?"

"She came every summer. She got us all hooked on *Doctor Who* and role-playing games. Man, she was the best dungeon master. She came up with the best campaigns. Never missed a detail."

"Campaigns?"

"It's like the mission in a role-playing game."

"Like a quest?"

"Exactly." He scratched his head. "Harriet always hated going back. 'You all are living one story up here, and I'm living my story down there, and then I jump into yours like time travel.' That's what she said. She wanted our stories to stay tied together, so she had this idea for a scavenger hunt that went through the whole year. She'd send clues and I'd make the cards and hide them and people would find them, and it all ended that June, when she came back."

"The cards are beautiful," I told him.

"Thanks." He grinned. "We talked about making our own game, Harriet and me. She would develop the story lines, and I would make the cards. It never happened, of course." He made a noise that was like a laugh, but also like a sigh. He turned around and took a small framed photograph off the wall. "Here," he said. "We called ourselves the Allegiance."

It was a group of teenagers, all boys except for one girl with hair dyed black and just a hint of a smile. The boys all had long hair—at least chin length. One wore a Pink Floyd T-shirt, and another wore a trench coat. "That one's me," he said, pointing to a short boy with a scruffy-looking beard that hardly covered up a nasty patch of acne. "You can see why I was always the troll." He laughed. "Harriet, she was always half elf, half human, descended from knights."

"Taryn Greenbottom," I murmured.

"That's right!" he said. "How'd you know that?"

Taryn Greenbottom. Harriet Wexler.

"That's Harriet Wexler," I said. It wasn't a question. I knew.

"Yes!" he said, still enthusiastic but confused. Then he slapped the counter. "You must have read her books!"

"One or two of them," I said.

He laughed again. "I always knew she'd be a writer. I don't know why she writes for kids. No offense. Her stories are fantastic, though, aren't they?"

I nodded. In the photograph, Harriet Wexler had one arm hanging down; the other reached across her body to hold it at the elbow. Her fingernails were painted black, and her dark hair had a streak of purple in it.

Harriet Wexler. Harriet Wexler had been a summer person.

"I sent her a letter once, but she never wrote back. Guess she forgot all about us folks back in Promise."

"What was your name?" I asked.

"It's Charlie," he said.

"No. Your troll name," I told him.

"Charlak Rapshidir," he said. But I already knew that.

"I don't think she forgot about you at all." I zipped my winter coat up. "I have to go."

"Wait!" he said. "Don't you want your final clue?"

He pressed a button on his old cash register, and with a clang and a click, the drawer popped open. He lifted the plastic cash tray and pulled something out from underneath.

One golden envelope.

THIRTY-ONE

Planning

I want a birthday party, after all," I said.

We were all sitting down together for dinner at home, which we hadn't done in ages. After the bee, we'd gone out to eat. Mum had made corned beef and cabbage, which is the only thing she knows how to make. Since she's Irish, everyone expects her to make it, even though they don't actually eat it in Ireland. But she learned how to make it. That and soda bread, which actually is Irish.

"A party?" Mom asked.

I chewed my salty corned beef and swallowed before saying, "Yes. A party. On Saturday. With boys."

Mom coughed, but Mum grinned. "Well, this is a pleasant turn of events!"

"Saturday is three days from now. We can't get the room at the hospital."

"I don't want to invite the whole class. Just five people. Lena, Coco, Adam, Dev, and Lucas."

"Brilliant!" Mum said.

"We need to get marshmallows," I said.

"For hot chocolate?" Mom asked.

"Sure. But also for a game."

"Chubby Bunnies!" Mum said, clapping her hands together.

"It's awfully late for sending out invitations," Mom said.

"My friends won't be busy."

I knew they were free because just like me, they were probably always free. And if they had some family obligation, they'd just have to get out of it. We were going to the final destination. We were going to finish this quest.

◄○►

I made the invitations on the computer. I used the font that looked like wizards and dragons and stuff.

Mum took me to school on Thursday, so I was early. I didn't have anywhere else to go, so I went into homeroom. Ms. Broadcheck was at her desk. Her shoes were off and her feet were balanced on the desk. "Ruth!" she said when I walked in. "Sorry. I wasn't expecting you. You're early."

"So are you," I said. "And you're always late."

She rubbed her ankles. "You noticed."

Everyone noticed. But I didn't say so.

She moved on to rubbing her feet. She was wearing the dress with the high belt again. "I suppose I can stop that ruse now. I was running out of excuses."

"What do you mean?"

She dropped her feet onto the floor. "You know your mum asked me to look out for you, right?"

"Sure. That's why I'm in this homeroom."

"Sometimes watching out, well, sometimes it just makes problems worse, you know? I wanted to give you a chance to sort things out on your own." Then she made a funny face and put her hand over her mouth like she was going to throw up.

"Are you sick?" I asked, taking a step back. I didn't do well with vomit. In second grade Charlotte threw up on the bus on a field trip. We were sitting together, of course, and some of it got on me. I cried the whole rest of the bus ride, even when the teacher wiped it off me with baby wipes. Mom had to come pick me up.

Ms. Broadcheck laughed. "Only in the morning."

I took another step back. Whatever Ms. Broadcheck had, I didn't want to catch it.

"I'm pregnant, Ruth," she said. "I thought you knew."

"Oh."

"Anyway. If I kept stepping in, telling kids to be nice to you, telling you where to go and who to be with, you never would have found Lena—because let me tell you, I did not see that friendship coming—or that gaggle of boys."

"So you pretended to be late?"

"Well, I was actually late a lot of the time. I mean, I gave myself some extra time in the morning. You know, the timing worked out quite well. It gave me time to yak before I came into school."

I didn't think teachers should use the word "yak." Lucas would probably tell her that a yak was an animal, and then he'd have some semi-interesting fact about yaks, maybe about their vomit.

"Thanks," I said. "I guess."

"You're welcome."

We could hear voices out in the hall. I shifted the envelopes in my hand. It had taken me forever to make all the little envelopes. We didn't have any origami paper, so I'd used wrapping paper instead. "I need to go find some people," I said.

"Sure, of course," she said. Then, laughing, she added, "Don't be late!"

I was almost to the door when she said, "Hey, Ruth, don't give up on Charlotte just yet. These things have a way of working themselves out."

There was a time when someone saying something like that would have made my heart soar. Now, though, well, maybe it would be nice. Someday. But I could wait.

THIRTY-TWO

Finale

We told my moms we were going sledding.

"Great!" Mom said. She hadn't stopped smiling since the first guest had arrived. "We'll have hot chocolate when you get back. It's from Dean and DeLuca, and it's fantastic!"

"And play Chubby Bunnies!" Mum added, tossing a marshmallow into her mouth. "Fubby bunnies," she garbled the words around the marshmallow. She swallowed and said, "I'll just be practicing until you get back."

"I don't like sledding," Adam said when we got outside.

"We're not going sledding," I said. "We're going to the fire tower."

"In winter?" Dev asked.

"Why?"

That's when I showed them the final clue that Charlie had given me.

No mountain of doom,
Just foothills of Ferdninand.
Towers of fire and glory as far as one can see.

*・********・**

"Another clue!" Lucas exclaimed.

"Where'd you find it?" Coco asked.

I explained about the book that Mr. Douglas had given me with the story and the map. I had the pewter figurine of the dragon deep in the pocket of my jeans. I told them how the library used to be where the comic shop was, and told them what Charlie had told me. Except about Harriet Wexler. I wanted to keep that to myself, I guess. You can't share all of yourself.

"And you're sure this is where it's supposed to be?" Dev asked, looking up at the hill filled with pine trees.

I unfolded the map, my fingers turning pink from the cold.

"This is the coolest!" Lena said. "It's our town, but you know, actually interesting."

I pointed to a small building in the hills. "There's a fire tower up there," I said. "'Towers of fire.'"

"And glory," Lucas said. "I told you quests were all about fame and glory."

"What are we waiting for?" Coco asked. "Let's go. The quest!"

"The quest!" we called back.

The hill was steeper than I remembered it being. Charlotte and I used to play around in the woods back here. She'd be a princess and I'd be a half elf, half knight. She'd pretend to be captured, and then I'd break her free. Or she'd break herself free. She was a very clever princess.

Maybe someday if I become a writer, I'll put a Princess Charlotte in one of my books and she'll read it and she'll know that everything is okay.

Lucas slipped and fell down onto his knees. I reached out my hand to pull him to his feet, and noticed Coco had fallen a little bit behind.

I waited for him and we fell into step with each other. Our boots crunched into the icy white snow. "I never thanked you for helping me," I told him.

"It was fun," he said. But his cheeks were starting to turn pink.

"Was your dad angry? With your sister?"

He shook his head. "No. It was really weird. We got home from school and Dad had all these board games out. Like old ones. Scrabble and Trouble and Operation."

"Oh, I love Operation!"

"Me, too! Anyway, we just played them all afternoon. And ate popcorn and drank soda. We never get to drink soda."

"Me, neither," I said. "Did he say anything?"

"No, just that when he was growing up they used to have family game nights and they would all end up yelling at each other about cheating and sometimes people would be mad for days. He called one game Full-Contact Pictionary."

"Weird."

"I know, right? Anyway, we didn't yell at all. He didn't say it, but I think he was trying to say that being competitive, that's part of who he is, but he got it, you know, that it didn't need to be that way for me and Emma."

"What about your brother?"

"Clint? He's more like Dad, overall, but even he seemed more mellow while we were playing."

A big pack of snow slipped off a pine tree and exploded in front of us.

"Oh, hey," he said. "I've been meaning to give you this. From my piano teacher."

From his coat pocket he pulled out a candy wrapped in

red foil paper. When I put it in my mouth, it was like sucking on creamy butter and sugar—like one of the elfish foods in Taryn Greenbottom's world.

"Listen," he said. "You know the Valentine's Day dance is coming up."

"Sure," I said around the hard candy in my mouth. I watched as the snowflakes were caught in the sun and twinkled like stars. It was enough to make you believe in fairies.

"I was wondering if you wanted to go with me?"

I turned my head sharply to face him. His whole face was red, right up to and under his knit cap. "Do people do that?" I asked. *Stupid. Stupid. Stupid.*

He took a step forward.

Was he going to try to kiss me like Lord Charlesmoore had kissed Taryn?

"Some people might," he said to the snow. "They could. Especially if they were, you know, together."

"Together? Like, together?" My voice sounded funny, and the words didn't form quite right with the candy in my mouth.

"Yes. Like together."

"I don't—"

"It's okay, never mind. I didn't figure you liked me, I just thought I would give it a shot. Clint said I should. And Dev. And Adam."

"I *do* like you," I said. And as I said the words, I knew they were true.

"You do?"

"Yes. I think so."

He grinned at me.

"I just don't think I want to be involved in that boy-girl stuff yet."

"Oh."

"Not in sixth grade," I said.

"Seventh?" he asked.

"Maybe eighth."

He looked up the hill at our friends. The redness was fading from his cheeks, and he was still smiling. "Well, all right, Ruth Mudd-O'Flanahan, but I'm not going to wait around forever."

And then he ran up the hill ahead of me calling, "Last one to the fire tower is a stinky troll!"

————◄○►————

The steps of the fire tower had so much snow on them, it looked like a luge track.

"Now what?" Dev said.

"We go up," I told him.

My foot cut through the snow and down to the step. I brushed off the railing as I went.

They waited a moment, but then they were behind me. Lena first, then Coco. Then Lucas, Adam, and Dev.

We didn't say anything as we climbed. Our boots crunched and cracked. Our breaths made puffs in the air.

Wind had blown the snow against the small structure at the top of the platform, leaving the other side of the platform clear. We could see all the way out to the ocean, all the way across the sea, it seemed.

I peeked in the window into the empty room. "My mom told me that during World War Two, women would man these fire towers. They'd sleep here and everything. The rest of the time, it was a man's job."

"There was a big fire here in the 1930s," Adam said. "My great-grandfather helped to fight it. They had to bring buckets up from the ocean, and they weren't sure the trees would ever grow back."

Dev stomped his feet. "So this is it?" he asked.

I spread my arms wide. "This is it. We did it!" I pointed at the railing. "This is where they stood in the picture Charlie showed me."

"We should take a picture!" Lena exclaimed.

A picture. Of course. Every quest needed a bounty at the end. How had I not thought to bring a camera?

Lena, though, pulled off her gloves and dug her phone out of her pocket. "I've never used the timer before," she said. "But I bet I can figure it out."

She balanced the phone on the windowsill. "Get close," she said. We all huddled against the railing.

"One, two, three!" she exclaimed, then scuttled over to us.

We heard three beeps and then a clicking sound. "Stay!" Lena commanded as she ran to check the picture.

Lucas did not stay. He went back to the structure and tugged on the latch of the door. It popped open with a creak.

"Paper wasp nest," Lucas said, and pointed into the room. There, as big and beautiful as the ones in Mr. Douglas's room, was a giant wasp nest. It was like a giant gray papier-mâché Easter egg, and I imagined the wasps with their strips of newsprint, dipping them in the glue and wrapping them around a balloon.

"Hey, look!" Lena said. She was pointing to something on one of the wallboards. Written in Sharpie were the words:

Not all who wander are lost.
The Allegiance, 1993

Robert   JEFF   Charlie   Matt
storm   Shaw   harriet
Jeremy

"That was them," I said. "Give me a Sharpie," I said to Lena.

She reached into her pocket and pulled out a black permanent marker.

"What else do you have in there?" Adam asked.

"ChapStick," she said. "And some artisanal chocolate."

"Really?" he asked. "What makes it artisanal?"

I ran my fingers over the words on the wall.

"J. R. R. Tolkien, right?" Coco asked.

I nodded. The first group had used the most famous book quote. What could ours be?

Harriet. I put my finger on her name. "That's Harriet Wexler," I said.

"*The* Harriet Wexler?" Coco asked.

"Uh-huh."

"That is so cool."

She had written her name in all lowercase letters, small and even.

I grinned and pulled the cap off the pen.

"What are you doing?" Dev demanded. "No one said anything about vandalism!"

I couldn't very well tell him it wasn't vandalism, because it was. "Sometimes it's okay to break the rules a little bit."

I started writing Taryn's words to Benedict, but changed them so it was for our whole group:

Without a quest, we were nothing.

I handed the pen to Lena, who signed her name and passed the pen to Coco. Then Lucas, then Adam, then Dev, who hesitated, but then wrote his name is small, neat letters.

"I ought to have just put my initials," he said. "It won't take them long to find the one Dev in this town."

I took the Sharpie from him and wrote my own name. I thought about writing like Harriet, small and lowercase, but instead signed it with a flourish.

Beneath our names I wrote:

The Allegiance Continues.

THIRTY-THREE

Epilogue

You probably want to know how the spelling bee turned out. I won the county bee. Charlotte got out in the third round on "censer." She didn't ask for a definition and spelled it with an *o*, like not letting people have access to something, not with an *e*, like the little container for putting incense in at church.

Everyone came to see me in the state bee. Well, not Charlotte, of course, but Eliot did, and Coco, Lena, Adam, Dev, and Lucas, who had to sit all the way in the back because he couldn't help but whisper the spellings of all the words. I got out in the fourth round. Adam called it the Curse of Coco, but he and I are already starting to get ready for next year.

As for Coco, he got into the program at Harvard. We all

wrote his recommendation together and called it "Everything Wonderful about Coco (A Necessarily Incomplete List)." Ms. Lawson said it was an exemplary essay, to which Lucas had replied, "Well, of course."

I finished *The Riddled Cottage*. Taryn and Lord Charlesmoore made their way through the Forest of Westbegotten and completed the quest. It certainly wasn't my favorite of her books, but it ended up okay. There was a dragon, and a dragon always makes a book a little better.

I took all the clues and put them back where they started, as best as I could. The town council made a temporary library in a strip mall just outside of the downtown area. Some of the books were gone, so I jammed the clues into the bookshelves, above where the book would have been. When the new library is done, I'll move them again. Dr. Dawes almost caught me putting the one back in the supply closet. I brought tape with me and taped the phone booth clue back into the book. Getting the clue back into the clock tower was the hardest. I tried three times to sneak back in, but ended up asking the town clerk if I could take a picture for a photography class. Luckily she didn't point out that there were no photography classes at Frontenac Consolidated Middle School.

I wrapped *The Riddled Cottage* in brown paper and tied it with twine. Then I stuck the golden envelope under the twine, like a present. I didn't bring it back to Pledge Allegiance Comics, though.

Instead, I hid it.

When I went to the post office to put the clue back in the post office box, I mailed two packages. The first I sent to Harriet Wexler, care of her publisher in New York City.

Dear Ms. Wexler,

Charlak Rapshidir, also known as Lord Charlesmoore, seeks the presence of your company. At the very least, he would enjoy a missive from your Isle of Solitude. He remains steadfast in Promise.

Sincerely,

A loyal reader, riddle solver, quest follower, and Member of the Allegiance

I put the twenty-sided die and the pewter figurine in the package, and hoped the publisher would not think it was from a deranged fan.

The second package was for Charlie.

The clue you gave is the clue you must seek.
The tale you will find is not for the meek.
Written for you, the troll and the lord,
A story is riches no man can afford.

Upstairs, downstairs, round and round.
Fish history in this town.
When you cannot climb the stair,
Under granite, find me there.

I put a print of the picture of the second fellowship in the padded envelope. I figured he could hang it up on his wall alongside the first photograph. We looked goofier. Lucas hung on the fence, and Adam scowled. Dev had his arm around Coco. Lena made a fish face. Me, I stood just like Harriet Wexler with one arm across my torso, cradling my other elbow. Her hint of a smile seemed waspish at first, but I knew what she was really feeling: what it means to find the spot where you belong.

Mom asked me again about why it was so quiet after a snow. I hadn't found out for sure. I finally got onto the army snow site, which was full of charts and graphs about acoustic waves. I thought maybe Mr. Douglas could explain it to me once I got to high school. I got the general gist, though. Because there's so much airspace between the snowflakes, the sound waves push down into them, and that lessens the sound energy. I like that phrase, "sound energy." Ms. Lawson would like it, too: the power of our words when we speak them aloud.

Anyway, I suppose all that is true. It is the army, after all. But I'd like to think the snow is quiet at first because it's remembering. It's thinking of its days before in a crystal lake or a muddy puddle or on top of a mountain, of being settled before melting and babbling through a creek down the hillside. When we finally finished with the classification system, we started learning about earth science. Mr. Sneed taught us how rain falls down and fills our lakes and streams and such. The water evaporates and goes up into the clouds. When the clouds are full and the atmospheric conditions are right, it rains again—or snows. The rain bears the traces of everything the water encountered on its journey, just like the whale's earwax. So maybe the snow is just taking a moment to reflect on where it's been before it settles down to the business of crunching under well-tread boots, crashing off schoolhouse roofs, and drifting down from heavy boughs.

It's the type of story that Charlotte would have drawn for me once, each snowflake with its own landscape of memories. Lucas wouldn't like it. He'd say that I was mixing science with fantasy, fact with fiction. He'd probably be right. But I know this: the weekend after my birthday, my moms and I went outside and we built the most amazing snow fort you've ever seen. We made hot chocolate and sat in our fort huddled together to drink it. Mum shoved eight marshmallows into her mouth, but one popped out, so we called it seven and a half—still greater than Adam. I poured a few drops of the hot chocolate onto the snow, then buried it deep. Wherever this snow went next—melted into the ground, floated back up to the sky—it would remember. Just like our footprints left their trace as we marched up to the fire tower, ready to be picked up and dropped off somewhere else. The snow would remember. And so will I.

THE MOTLEY CREW

Like Ruth, I've realized that I need to rely on others to help me get the work done. I owe a debt of gratitude to my own motley crew.

I first came to love spelling bees while working at Berwick Academy. Janet Miller was the driving force behind the bees at BA, with assistance from Lisa Wagner and Rosemary Zurawel. The spellers of the school inspired me with their knowledge, dedication, and memory tricks.

The Scripps Spelling Bee is the national spelling bee, and its website has a wealth of information for spellers both secret and known (www.spellingbee.com). Merriam-Webster partners with Scripps to provide study help in the form of their Spell It! website (www.myspellit.com). The site provides word lists, games, and more for students interested in participating in a bee—and for writers who want to write about them. Poring over this website not only increased my vocabulary but also helped me to choose the words for the chapter titles and the words the kids study in the book. The Scripps Spelling Bee uses the Webster's Third New International Dictionary as both the source of words and the final authority of their spelling. In this book the definitions for "trajectory," "ninja," "inane," "gusset," "banzai," "vendetta," "keelhaul," "mizzle," "pachyderm," "shrieval," and "perfidy" come from the Merriam-Webster online dictionary. These definitions are used by permission from *Merriam-Webster's Collegiate® Dictionary, 11th Edition* © 2014 by Merriam-Webster, Inc. (www.Merriam-Webster.com).

To better understand the world of role-playing games, I got feedback from Jeff Weir, Matt Frazer, and Lisa Shaw Frazer. The librarians at the Kennebunk Free Library put me in touch with Robert and Storm Madore, who spent an afternoon explaining the ins and outs of Dungeons & Dragons to me. If I misrepresented the games in any way, the fault is mine.

I have had the good fortune of having Bloomsbury Children's Books with me on my last three quests—er, books. They are the best team a writer could hope to work with. Cindy Loh, Beth Eller, Cristina Gilbert, Erica Barmash, Lizzy Mason, and Linette Kim are not only top-notch at their jobs, they are a lot of fun to be around. Also, they like sweets, which is key on any good quest. Thank you to Erin McGuire for the front jacket illustration, Nicole Gastonguay for the book design, Andrea Tsurumi for the interior and back jacket illustrations, and Patricia McHugh and Regina Castillo for copyediting and finding all the mistakes I never seem to see. Mary Kate Castellani, editor extraordinaire, made sure the journey didn't go off course, and helped me to see my own vision and goals more clearly. I am forever grateful to both Mary Kate and my agent, Sara Crowe, for their unwavering faith and willingness to see where the story goes next.

Finally, writing would simply not be possible without my family and friends: the Frazers, the Blakemores, the Weirs, the Faronis, and the whole Pikcilingis crowd (a motley crew if there ever was one). Special thanks to Eileen Frazer, Joseph Frazer, Susan Tananbaum, and Ed and Audrey Blakemore.

My dear husband, Nathan—I'd kiss you even if you were a troll, because I always see the prince beneath. Thank you for always standing by me, and for helping me to raise our own little elfin army. Jack and Matilda, you are the stars that light my way.